# UNDER LOCKE & KEY

## TRISTEN CRONE

This is a work of fiction. Any resemblance to actual persons, living or dead or actual events is purely coincidental. Although real-life locations or public figures may appear throughout the story, these situations, incidents, and dialogue concerning them are fictional and are not intended to depict actual events nor change the fictional nature of the work.

First published in the United States of America 2025 by Lake Country Press & Reviews.

Cataloging-in-Publication Data is on file with the Library of Congress.

ISBN: 979-8-9922275-6-7 (Paperback edition)

ISBN: 979-8-9922275-7-4 (Ebook edition)

Author website: https://tristencrone.com/

Editor: Tara Sexton

Cover Art: @vivsketchess

Cover Design: Rae Valtera

Formatting: Juliet Bridges

# Lake Country Press

Publishing & Reviews

*To everyone who has felt like they had to earn the right to be loved—you don't need to prove a thing. Who you are is enough.*

## AUTHOR'S NOTE

Thank you so much for giving this book a chance! I want to ensure that you have a pleasant experience while reading, so please find a list below of content that might be potentially distressing. My hope is that it will help you protect your peace and enable you to enjoy Bryce and Rachel's story to the fullest.

This story contains the following:

- Alcohol Consumption
- Sexual Harassment
- Misogyny
- Divorce
- Panic Attack
- Explicit Language
- Explicit Sex
- Adoption
- Strained Parental Relationship

# CHAPTER  1

SMILE. THE MENTAL REMINDER BURNS THROUGH ME EVERY TIME I FEEL it slipping until my cheeks ache with the strain. Keith accepts every pat on the back, tapping his to-go coffee cup against others in the office with their congratulations. Inside, I'm a mess of confusion and anger, but I swallow it until it's nothing but a sick twist in the pit of my stomach and my smile covers up what I'm fighting against.

Andrew lifts his hands to quiet the group before speaking, practically beaming.

"I'm so pleased to have Keith as our new program manager on the developer side! He's put in the work and I know he'll be a great asset and awesome leader!" Andrew urges us to clap and my hands sting at the force of my false enthusiasm for the man who just stole what I've been working towards for the last eight or so years—the man who's only been here for two and does half the work I do.

Keith makes a half-hearted attempt at looking sheepish but it lasts for only a second before he's soaking it all up. Smug asshole.

"I appreciate the opportunity and I'm really excited to keep working with my team. We've got a lot of strong people and hard workers. I know you'll make me proud," Keith says and goes back to shaking hands with our colleagues until his little parade is done and we're at our desks.

I stare at my screen until my eyes blur, my hands clutched together on my lap, unable to move.

"Hey, Rach. You gonna sit there all day? Will you have that code for Morrison's done by the end of day or what? I'll be checking whatever you have before you submit it to Andrew." Keith looks over the cubicle wall at me, arms crossed over the barrier that we've shared for the last two years.

Aside from the fact that we've never had to have our work "checked" before sending it over, I resent the way he's immediately let this go to his head considering I was the one that mentored him when he got here. Plus, I fucking hate when people shorten my name.

"It'll get done." It always does. I have nothing else to say to him because if I do it'll be bitchy, and although I have a reputation of being single-minded in my job, I've been careful to not be seen as an emotional and bossy "female." God, I hate the verbiage. I hate the delineation of "female" and "male" and the way it's used to be "scientific" fact about my apparent lacking.

I push back my wheeled chair, locking my screen and slipping my phone into my blazer pocket before I march over to Andrew's office. Every step pushes the rage I tried to suppress to the surface. Hand poised over the wood of his door, I tap against it three times and wait.

"Come in." Andrew's voice is muffled.

Stepping inside, I shut the door behind me and take a deep breath.

"Rachel," he acknowledges but doesn't invite me to sit. Instead, he looks like he's bracing for something.

"Can we talk?"

Andrew sighs. Audibly sighs at me and I wish I could rage and rail. It's long-suffering. It's annoyed and superior, and tells me that I'm wasting my time before I've even started.

"If you feel it's necessary then I'll hear you out."

Oh, *thank you* for deigning to give me your time. *Asshat.*

"It's more a question than anything else. You know how much I care about performance and doing my best. I was wondering what it was that counted against me with the program manager position." I bite through my smile.

"Honestly, Rachel, I can't discuss that with you. There are policies in place . . ." Andrew shrugs with a big show and if he puts his wrists together to say his hands are tied I'll throw his stupid fake bonsai tchotchke at the window.

"Andrew, I haven't made a fuss. I've been here longer than you have and I haven't taken a single complaint to HR. I've worked my way around things. I've pushed through them. For the last eight-ish years, I've done whatever I could to be successful at my job. If there's something I can work on, I feel like it would be unfair to deprive me of an opportunity to improve."

During those eight years I've also learned what the right thing to say is in order to get what I want. Plump up their egos when the time calls for it. Cut them down when they overstep too much. Stay focused throughout it all. Whatever developer skills I've honed in my time here, I've spent just as much time studying the social play in this environment.

I thought I had it down to a science. My entire image has been centered around being capable but approachable, driven but not divisive. Networking and embodying the company values like they are a checklist—the same way I've approached any challenge, big or small.

Andrew grimaces and I sit so that I'm not looking down at him. He steeples his fingers on top of the desk like he's considering his words carefully.

"Keith is the better candidate for the position, not just because of his qualifications now, but primarily because of the level we know he'll be performing at and the work he'll be able to provide in the future."

There's an underlying message here, but for the first time in a while I'm not willing to root through all the options to make it easier for Andrew.

"Why would my ability to perform in the future be a question or concern?"

Andrew sucks in a breath through his teeth and it's like he's toeing the line between what he wants to say and what HR would crucify him for saying.

"Rachel . . ." He gestures at me, as if my person is reason enough.

I just raise an eyebrow in response.

"We wanted a more experienced candidate."

"But I'm only three years younger than Keith and I've worked my way up the ladder since I got here?" Surely my time at the company should be enough to counteract that.

Andrew looks so uncomfortable it makes me think of one of my short-lived relationships, where the guy was near disgusted when I said I was on my period and didn't want to hook up. It was as if the mere mention of the way my body functioned made me a pariah.

Wait. No fucking way. That can't be it, surely? I've heard rumors but never actually seen it in person.

"It's not that I'm twenty-nine. It's that I'm a *woman* who's twenty-nine."

He shakes his head. "No. No. This is *not* because of your sex or age."

4

Cause that would be discriminatory and if he said that it would be a liability for Lakin-Cole. I keep going though, my anger at the unfairness peeking through the carefully constructed persona I've curated.

"The quality of my future work is in question because you believe at my rapidly deteriorating age, the incessant ticking of my 'biological clock' will leave me beset with a sudden urge to procreate, and that would put my dedication to the company in question. Even though if Keith were to have a kid he'd be just as much a parent as I would, it counts against me but not him."

Wiping his hand across his mouth, Andrew takes a beat before his own corporate mask slips onto his face to cover the discomfort.

"Keith is the preferred candidate. He's dedicated to this company and we are confident he will provide what we expect out of a leader. I'm sorry you're unhappy with the outcome but that's the reason. He's your superior and I suggest you accept that sooner rather than later. We don't have time for employees who let personal pettiness impact their work. This is a large-scale contracting company and professionalism and teamwork are a requisite for working here. It's your choice."

Take it or leave it but either way I'm the loser here. If I speak up, I'll be giving in to every stereotype I've been trying to avoid. If I sit back and let it happen I'll be trampled under what I've been working to break through.

"I know you're disappointed, Rachel. I hope it's a consolation to know we think you're indispensable where you are now. We can't afford to lose you as a developer. No one can do it like you can and we do see the effort you put in."

Rising from the chair, I nod at him before leaving, my thoughts a maelstrom in my head.

"Hey, Rach," Keith calls out from the water cooler when I emerge from Andrew's office.

I acknowledge him with a little wave.

"After work celebratory drinks at Public at six. You better be there!" Keith says to the whole office more than just me, and there's a little cheer among our colleagues at the prospect of Thursday night drinking.

After work, drowning-out-the-rage drinks at Public Service sound great. And Ángel will be there. One upside to this whole mess.

IT'S GIN. I FUCKING HATE GIN. IT TASTES LIKE CHEWING A TREE LEAF— a pine needle stuck between my teeth and burning through my chest when I swallow. But I take a swig and bite out a smile in the direction of my mysterious benefactor. Turning back to Ángel— the bartender and my best friend—I sit with my back to the rest of the room. I catch a distorted glimpse of myself behind a wall of bottles and consider my options.

The gin sucks but today sucks even more.

"You don't have to drink the rest of it." Good ol' Ángel, kind as always, and well aware of the face I make when I find something disgusting.

"It's free. I'm having a bad night."

"It's *gin*."

The sigh shudders out of me. "I know. But if I turn it down he might get nasty."

We both turn to take a quick glance at the man who sent the drink again and I get a brief look at a baby blue button up and perfectly coiffed blonde hair.

"What do you think?" I ask.

Ángel and I play this game every Friday night, taking bets on which sector these guys might be working in. When I lose, I owe

Ángel a twenty. He puts it toward his Paris fund. He wants to walk the streets of Montmartre and feel like a "real poet" even when I tell him that writing poetry makes him one, not the location. He's firm. So far, I've helped him save up a couple hundred dollars over the last few months. When he loses, and let's be honest I lose on those nights as well because most of the time I stay here until they close, Ángel takes me to get something greasy to soak up the alcohol.

Raising a newly-bleached eyebrow, Ángel has more opportunity to look without being obvious. "I'm going to say Capitol Hill. He's slinging his jacket over his arm. Looks like he's heading over here."

"Oh *come on,* that is such a cheap shot. Half of the people in this bar probably work on the Hill. Hurry. Give me something real to work with." I take another swig of the disgusting liquor for some courage.

If he really is heading over here, I need to try and get in the right mindspace.

"Fine. Assistant or intern of some kind."

I roll my eyes because, again, that's such a fucking cop out. But we're out of time. That brief impression of the stranger knocks around in my mind and I settle on, "Finance. Contractor, not government."

Ángel turns pensive, and nods once in a way that I know means it's a solid guess.

The stool beside me scrapes against the floor as Mr. Gin settles in beside me. I shouldn't be able to hear it over the music but I feel the vibration in the seat of my own stool and I steel myself.

Flicking my long black hair over my shoulder, I greet him with a pinched smile I've spent hours practicing. Not too obvious, not too open. Something that says "thank you for holding the door" or "no, you go first" without drawing attention.

He returns it, and I blink through the haze of my last three drinks to get a proper look at him. Blonde hair with more product than I have in mine. It's subtle but I've dated enough high-maintenance people to know how long it takes to get such an effortless style to look that way. The top two buttons on his shirt are undone. Ring finger is naked.

"Hi." He holds out his hand for me to shake and his palm is smooth against mine. Office then, for sure. "I'm Austin."

"As in the city?" I ask and kick myself immediately.

"As in Powers. Like the movie."

Ángel chokes out a scoff and when I give him side eye he has the grace to go fill someone else's drink before he returns, with his humor under control.

"Oh, wow. Okay, that's cool." *Is it though? God, this is awkward. When did those movies come out anyway?* I squint a little harder through my buzz and he does look young. Younger than my twenty-nine anyway.

"So, what do you do for a living?" he asks and I could kiss him right then and there for hurrying up this little charade. This is about the bet. I decided at the start of the night I'd be going home alone.

"I work for the Senate." He beams, actually beams. Bright white teeth that his parents must have spent a fortune on. I let the silence stretch just past the point of comfortable before I answer.

"Oh, I'm a software developer. Your job sounds exciting. What do you do up on the Hill?" I'm near choking to inject fake interest into the sentence but flattery gets me there quicker and I'm so ready for this interaction to be over already.

"I'm just an intern right now but I'm hoping to get a job on the press side."

*Fuck.* I might as well reach into my purse and slap the twenty on the bar right now. But Ángel doesn't like the camera picking up my extra tips when he'll just have to split them. So I'll save it for the end of the night like usual.

He's an intern, named after a movie that came out in the late nineties (if we're talking about the first one) which can only mean . . . Oh god.

"How old are you?"

Austin flushes. Never a good sign. "How old are *you*?" He lobbies back and this is a fucking nightmare.

I drop the practiced smile and level him with one of my "don't test your bullshit on me" looks. His blush fades into a pale terror.

"Austin. How old are you?"

Ángel is back, and if he were a dog his ears would be upright and turning toward us like a fucking antenna searching for signal.

"Twenty-two."

A veritable baby. God, am I in cougar territory already? Sure, my knees hurt sometimes when I've been sitting at my desk for too long but that's from disuse, not age. Ángel snickers and pours me a glass of water, setting it next to the offending gin. What kind of fucking twenty-two-year-old sends *gin*?

I'm sure there are some mature guys in their early twenties, but, from my experience, the men on the Hill are no better than frat boys at that age, and I really don't have it in me to train one again. The last one ended with a whimper and pushed me toward the worst relationship I've ever had. A reverse Good Luck Chuck and just as terrible.

"Look, it's very kind of you to send over a drink. I appreciate it, really. I'm just a little too old for you, I think."

*Gentle. Make it about you.*

"It's okay. I don't mind an older woman. My ex was twenty-five."

"Yeah, well I'm twenty-nine. Bit of a bigger difference there. So, unless you're interested in getting married and *having kids* sometime soon, I'd recommend you give me a pass."

The word *married* makes him swallow—hard. The word *kids* has him looking downright sick and I can't help but empathize.

God, I'm still so angry at Andrew and the implications he didn't have the balls or stupidity to admit to.

"I—you—" he stutters. "Have a good night." Austin rushes away, back to his table of friends and I can already hear them laughing at his rejection. It's good-natured ribbing at least. He'll get over it, or under someone younger.

"Now, why did you go and lie to the boy? You have no interest in marriage and as far as I can recall you said kids were quote, 'nice for some but definitely not for me, and so far off my radar the concept might as well exist on another planet.'"

"*Twenty-two*," I hiss in response and he takes the gin from me, pouring it down the drain and saving me the torture.

"Speaking of twenties. I expect mine when we leave." His smile is sly, and I wish he still had his longer dark hair so I could ruffle it. This shorn and bleached look works for him, offset against his golden skin, but it's way less fun.

"Have I ever let you down?" I ask.

"Not unless we're counting that first night."

I sigh again, second time tonight, and it feels a little excessive to be this annoyed by small things when other—bigger—things are what drove me here to drink in the first place.

"How the hell was I supposed to know you were going through it? It wasn't until we were in bed and you were crying that I realized I was just a rebound. The only way I let you down was by not being Jesse—something you were super kind about at least."

His smile drops into something more regretful, "And thank goodness for it because he was a mess. One I was tired of cleaning up. Plus, we work so much better as friends." Pushing the glass of water closer to me, Ángel urges me to drink.

I swig the liquid back, my stomach so pleased it doesn't burn on the way down. Ángel heads over to the other side of the bar to take care of another one of my colleagues.

And then I feel the heft of an arm slung over my shoulders and the acrid smell of alcohol already leaching through Keith's skin. He's put his drink on the bar beside my glass of water and effectively boxed me in with his body. The heat is unwelcome and the smell in conjunction with the gin I've failed to wash away the taste of is enough to make me want to gag.

"Rach, Rach, *Rach*. What did you say to scare off the little cub? It took quite a bit of bolstering from us to get him to approach you. You're not getting any younger, you know. You've got to grab life by the horns before it's too late. Then again, maybe you like your men a little bit more"—Keith bends down, taking the invasion of space from uncomfortable to unbearable—"experienced." The last word is a rasp against the shell of my ear and I shudder. And the fact that it echoes what Andrew said earlier makes me feel sick.

Stroking his fingertips over my shoulder, I shrug him off of me and slide to standing in order to put some distance between us.

"You're drunk. I think you should have some water and sober up."

"You're just upset about the imbalance between us now. I've seen the way you look at me. I know what that intensity means."

*It means I hate your fucking guts.*

"I won't tell anyone. You don't have to worry about getting in trouble at work if we do. Just because I'm your boss now doesn't mean we can't have fun outside of the office."

He's encroaching on my space again and I take a step back, bumping into the barstool beside me. Part of me wants to lash out but the smarter, more careful, part of me reminds me for a second time tonight not to antagonize them so that I don't have to worry about retaliation, either physically or at work.

"There a problem here?" Ángel asks and I sigh in relief. Keith's attention is diverted.

"This is none of your business." Keith's rudeness would have been red-flag enough even without all the unwanted attention.

"If you're harassing one of my patrons then it's my business. Now, unless you want to get cut off and kicked out, you'll back off."

Keith sneers at Ángel but grabs his drink, sloshing some of it over the side before he walks away.

"Just in time. Thank you." My relief is a little too acute to dismiss as no big deal and Ángel can tell I'm shaken.

"Now, we have about fifteen minutes until Shelly will be here to relieve me. Think about where you want to eat and then we'll talk about why you *really* came here tonight, since it's not your regular Friday, and because I know it wasn't to get picked up by Mr. Austin Powers."

Returning the now-empty glass of water, things feel a little clearer, but no less bleak.

"Deal. But you know my answer never changes." Creature of habit down to the core.

Walking to the Metro, and then down the sidewalk as the early spring air leans just a little too cold for comfort, I cross my arms to keep warm and hustle to get inside.

Our booth in the back is empty and we slide across the slightly cracked leather to take our regular spots. The hole-in-the-wall burger joint I found during my sophomore year at Georgetown isn't much to write home about where appearances are concerned. Ángel is appalled that I keep coming back here when this place takes grunge beyond trendy to downright questionable. But the building is so old it feels like a person greeting me when I step through the creaky door, and the food is always good.

Although I don't need to be as frugal as student-me used to be, it's a bonus I appreciate. Coming here makes me feel closer to who I was back then—excited, ambitious, and so sure of her success that the roadblocks barely registered.

But that was eight years ago, and the roadblocks turned into dead ends.

"So, you going to tell me what this is really about?" Ángel sips his diet Coke from the paper soda cup that will start leaking from the bottom in about thirty minutes, and winces against the cold.

"Remember I told you about that promotion I've been working toward since last fall? The one I thought I'd be a shoo-in for after Andrew made me do the presentation alone and kicked Sebastian off of it?"

God, it feels like such a long time ago, and at the same time very little has changed. Just hours upon hours of staring at a screen and tipping some eyedrops in every now and then when my eyeballs feel like sandpaper from not blinking. I glance at the menu that's a little too sticky for comfort even though I know I'm going to get the same thing I always do.

But it's a ritual. So I do it.

The waitress interrupts our conversation and we order our usual, handing back the menus and waiting for the clip of her shoes to fade.

"Yee-ess," Ángel stretches the word out into two syllables.

"They announced the program manager appointment today."

"Congratulations?" It's cautious. He knows my mood well enough to know the difference between celebratory drinks and drowning my feelings.

"Congratulations to *Keith*," I spit the name out like it's a curse.

Fucking Keith. Just because he's "personable", as if that's what you need to be a good developer and program manager. I get shit done. I always get shit done and outpace him every time. Of course when I brought that up to Andrew he just bludgered me with a "you're indispensable where you are now. We can't afford to lose you as a developer. No one can do it like you can."

As if that made it any better.

"Not ballroom bastard Keith?" Ángel injects the correct

amount of appalled into the question and it makes the edges of my mouth quirk up into the ghost of a smile.

"One and the same. The guy you chased off at the bar tonight. You know, he had the gall to say just because he's my boss now doesn't mean we can't *have fun* together." My face is twisted in disgust and even the thought of it is almost enough to put me off of my meal.

"Oh, hell no. You cannot keep working there."

I slurp some of my Sprite, somehow always better from a fountain than a can, and steal some fries from our communal order.

"That's almost not the worst part. When I confronted the general manager about it he 'couldn't exactly say why' but the reason I wasn't hired was because they're worried I'm not dedicated enough. They think I'm going to get pregnant as soon as I get the job and then fuck off and waste their time."

"So that little comment to the Gin-tern was—"

"—me being pissed about the image they have of me in their minds. Yes. If they knew a thing about me they'd know it's a non issue. Which, it shouldn't fucking matter whether I do want kids or not. It's such outdated bullshit. I don't know what to do. What would *you* do?"

Ángel shakes his head, a rueful smile on his face. "Rachel, I'm a bartender in my mid-thirties that writes poems that no one will ever see, and my aspirations for anything more died a long time ago. At this point I'm happy if I can make rent and get groceries for the week. We are opposites, you and I. I've never wanted to conquer the world. I'm just glad to experience the little things."

The sigh that leaves my lungs is so heavy it hurts.

"It can't all be for nothing. Years of this, for it to be *just this*. Is it wrong to want more? To want to be acknowledged?"

"If that's what you want to get out of your work environment —if what you need to keep going is being valued and not just

14

being paid—then maybe you need to rethink some things. You mentioned Sebastian got out of there. Have you thought about doing the same?" he asks.

I shrug and we dig into our food, the rich taste of garlic aioli spreading across my tongue. The burger soaks up the last of my drunken sorrow and Ángel has given me something else to ruminate on besides being upset.

Should I consider leaving?

"Would that be giving up?" I ask, my doubts sneaking out. Only with Ángel. He's the only one who's seen me at close to my worst and I know he won't judge me for my moment of weakness.

"Does letting go of something that's no longer serving you equate to giving up? I don't think so. You're not the kind of person to slowly atrophy sitting at the same desk for years just because you're somewhere familiar. Sometimes you've got to keep moving to keep the blood flowing and your spirit alive."

I chuckle. "You really should get back to the poetry book. It doesn't feel fair that I am the only one benefitting from that brain and those words of yours."

His tan skin flushes, just barely visible but I know the tells by now.

"You first. I'll follow your lead."

"I'm taking that as a legitimate agreement. I'll look for something else and then you need to look up some agents again. We'll be brave together."

Sticking my hand out across the table, his palm is warm against mine and we shake on it. Silly. But it feels like a start, the bleakness of being overlooked again not aching as badly knowing someone has my back and believes in me.

"We'll look together. I need you to keep an open mind though and trust me. If I find something I think will be good for you, you have to at least apply. Okay?"

I roll my eyes but agree and we scroll through Indeed in

silence. My heart's not really in it though. I'm too pissed about potentially having to take a step back to get hired. Mid-level positions are so much harder to find since most places hire from within.

"Here," Ángel says, sliding his phone across the table.

"Escape Room Developer?" The skepticism drips from my question. What could they possibly need a developer for? All I can picture is a dinky room with bad props and poorly thought out clues, with a deadline taunting you.

"Keep reading."

"It's not even in D.C." An escape room in some town I've never even heard of before now. God, what a downgrade.

Ángel hits me with his no-nonsense stare, the same kind he gave Keith at the bar and the reminder is enough to make me return to the job posting. Anything would be better than slinking back to Lakin-Cole's toxic "male"centric environment.

Immediately hiring candidates for now through December— possibility for a permanent position thereafter. Daily flat rate. Must be able to work on-site in Dulaney, MD.

Seeking a developer and collaborator to bring an edge and new take on a beloved activity. 'Locke Box' will be an escape room experience that's more interactive and higher-tech for visitors while adding a fun addition to the charming town of Dulaney, MD. Its unveiling will be at the town's December Fest and it is imperative that a candidate be able to function under a deadline. You'll have the chance to put your creativity to use in addition to your tech skills.

This would be perfect for a candidate looking to branch into freelancing or something outside of the typical corporate landscape. If you are detail-oriented, good at problem-solving, and eager to put your mark on the escape room industry then this is your chance.

**Come for the challenge, stay for the fun.**

Collaborating instead of just doing what I'm told feels like a buoy in a storm—a hand reaching out to pull me from the corporate hellscape I inhabit every day on my rolling chair. But the risk of relocating and a daily rate instead of hourly gives me pause.

"Come for the challenge, stay for the fun" echoes through my mind and I can't help but think that would make the perfect tagline. Not that I'm already thinking about how to make this work or anything.

"I can see the gears turning. Apply. Now. You won't call it chickening out but I know you'll logic your way out of having to do it. Apply and go from there. If you do it I'll reup my Query Tracker." Ángel dangles it in front of me, knowing I'll do it for him after the countless saves at the bar, and the kind ear whenever I cry about work or the pressure of trying to live up to the image my parents have in their minds of who I am and what I should be capable of.

"That's coercion and we both know it."

"I'm not above that to get shit done. You play by the rules. I don't. Maybe it's time you make your own."

Rule-follower. Teacher's pet. Perfectionist. The qualities I've prided myself on have gotten me passed over and harassed. The game is rigged against me and those like me, maybe it's time I try something where I can level the playing field.

"Pull up Query Tracker and your old query package. You're doing a lot of big talk for someone with no skin in the game."

Phones in hand, we take the leap. I apply and put every ounce of yearning for something better into it. I haven't had to do this in years and I can only hope that my promise shines through. The alternative is too depressing to consider and I worry that if I don't go elsewhere soon I'll be permanently glued to that rolling chair—

the scratchy fabric against the back of my knees embedded into my skin.

There has to be another way.

"I'm proud of you, kiddo." Ángel says.

I scoff. "You're barely older than I am, and you know I hate nicknames."

"No." He wags his finger at me, his face mock-serious and I can't help but giggle at it. "No, you hate being called 'Rach', you don't hate nicknames. I am geriatric. You need to get out there for my sake."

"Okay, old man. If I'm going to actually go for this, there are way too many moving pieces. Don't get your hopes up."

His expression turns serious, "Or do. Do get your hopes up. Take a risk for once in your damn life. You can't be this perfect person all the time. You're so used to molding yourself to a situation to do what everyone else expects from you. Who are you outside of that? Away from trying to be the best for your parents and not pissing off the wrong people at work, and being too kind to drunk assholes at a bar?"

We stare at each other for a moment and intense gratitude wells within me at my friend. For knowing me and when to push.

"Thank you. You dragged me back onto the path. When I got to the bar tonight I was so angry and bleak. Discouraged. Thank you for keeping me sane."

He shrugs as if it's no big deal. "Thank you for singlehandedly funding my Paris trip with your terrible guesswork. I thought I was bad with men but you've got me beat."

"See. I give you a compliment and thank you for tonight and you insult me in response."

"You know I don't do well with sappy. I'm allergic to feelings and you hide all of yours. That's why we're such good friends."

We share a smile, put money on the table, and walk out into the spring night. Cool, a bit of a bite, but there's promise there in the scent of flowers and the green leaves unfurling overhead as we walk back to the Metro.

"I'll see you next week?" I ask. Fridays are kind of our thing and somehow showing up to the bar two nights in a row feels wrong.

"I'm off on Friday but I'll be back the week after. Depending on if you're still in the District or slumming it in a cute Maryland town."

"You know, we *can* meet up to hang outside of the bar."

"I know. But I enjoy watching you swat men away, and getting fantastic tips. Don't take away the one night at work that I don't hate."

Scoffing, I give him a quick hug and head back into Mt Pleasant. Unlocking my basement apartment, I drop my purse by the door, kick off my heels, and head into the kitchen. One giant glass of water later I trudge into the bedroom. Collapsing on the bed, I promptly pass out.

My inbox pings around 2AM, and I crack open one eye to make sure it's not an emergency. Small text is illegible when put up against sleep and bleariness but the subject line is bigger and in bold:

**Rachel Mackey — Locke Box Interview**

Rubbing the fuzz from my eyes, I blink a few times to clear them before reading on.

**Hi Rachel,**

**I appreciate your prompt response. Your resume is impressive. I would love to schedule a time to discuss the prospect of having you join me in making Locke Box a reality. It's a passion project for me and to say your cover letter intrigued me would be an understatement.**

**Please let me know whether next week will work for you. I really want to get the ball rolling on this project and I'd like to get a feel for you and your style before I offer.**

**I look forward to hearing from you.**

**Good night,**

**Bryce Dawson**

I don't know why the short message affects me the way it does but something warm shoots through me at the words "impressive" and "intrigued" and "please." It's been such a long time since someone asked me please and didn't just demand it. The "Good night" feels strangely intimate even though it's appropriate given the hour.

Before I can "logic" my way out of it like Ángel said I draft a resignation letter for Andrew and shoot off a reply to Bryce.

**Hi Bryce,**

**Next week will be perfect. Just tell me when and where.**

# CHAPTER  2

IF THESE WALLS COULD TALK, THEY'D CURSE STEPHANIE DAWSON. OR maybe I just wish I could. Does she even *go* by Dawson anymore? Or is it just one more thing she's content to leave behind along with me?

I follow the hollow clacks of her shoes against bare floors—the rugs rolled up and stowed away with sticky notes on each denoting their loyalties. It's so faint the new owners will miss it, or paint over it if they do notice, but there are little shapes bleached into the walls from the sun on our photographs and a larger one from the giant canvas we did that photoshoot for.

With a dog that wasn't even our own.

The silence between us stretches five years, a canyon of words unsaid that might have made a difference at any point other than this one, 'cause they're useless now. The lawyers have been paid. The papers are signed. Our lives intersected and cleaved from each other with the flick of ink on a dotted line. I've never hated the sight of my name more than I do in those documents.

There's so much said about the stages of grief for when someone dies, but can you grieve someone who is very much alive? How do you mourn the death of what lived between you? How do you feel their loss when their high heels click in front of you and you know the shape of their calves and the feel of their skin beneath your hands—skin that's closer than it's been in almost a year and no longer yours to touch?

"I'll take care of the cleaning fee." Stephanie has no idea where my mind's at, or maybe she doesn't care.

It's not her job to care anymore.

I'd like to get angry, to lash out and say that I busted my ass packing and moving and cleaning this place from top to bottom by my kick-out date, but it wouldn't do anything. Holding my tongue has been a constant almost as long as the stupid combination robot vacuum mop that never worked but Stephanie insisted we needed.

"Thank you." My voice is rough with misuse. Between boxing up the last of my stuff and getting it in a storage unit by the date she wanted to start showing the house to other people, I haven't spoken to anyone.

My parents call. Of course they do. But I haven't answered them beyond a few short text messages for over a week. I feel bad. I should. I've barely seen them over the last few years since Stephanie preferred not to go visit them. I've been busy—watching the last part of my marriage and my life disappear with each piece of furniture until it's just me and her and the walls that are as quiet as I am. I hate that I'm slinking home a failure when all I've ever wanted is what my parents have. It just goes to show that signatures on a paper don't make a marriage, and that a document doesn't denote a true partnership.

"The agent will be by in the morning but I wanted to get a look at it before I brought her over." She's rambling, I realize. The closest she gets to it. Stephanie is ruthlessly efficient and stalling for time with little bits of conversation is beneath her.

I say nothing. What can I? *I hope our life fetches a good price so we can both sit flush but alone out in the cold?* Does she already have someone new? Nothing about her looks any different than it did nine months ago.

Her blonde hair is sleek and blown out to within an inch of its life. I know because I watched her do it a thousand times, her knee bouncing as she dragged the big round brush through golden strands that cost a couple hundred every month. She's got her same immaculate makeup that I jokingly called war-paint on the night she met my mother for the first time and has no smudging or streaks. No tears shed.

My sorrow has been abundant. It echoes within me even now —although muted with time. But I can't cry anymore, not in front of her. I won't and I shouldn't—not when the death of our marriage was slow and painful. And as I watched our relationship wither and die—a bystander to my own life—I can't help but wonder if there were moments where we could have revived it and we just didn't. Why is that? If we wanted it, wouldn't we fight for it? Instead of just fighting each other?

We haunt the living room and wander further, and the kitchen countertop is cool beneath my fingertips when I ghost my fingers over the surface. Stephanie inspects it through the eyes of all the newcomers who will walk through here with dreams in their eyes a week from now. I drink in every memory I'm leaving behind until I'm drowning in remembrance for the sake of it—with only hurt to show for my efforts.

Steph's delicate hand wraps around the metal bannister—that I insisted was too cold and she insisted was a better alternative than the dinky old-fashioned wood I preferred—and her bare ring finger doesn't have a tan line or indentation of any kind.

Nine months is all it took for it to fade away.

I refuse to look at my own hand. White gold has embedded itself into my skin and I don't know what my hand will look like without it—a final holdout of delusion and grasping for what is comfortable and known. Although I can't help thinking that even pain can be comfortable when we've grown used to it.

The sound of our breathing and footsteps ricochets against the narrow walls of the corridor between bedrooms. At the end of the hall, door splayed open and welcoming, we step into our old bedroom and I want to rip the carpet up with my bare hands.

Cream. Thick and lush and more expensive than my first car was. There are indentations in the carpet where our bed stood. No matter how much I vacuumed and scratched my fingers through the weave, it refused to leave. Without the bed the room feels cavernous with just the two of us there to fill it.

What a sorry pair we make.

Staring at the bottom indentation, I let my gaze blur and the room as I know it fills my mind. End tables, hers near-empty with whichever self-help book she's reading, the retainer in its container she'd die before admitting she still used—a bottle of Voss that she gets imported by the crateload. Mine, fiction piled upon fiction, and my glasses only half-closed so I can grab one of the legs in the morning when I'm too bleary to make them out properly. It's the only way I can avoid accidentally touching the lenses.

"Are you going to say anything?" Stephanie pulls me from my mental catalog and I turn to face her, framed by the doorway with the sunset dappling onto her face.

Arms crossed, over her stomach more so than her chest, she looks vulnerable and it's not something I'm ready for. The only way I've kept myself upright—moving and breathing, and somewhat human—has been picturing her indifference to all of this. Somehow it's easier for me to accept this outcome if I think she made this choice in a detached and cold way.

But if she breaks, I do.

"What do you want me to say?" Is there something I *can* say that would take all this back? Will my words douse the flames we went down in even though we're just ash now?

She scoffs, or perhaps it's a bit of breath caught at the back of her throat, but either way it's not a happy sound. Her lip curls in disdain and I want to sink onto the carpet and decay into it.

"*Anything,*" Stephanie hisses. "Say anything. Fight. Scream. Do fucking something!" Her voice rises until it echoes around me in the empty room, the carpet not enough to dampen the sound. She wants a "fuck you" fight but I've never been that guy and she knows it.

"It won't change anything. I could tell you I don't want this but you already know that. I could tell you that I love you and I meant it when I promised the rest of my days to you, and I always keep my promises, but it would be redundant. Nothing I say now will make a difference to what's left here. *You* made that choice for the both of us."

It's the closest I've gotten to trying to hurt her since this all began. First was denial, like those pesky stages of grief. I skipped disbelief; it made sense to me in some sick way. From the moment I took her out on our first date, I've been outrunning the feeling of not being good enough. Stephanie leaving me felt like an inevitability.

"What did you expect me to do?" Stephanie asks.

It's the stupidest question. There's a hysterical edge to my laugh when it bubbles past my lips—pained and dry and the furthest thing from funny I've ever heard.

"I expected you to love me. I expected us being together and married to be enough for you. God knows it was enough for me."

"Bryce." It's long-suffering. As if she's already explained it to me multiple times even though nothing even close to a reason has crossed her lips since that night almost a year ago.

"Why, Steph?"

She swallows, my eyes caught on the column of her throat, blurred with past and present—tiny marks from my kisses and my stubble, and now the nervous movement of her gulping back her feelings. This is my last chance to ask. I'm not just saying goodbye to our house today. This is it for us.

"I told you why, Bryce." She hugs herself, eyes flicking away from mine as if she can't bring herself to look me in the eye while she lies. Which is ridiculous. Stephanie is the best liar I've ever known.

"No."

Her hair flips over her shoulder as she pivots to face me fully, her eyes blazing with something I can't put a name to and I don't want to try anymore.

"No, what? You're calling me a liar?"

"No. I just—there's got to be more to it than you leaving because you're tired of us. You don't throw away five years of marriage because you're tired. I've seen you run yourself ragged for work, over and over. I've seen you make yourself sick after you pushed yourself further than you possibly could go."

"So what? You want me to exhaust myself for you? You want me to *hurt* myself for your sake?" She takes a step toward me, her shoes silent against the carpet now. Almost close enough for me to pick up the notes of her perfume.

"No! Of course not. I just—" I look down at my empty hands, trying to gesture and explain while at a loss for the words. How do I ask her why I wasn't good enough when it's all I've been able to think about through these nine months of separation? The words die on my tongue before I can form them and my heart aches at the thought of even asking. Because I know I'm not good enough and I don't know if I could handle the why.

"I was trying my best to keep this *amicable*, but you won't be happy until I've been mean. Is that it? You want me to be mean?

You need someone to blame?" Her expression twists between anger and pain and I don't know what to do when I no longer have the right to pull her against my body to absorb it all.

"Steph, please. You know that's not what I mean—"

"I didn't leave *us*. I left *you*. The truth is, I thought you were a different kind of guy than you actually are. We started along the same road and then you just . . . stalled. I can't keep slowing down for you."

I just watch as she starts the flaying process. The words kiss my skin with a blood-drawing bite and I feel like I'm rubbernecking outside my body when the accident is me.

"Even now you're so—compliant. I blow up our lives, I break up our marriage and I sell this house out from under you, and you just stand there and take it. You're *meek*, Bryce. You convince yourself it's because you're nice but really it's because you don't have the backbone for anything else."

Her blue eyes are bloodshot, tears gathering, but all I see is anger and all I feel is her rage as her voice hits my body.

"My father gave you a job at the company and *still* you didn't progress. Even with nepotism on your side you were content to sit back and let everyone else make the decisions. So, *I* decided. I decided for us because you sure as hell weren't going to. You can't pretend nothing was wrong. You're a coward but you're not stupid."

Little pieces were wrong, one or two missing from the puzzle, but nothing catastrophic enough that I couldn't still make out the picture. Maybe I was the only one building the puzzle. Maybe Steph wasn't even in the same room.

"I was trying to be stable, dependable." It sounds pathetic even to me.

"I didn't marry a fucking dining room table. I needed more from you." The curse word hits me harder than I expect, neither of us prone to swearing—Steph even less so since she considers it "crass."

The sun shifts across the floor, the cream fading to something closer to beige and some of her face is in shadow now, unreadable.

"Then why didn't you say something?"

"I *did*. Every day. It may not have been overt but I asked in all the ways I could. Sending you job applications for positions a little better and mentioning all the places I wanted to go to dinner at where you could have dressed up a little. Anything I could think to force you to be more, to be bigger, to be a better man."

Adrenaline is the only thing keeping me standing. But it can only do so much and if this carries on any longer I'll be dropping onto my knees with the weight of this feeling.

"I . . . didn't know. I was just—the man you married."

I was who I have always been and if I had less pain and more impartiality I might be able to ask why she was okay with it then but has only been wanting to change me since. The truth settles between us, the fissure widening into a chasm of me not being what she wanted and her resentful that she couldn't melt and meld me into someone I'm just not. Something flashes across her face and I know what I've said just screwed whatever "amicable" thing she thought we could be in her mind. I've cast my own blame and Steph has never been able to take as good as she gives.

"And now you're just the man I divorced."

She turns on her heel and I wait twenty seconds. Keys jingle as she pulls them from her bag. Footsteps get quieter until they're gone, the exclamation of her last word reverberating through the sound of the front door slamming.

Moving on autopilot, I walk off the fluffy carpet, each step down the stairs feeling heavier than the last. Spinning around one last time at the bottom, I can barely see who we used to be here. Someone else will move in and paint over the chip from my DIY mishap a year ago. The scuffs by the front door from my shoes will be buffed into nothingness. And Stephanie won't think twice about it—or me. Perhaps I should be the same.

Closure isn't all it's cracked up to be.

I shut the front door behind me and turn to lock it before I realize I no longer have the key for this place. We had to turn in our copies when we signed the final paperwork and released all our assets to be divided. Stephanie must have gotten a new copy or asked permission to use an old one.

Maybe she kept a spare and didn't tell them.

There's nothing I can do though but hope no one trashes the place. Then again, perhaps they should. Settling into my car, my headlights flicking on and bathing the front door in white, all I feel is empty.

> Leaving Philly now. I'll be back in Dulaney in around two and a half hours.

I send the text to both my parents and my best friend, Logan, like I promised, before I ease out of my old driveway and onto the road.

The radio is set to nothing, snippets of songs and talking cutting between static and white noise but I don't care enough to fix it. The drive between Philadelphia and Dulaney is broken up by stations fading in and out—country and talk, and then finally 97.9FM Dulaney's hits station.

My indicator clicks as I wait for a row of cars to pass so I can turn into South Grove and night has swallowed the neighborhood I grew up in. Even without the sun, memory guides me despite the changes over the years.

The Baker's big tree in their front yard is gone. The Niebecker's house has new siding, much darker than before. The only consolation to me now is how "same" my parents' home looks, even after the last few years. Steph hated coming here so my parents usually came to us. It's been two Christmasses since I was home in Dulaney.

My headlights flick off, hands gripped around the steering wheel so tight for so long they've gone a little numb, same as my ass. The motion detector by the back door floods the yard as my dad slips out of the kitchen door to let me into the garage. His little wave sends a twinge through my chest and although his smile is balm on my soul the lines sweeping out beside his eyes and mouth at the motion are less familiar.

He's older than I pictured him in my mind. I forget how that happens. The years don't just affect me but them as well. My father's forehead creases when he catches sight of me, bushy salt and pepper brows fixing down over the quiet brown eyes I inherited from him.

I shut the car door. The garage still smells vaguely of oil and engine even though he keeps it pristine. My father gathers me into a huge hug and ushers me into the house as if I'm a stray animal he's decided to keep, one he's worried will strike out at any moment.

My mom's in pajamas. If I know them at all they've been sitting on the sofa trying to stay awake past their 8 p.m. bedtime, and just listening for the sound of my car turning up into the drive. Her kiss is kind on my scruffy cheek and I'll need to shave soon. Steph always preferred me clean-shaven so I've been letting it go until it starts to irritate me and then trimming it, but not clean. Not anymore.

"We've turned your room into a guest room/sewing room since you were last here, and you can sleep there as long as you like. But we have the garage apartment set up for you to settle your things in whenever you're ready." My mom looks like she has more to say but thinks better of it.

I'm weary. My body aches in a way it hasn't before. Fatigue leaves me feeling far older than I should and apathy hardens like cement in my veins, sapping me even further. But I can't let the day end like this. Thirty looming ahead of me—a milestone that was supposed to mean I had it all together—and all I have to show for it is me falling apart.

"Thanks."

I trudge up the stairs, my hand on the wooden bannister to help hold me up when all I want is to sleep for a week straight. It smells the same, welcome and forgotten, and everything I never needed until right now.

My mom's perfume and her scented tea candles follow me up the stairs. The bedding in the guest room smells like the detergent they've used all my life and I want to breathe it in until my chest loosens around my stone heart. Instead, I stare up at the ceiling still fully dressed. Night washes over the room, only the barest of impressions of furniture around me in the dark. A golden sliver breaks up the black from under the door. The hall light is on and my parents putter through their evening routine. With the threat of an entire existential crisis looming, I check my phone.

LOGAN

Come out with us tonight! It's half-off draft night. You're home.

You deserve to get away from it for a bit.

I can't sleep. It's too early anyway, even though I haven't slept well in months. So although I don't feel like it and the idea of having to recap my failed marriage to my high school best friend fills me with dread, lying here is worse.

Where and when?

It's barely a few minutes before I get a response.

I'll pick you up and play DD so you can actually loosen up. Be ready.

The prudent part of me that's ruled my life the last decade says this is a very bad idea. The angry and heartbroken part of me just wants it to stop for a little while. So I agree to Logan's plan despite knowing none of it and he's at my parents' front door in under ten minutes.

I jog down the stairs, shoving my wallet into the back pocket of my jeans and my house keys in the front with my phone. My dad's drinking orange juice straight from the carton in the white light of the fridge and he stops mid-sip to glance at me behind his own owlish glasses.

"I'm heading out for a bit. Logan wanted to catch up now that I'm back."

"Be safe, you two." It's as serious as he can look and I give him a ghost of a smile and a nod before I'm out of there.

Logan's truck is still running, and he waits leaned up against it.

"Well, shit. If you aren't a sight for sore eyes!" His accent is thicker than mine, the twinge of a Baltimore twist to it since he grew up near the city before they moved to Dulaney in our sophomore year.

He gathers me up in a back-slapping hug, eyes assessing me before he nods to himself.

"Definitely due a night out. You look like you haven't left your house in months."

Logan isn't wrong, except for having left for work, but I'm not about to admit to it. I just grunt and we climb into the truck, my hand wrapped around the grab handle as he peels away from the driveway and out of the development.

"You sure Gabrielle is okay with this?" I ask.

"She's just excited to get a chance to binge more Grey's

Anatomy. That shit is too bloody for me. Plus, she knows how bad you need to get out for a bit."

I'm a little surprised she's not joining but then again, they're the thoughtful kind of people that might have decided seeing a disgustingly-in-love couple wasn't the best way to help me deal with my divorce.

"So, where are you kidnapping me to?"

"It's kind of like a Dave & Buster's thing between Rockville and Silver Spring but instead of an arcade it's an escape room-type experience."

The mixture of starlight and headlights on 270 flicker over the car, the whoosh of tires loud against the asphalt. So ironic.

"That's kind of heavy-handed, don't you think?" I glance over at my friend, at his bushy dark curls and the boyish mischief on his face that he never quite outgrew.

"I have no idea what you're talking about."

"Hmm."

Logan turns on the radio, the car filling with some indie song I've never heard but that he's likely ahead of the curve on. The silence between us is familiar—comfortable—and it's such a relief not to have to scramble to fill it.

Nearly two decades of friendship smoothes any rough edges of expectation and I let my mind still as we leave Dulaney behind for something busier—closer to the capital. When we pull into the industrial building that's part brewery, part entertainment, Logan turns to me and I prepare myself.

"I might have invited a few people."

Oh no.

"How many?"

I don't need to pretend in front of Logan but the thought of having to put on a brave face in front of others holds no appeal.

"Two. James from college and our neighbor, Kate."

James was pretty chill from what I remember. Kate is a new

entity entirely and I can only brace myself before we enter. They've got a table already, laden with nachos and a flight that I find out is mine.

"We didn't know what you like so we figured we'd get a variety." James's smile is kind, cutting into his bronze cheeks. I haven't seen him in about a decade since Logan's wedding but he's not too different from what I remember—the only change is that all of us look slightly less nerdy. Or perhaps nerd culture has become less of a deterrent as we've aged.

Between myself and Logan, and our weird interest in close-up magic and sleight of hand, we were given a hard time at school. College felt like a whole new world where we didn't have to befriend whoever was in our class and could actually choose to hang out with people that had similar interests—not just a question of proximity for five days a week.

"Thank you. I appreciate it." Sipping the first—a sour with a fruity undertone—the cold beer snakes down my throat and silences my mind enough that I can enjoy this moment.

Nachos and beer, and the rest of them chatting in a comfortable groove tells me this isn't the first time they've all hung out together. I am the outlier here, looking in.

Within thirty minutes my flight is done and the beer has started going to my head. We've polished off the nachos and I've learned a few things about the group I've been dragged into.

Kate's ex-girlfriend is now dating one of their mutual friends. James is thinking about proposing to his college sweetheart and when Kate hits him with "What the fuck, dude? You've been holding off for over ten years?" I can't help but agree.

But then again, jumping in quickly just ended in divorce for me, so who am I to say what works and doesn't.

"Logan told us a little about your situation. Tough break, man." James lifts his glass in commiseration for me to clink my own against—though mine is mostly just froth at this point.

"Yeah . . . I didn't really see it coming and we just had our final walkthrough of the house, which was brutal. She kind of laid into me saying how meek and disappointing I was."

I shrug because it's not far off. "She's right."

The words taste bitter on my tongue and it has nothing to do with the alcohol. Saying it out loud is harder than I anticipated.

"You are so much better than she deserves. Don't let her win. She doesn't get to define you. If that's not who you want to be, then fix it. Be successful without her and then rub her damn face in it." Kate's words are harsher than I've considered. Revenge wasn't high up on my list but as the night drags on and the drinks hit me harder, the anger outweighs the depression.

Kate's got a point. Stephanie doesn't have to win. I can turn things around for myself. With or without her.

Before I can get too in my head about it, our server closes out the tab and ushers us toward the "fun" side of the space.

There are air hockey tables, a couple of old arcade games, and a hallway that leads down toward the escape room.

"You are stuck in a snowstorm—your car is out of gas—and come across a cabin in the woods. Once you got inside the door shut and locked behind you. If you don't find the key to get out and the tank of gas to fill your car with, you'll be frozen inside." A bored employee drones on about how we have sixty minutes to escape, three hints, and if we need help (or mess with their equipment) they will speak to us through the intercom. We step into the room and the door clicks shut behind us, and although we've been assured it's not actually locked, my anxiety ticks up.

The room is small, vinyl floors that have been covered up with a plain carpet to make the space less obviously industrial. Wallpaper murals of logs line all four walls to make it look like we are in a cabin but one wall has started to peel in the corner, exposing a Pepto-Bismol pink paint beneath it.

"Okay. Let's see what we can shake loose," Logan says and

each of us heads into a corner of the room, tugging at box lids and drawers.

"I have a lock here but no key! It's a combination, like for a locker." Kate tugs on it but the metal makes no move to release. "If anyone finds any number clues, let me know."

And so it goes. I stumble around the room, drunker than I expected, as I search for clues but all we find are more and more locks and deterrents. One or two clues come from the fake notebook on an end table, and another from within a drawer, but given how little is in the room, it should've been simpler to find stuff.

We use all three of our clues and it's ridiculous how silly they are. One says we should lift up the coffee table and underneath is a sheet of paper with one of the combinations. The solutions are in such weird spaces, not intuitive at all, and I get that this is supposed to be hard but not so much that four grown adults (most of whom are a functioning level of drunk to stone-cold sober) should be able to solve it in time.

Unfortunately, even with all our clues used up, it's not enough for us to find the final one—under the mattress of the fake cot they have set up in the room.

The employee lets us out and we leave kind of deflated, the evening coming to a halt soon after.

"Thank you guys for taking me out. I really appreciate it!" I say and I find that I actually do mean it. Getting a break from myself, my mind, and my misery is a nice change of pace.

"We'll do it again sometime," James promises and sticks out his hand for me to shake.

Saying our goodbyes, Logan and I head back to his truck and I clamber inside. The spring breeze is cold and I should've brought a jacket or something other than just my plain henley but my priorities have been kind of skewed tonight.

Kate's words dance around in my mind, mixing with memories of me and Logan in high school practicing magic in our spare time, and that shitshow of an escape room.

"Penny for your thoughts?" Logan asks and when my eyes refocus I realize we're already back on the highway.

"Just trying to make sense of my life now. So much of my time and energy went toward Steph—first being together and then the slow process of us breaking apart—and I'm stuck between wanting to hate her and prove her wrong, or hating that part of me still wants her approval. I have no idea what to do with myself now. I had to leave the job with her father's company, and I haven't started looking here yet. The house money and my savings can float me for a while but I'd rather not piss it away on rotting on my parents' couch."

Logan makes a little humming sound in the back of his throat as he considers my words.

"If Stephanie wasn't a factor in all this and you could do whatever you wanted, what would you pursue?"

My mind races back to high school and college, Logan's and my plans to open a hobby shop. Though looking back on it now, we mostly just wanted to own those things, not sell them. Still, I got my MBA and he got his Marketing degree.

"I keep coming back to that idea from back in the day but I don't think I'd want to run a store now. Retail isn't appealing and I haven't touched my magic stuff since before I even met Steph while I was trying to get 'serious' about the trajectory of my life."

Logan's chuckle fills the cab of the truck. "We had big dreams back then. Though you're right, I don't think I'd want to own a store either. If I was going to take the risk of running my own business it would have to be more fun than that."

"I don't mind the idea of running my own business but I agree. It has to be worthwhile, something Dulaney doesn't already have. Like this escape room thing. We had to drive over half an hour to go to one that's terrible."

Not that I'm sorry we came. It's just a pity the night ended on a somewhat sour note. I'm still not sober enough, the drive feeling like I'm being rocked closer and closer to sleep as my vision blurs at the edges.

"Oh ho ho. Strong words for someone so 'meek.' You really think you could have done better?"

The term bristles again, more and more as time passes. There's nothing wrong with being a more quiet type of person. Picking your battles is smarter than running into every fight recklessly. Why should I have to be mean to people to prove my efficacy?

"Yes. Yes, I do." Pushing my glasses up the bridge of my nose, I sit straighter in my seat.

"How?" Logan asks, and it's less of a challenge than it should be. There's an undercurrent I can't fully pick up on in my inebriation.

"The set up for one. The best they can do is bad carpet and peeling wallpaper? One room only for the whole operation. I get that it's not a whole escape room business but if you only have one shot at pulling it off then you should do better."

"I don't know, man. What could they have done instead? It's an offshoot of a brewery, not Medieval Times." That tone again. Soon I'll parse it out. I'm just too busy trying to prove that my opinion is valid.

Logan is the only person I've ever really been able to debate with, so I feel fine pushing my opinion.

"It wouldn't have to be much. Switch out the harsh overhead lighting for a soft yellow or warmer tone to give it a cozier feel. Play some ambient snow storm sounds instead of having it be silent. Small things to set the mood, even if you didn't have better decor. Although no matter how good it looked, those clues were ass."

My best friend's guffaws spill through the night air and I join in, the first time I've felt like laughing in months.

"They *were*. First of all, the clues should be accessible. What if someone is super short and can't reach the top of things? What if they are in a wheelchair or have a disability that prevents them from lifting a whole mattress? That seems like poor planning on their part. Besides accessibility, there's the question of assuming everyone has the same level of experience or skill. Why limit it to three clues? Let people decide how many they need. It should be fun, not demoralizing. It's not just an escape from the room, it's supposed to be an escape from reality." My tirade continues and it's surprising to note how much I *do* actually care about this.

"Sounds like you've given it a lot of thought already. If anyone could pull it off, it would be you. Remember when we did our magic for the talent show and you were the one that insisted on having a whole routine because it would help with the immersiveness? Start with smaller tricks so by the time we do something risky the audience is already invested? You've always been way better at that sort of thing than I have."

His words whirl around my confused and tipsy ramblings and somehow congeal into something resembling an idea.

*If anyone could pull it off, it would be you.*

Stephanie would have thought this whole thing was stupid. She never would have been caught dead at an escape room, let alone one attached to a brewery.

The further I get from Philly and her, the more I wonder just what I was waiting around for? Without all the shine of a new relationship—of being *seen* for the first time—and now a step away from the wreckage of us, it's hard to figure out why I wanted us to fit so badly.

Logan drops me off at home with a "Think about it some more, okay? There might be something there." Then his truck is gone and I'm left in the darkness of the development, someone's little dog yapping in the distance when Logan rounds the corner.

My keys jingle as I deposit them on the key rack. There's nothing but the light above the stove left on.

I plop down on the spare bed, fully clothed, staring at the ceiling and all the loneliness floods back. The next year stretches out before me and I can picture it in my mind: me driving myself insane trying to piece together what I should have done differently and trying to figure out where to go from this when my whole life was tied up in Stephanie.

My notice at her father's company was accepted and my last two weeks were over a month ago. Staying with my parents is temporary, for sure, but I'll have to think of something permanent soon.

As aimless as I feel right now I can't justify throwing away the money I have from before we got married and soon my half of the house. Minutes bleed together until time doesn't feel real anymore and all I can focus on is how tired I am but I'm too wired to slip away into sleep. Unpacking my duffel seems stupid when I'll just have to redo it tomorrow when I settle into the garage apartment.

So, I turn on the bedside lamp and shuffle over to my old closet. Inside the doors still have tacked-on scotch tape that used to house posters of things I cared about. The shelves are stacked with old school folders and memories I haven't touched in years.

The middle shelf holds my high school obsession with all things illusionary. Books on escape artists and prestidigitation, and a way to bring magic into the world through lies. So much wonder that spiraled down the drain with each passing year and each step closer to the complacency Stephanie accused me of.

I used to be whimsical, silly. I used to have fun just for the sake of it and not because one of her parties demanded it. But this was never high-brow enough for her. Childish things should stay in childhood. The present had no space for a weird boy from Dulaney that put on magic shows for his family and accidentally locked himself in the garden shed for hours before my family realized I wasn't just out. It's been so long since I've been able to let that person out—to enjoy time and a beer with friends without feeling like I'm misstepping somehow . . . wasting time on relationships that don't serve another goal the way Steph has cultivated her friendships into networking opportunities.

My fingertips cross over the embossed title of the book in my hand, old leather and gold foil. It was the most expensive thing I owned at that time, purchased with my own allowance. In the intervening years I spent so much time on helping other people be financially sound, on making their businesses succeed, that I forgot my old dream.

The hobby shop might be a stupid idea now. I have no interest in flogging wares and there's no money in hobby shops anyhow. No amount of dreaming can counteract the prudent man I've grown into.

*Escape*, the book taunts and I want nothing more. My conversation with Logan in the truck backs it up until my mind is full of possibilities and questions, and the "what if" of it all.

I fall asleep with the book clutched against my chest as if it can protect my heart from the outside. As if I'll be sucked back in time through osmosis or just turn into the version of myself I used to like.

And when I wake it's with the other stage of grief yapping at my heels and nipping at my ankles—anger. Staring up at my old ceiling and barely able to make out where the glow-in-the-dark stars used to be, I am enraged down to the marrow of my bones.

How dare she? How dare she blame me for being what I had to be to keep her. Steph was used to a certain level of living and I had to provide that. Long nights in the office and stressing over balance sheets, profits and loss. Tucking away the silly parts that she sneered at to be more serious. All of it to be the kind of man who can indulge someone like her. Only for her to throw it up in my face.

*Escape.* The book whispers in my hand, still there after the whole evening, though it feels like the ridged spine has left indentations into my palm.

I'll show her. She says I don't take risks. That I'm boring and happy to let life pass me by. Well, I'm not. I'm *not*. I won't be anymore. It might take some mistakes but I doubt anything will ever feel as dire as this—as empty and looming and endless.

My mind loops through two thoughts: *Escape* and Logan's *"If anyone could pull it off, it would be you."*

The explosion of all my paraphernalia on the floor clicks together in my mind in a way that I should probably consider alarming and manic, but all I feel is a surge of something other than pain and anger.

I'm going to do this and she'll be wrong about me. I will make sure of it.

It isn't until I've spent all day drafting up a business plan— going so far as to call up the banker Steph and I knew back in Philly to ask questions about the start-up capital needed for a new business, and the steps required to establish one—that it sinks in. It takes me typing up a job description for a collaborator for a job that technically doesn't even exist to realize what's driving me through this whole endeavor.

Spite.

Spite burns through me and fans the flames of my anger. God, I've never felt more capable, more determined to see something through. I stay in that room all day, breaking when my mom knocks to leave a sandwich outside the door and my father whispers, "Leave him be, Theresa. He'll come out when he's ready."

I type until my wrists ache and my eyes blur, and I never want to sleep again.

And then my email pings.

Rachel Mackey with an immaculate resume and an impassioned cover letter that smacks of the same kind of desire that burns within me now to succeed. There are moments of overlap between us.

> I am currently transitioning out of a corporate environment into something I hope will have more of a community feel. I learned a lot during my time at Lakin-Cole, but my favorite part has always been getting to work with the people behind the projects. As I move away from an environment that places little emphasis on interaction, I am eager to step into a position that would allow for a more personal and impactful experience.

I think of those miserable cubicles again, and driving home so late the sun's already gone. Meal delivery because we're both too tired to cook, and barely watching a show in silence because we're so mentally exhausted there's nothing to say.

> I am the kind of person who pushes hard to do good work and am determined to prove my worth. I know I would be an asset to your company and this endeavor because even though I do not have experience with escape room design, I research extensively for every project I undertake. Failure is not an option for me and I am not afraid to work hard for the desired outcome. Corporate culture has honed those skills but doesn't offer any reward for them, so I hope I might be able to have what I bring to the table mean something.

Overlooked. Underestimated. Eager. Hungry. Angry. So angry.

Lost. So tired of being defined by the vision of myself that Stephanie wanted that I would never be.

Let's see if Rachel Mackey will be the person who will help me across the finish line, and even if she isn't it'll be good practice for more interviews. I set it for Wednesday, to give myself time to pull myself together and actually put this business endeavor into practice. Mind spinning even though it's running on empty, I press send before I think better of it, and then sink into a fitful sleep with all the parts of my life colliding.

I may not have had the courage to say it while I was at our old house, or at the divorce meeting where we divvied up pieces of ourselves, but this will be my last word. Damn you, Stephanie Dawson, and your idea of me. You'll be sick at the loss of me before I'm through and when I'm done you'll live with the regret for the rest of your life.

The best course for heartbreak and disappointment is resounding success so loud that it drowns out all the hateful words and the silence, and the empty space on the other side of the bed.

This is not where I end. There was a Bryce Dawson before Steph, and I'll make it out on the other end—the kind of person I actually want to be.

# CHAPTER  3

I MAKE IT APPROXIMATELY SEVEN HOURS BEFORE I START FREAKING out. I've been offered an interview, in a town I don't live in, for a job I've never done before.

*Breathe. Just breathe.*

My parents loom at the back of my mind, along with every sacrifice they've made. All their time, all the money they had and didn't have that they're still trying to help me pay loans on. Even though they've never outright said it, the expectation was that I would use my degree for its intended purpose in the most lucrative way I could. When you grow up without the safety of a backup plan or trust fund, there's only one option: to succeed.

They want me to be happy—on the surface I know that—but they also want me to reach my potential and those feel like very different things. They want me to be the version of myself they've always envisioned, the Rachel they hoped for when picturing a child and helping that child grow into success. How do I go about this without feeling like I'm taking a step back, in pay and in prestige? Would they even understand my desire to?

Ángel doesn't get it, and he's said as much. The pressure to perform just doesn't factor into his life. Rachel Mackey, as my parents and the world know me, isn't a risk taker. Employed at Lakin-Cole since before graduation, living in the same apartment for years—I've built a life on being consistent and all it's gotten me is exhaustion and misery.

Ángel doesn't have the firsthand experience of being done dirty by Lakin-Cole but there is someone else who might get it. At least partially.

I shoot the text off before I can second-guess myself.

> Hey, Sebastian. It's Rachel. I was wondering if you had some time to discuss something work related. I wanted to pick your brain on some options outside of Lakin-Cole.

I don't have to wait very long for a reply.

SEBASTIAN

> Finally realizing you're better than they deserve?

A laugh bursts out between my lips and it's a relief, knowing there might be another path for me. I'm not committing to anything. Monday is another workday and I'll be there again, same as always if I don't take that chance in Dulaney. But having a contingency for when I lose my patience is a good plan.

> Keith got Program Manager.

Nothing else needs to be said. I know he'll understand.

> If you're not busy tonight, you're welcome to come join me and Farren for pizza and you can vent all you need. You know I get it.

> Sounds great. Just send me the details.

THEIR PLACE IN ALEXANDRIA IS DISGUSTINGLY CUTE, A WHITE townhouse with cute black shutters and a flower bed that will soon be bursting with blooms once the heat catches up.

Knocking three times, I wait. My clammy hands are wrapped around the neck of the wine bottle and I hope I've made the right choice in what to bring. It's not a housewarming, it's a "thank you for indulging an old colleague and helping her get the courage to escape a soul-sucking environment" kind of gift.

Farren answers within a few seconds, her smile welcoming and warm. She has curves that won't quit and when the light hits her curls they glow golden. I feel overdressed in my dark jeans and blouse compared to her leggings and "You Either Catan or Catan't" shirt and fluffy socks.

"Rachel? Hi. Please, come in." Farren steps aside for me to enter and I try not to wonder just how they found this place in this market.

Following her lead into the kitchen, she takes the bottle of wine and pops it into the door of the fridge to chill. "This is so sweet of you. Thank you! Sebastian is just out picking up the pizzas but he'll be home any second."

Part of me pipes up that I should be uneasy about meeting Farren without Sebastian as a buffer. We are technically strangers, after all, but something about her calm warmth dismisses the thought before I can dwell on it.

The wood floors are pocked and scarred with age but gleam as if they've been polished. The interior is a mixture of cool neutrals with hints of color that brighten up the space and make it feel homey. Fairy lights strung up and wrapped around the curtain rods give the space a gentle glow that an overhead light would've killed. The cocoon effect is continued in the warm white of lamps next to the sofa, light blue and teal throw pillows on the seats, and a chunky-knit cream blanket folded over one of the arms.

Farren settles down on the plush sectional with one leg folded underneath her and I join, my nerves melting away under the comfort of the huge sofa. I mirror her position, my leg tucked under the other, holding the throw pillow I displaced in my lap.

"Comfy, right?" She smiles as if she's had this conversation before.

"Super comfy. You've got a beautiful home."

"Thank you. We lucked out. Sebastian had a big chunk saved up so we were able to put in a down payment. Most aren't that fortunate. It helped that it was a private sale too."

I think of my parents who made sure I had the best even though it put us all in an uncomfortable position. Even with the scholarship to Georgetown, we're still paying off the loans to cover the rest—the interest rate killing us. The payment deducts every month, half from me, half from them. Even with my salary at Lakin-Cole it's slower going than I'd like. D.C. is not a cheap city to live in and I'm the kind of person who prefers to enjoy the money I've earned. Bills first, of course, but Friday night drinks and a show at the Kennedy Center now and then—every little luxury adds up.

"So, you're considering getting out?" Farren asks after my internal rambling stretches too long, saving me from formulating a response.

"Mm, I think it's time. Keith got the promotion I've been working toward."

Farren rolls her eyes, "Ugh, fucking Keith. He's the ass that took up ballroom lessons, yeah? As soon as that wine is chilled we're going to enjoy a couple glasses and get your mind off it. Sebastian might not be as forthcoming about his circumstance before he left but I'll tell you, Lakin-Cole did a number on him. Time away from the company, setting his own hours and picking projects he actually enjoys has made such a huge difference already. He's so much more relaxed."

Farren's expression flits from anger, to concern, to nauseatingly in love as she talks about the situation and Sebastian, and I get it. I can see exactly why Sebastian is all tied up in knots about her.

She's open. What you see is what you get. And despite myself and my tendency to hide behind my careful facade, something about her feels safe enough for me to be wholly honest.

"I've given them everything. Years. All I got for it was them being vague about why they didn't give me the job and then Keith hit on me at the bar when we were out celebrating afterwards." Picking at the texture of the pillow in my lap, the statement is more choked than I expect it to be.

Farren pats my hand and stands.

"This is an emergency and I hope you don't crucify me for it but that wine can't wait. I'm throwing in an ice cube or two. You sit right here. Give me two minutes."

I choke out a laugh and nod. Ángel would cuss me out if I did that, but he's not here to see and I'd take the fuzz of a little bit of wine over decorum right now.

Glasses clink against the countertop and I hear the soft pop of the bottle being opened. The front door whooshes open and shut, the clang of keys tinkling against each other sounds as Sebastian tosses them into a bowl of some kind.

"I'm here!" he semi-shouts.

"Kitchen!" Farren responds and I'm super aware of his socked feet padding toward her.

Staring over my shoulder, I watch as he puts the pizza boxes down on the island and gathers her up into an embrace. His chest to her back as she pours, he smooches the side of her neck and she giggles, pushing him off of her.

"Your guest is here."

I've never felt like more of an observer than right in this moment. Some of Sebastian's ease drains away and he turns to give me a smile—genuine but guarded. He looks different. It takes a moment for me to put my finger on it but it's clear.

"Hi, Rachel."

"Hi." I give an awkward little wave from the couch.

The dark circles and deep brackets beside his frown are gone. His shoulders aren't bowed like they were before, the world on them and weighing him down. The last time I took him to coffee and gave him a pep talk, urging him to quit, he looked like a man on the brink of something dire.

This man looks healthy, happy, and smitten when he glances back at Farren.

"Sorry." Whether he's apologizing to her or me is unclear but he does have the grace to look sheepish at his display.

Farren walks over with our glasses, holding one out to me and we tap them together in cheers as she sits down onto her perch again.

"Babe, bring the box and some plates. We'll eat over here."

I'm back to being thirteen, at a friend's house and totally alarmed at the fact that they get to put their feet up on the sofa and eat in the living room. Even though I've lived on my own for years, and eat wherever there's a free surface in my apartment, something about being a guest here reverts me back to some long-dormant state where my parents' rules sit on me like the coat they insisted I wear out lest I catch my death at the lightest breeze.

We bite into bubbly mozzarella and crusts flecked with the kiss of high heat and flame. In between sips of wine, Farren bridges the gap between the Sebastian I knew and the one he's been able to grow beyond.

"How did you do it? I mean, I know I pushed you to quit, but the aftermath . . ."

"I won't lie and say it was easy; it's taken me a couple months to build up a clientele. Word of mouth goes a long way in the free-lance space—not that you have to go that direction—but that was my experience." Sebastian shrugs.

"I just—I'm conflicted. What if I've wasted the best years of my life there and now I'll be starting from scratch?"

Farren takes this question, her smile kind and understanding. "As someone who has had a slew of jobs as long as my arm and am only now finding my groove juggling substitute teaching and game design part-time, I can say definitively that no time is wasted if you can learn from it. Take what you can from your stint at Lakin-Cole and use it. Even if you don't employ the same skillset, use the way they make you feel and make a promise to yourself that you won't let anyone do this to you again."

All my programming revolts against the concept of letting a mistake just be a mistake because as long as I'm in it there's a chance I can fix it and not be a failure. I balk at the idea of stepping away. But she's right. I cannot keep going like this and I should have seen the writing on the wall before now but I thought my time and effort made me immune. Sebastian wasn't weaker than me. He had the strength to put himself first.

I'm not sure I know how to do that when all my worth has come from the mouths of others.

"I—I don't have the funds built up the way you did. If I leave Lakin-Cole, I'm screwed. D.C. rent is no joke and even though I have a job interview lined up, it wouldn't be enough to cover my current expenses." My faults are piling up. Admitting anything even relating to money feels wrong, another way I'm stepping off the path laid for me. Money talk is crass.

"Is it in D.C. or would you be willing to try something else—somewhere else temporarily—to ease some of the financial strain?" Sebastian asks.

"I'd be willing to try but I want to stay close to the area. Maryland or Virginia is okay, though I wouldn't want to go much further. My parents are getting older and they live in Delaware, so I need to be able to get to them if they need me." Though I doubt they'd reach out even if they do. I learned the mask of perfection from them after all. Admitting need is tantamount to admitting incapability.

Farren has a sharpness to her gaze as if she's latched onto something I'd prefer stayed hidden and she asks, "Any reason Delaware isn't on one of your relocation options?"

"Delaware is a place I worked hard to leave. I'd rather not bruise my ego even further by slinking back."

They both nod, a shared understanding. I sip my wine, more melted ice than anything else now but it gives me something to do rather than talk for a second. If I start I might not stop and I've done such a great job of keeping the different parts of my life separate. Combining them is just messy and allows too much leeway around my boundaries.

Eventually I condense it down as impartially as possible.

"The interview I have is for a longer-term position—so not a one-off—and it's in Maryland, about an hour from D.C. It's something I would do if I wasn't living here, and unfortunately commuting at least an hour each way isn't for me. I'd have to move."

"Where?" Farren asks.

"Some place called Dulaney. It sounds like a fun project too, but I'm torn."

Farren bites her bottom lip as she thinks for a moment. "Show me. Let's take a look at the town and see if moving there is a possibility for you."

"But . . . my lease—"

"Can be dealt with. Trust me." She pats the top of my hand and I let a rush of air out, relieved that someone else is here to help.

I pull out my phone, search underway and it's a charming historical town. Victorians and Colonials and a quaint downtown surrounded by suburbs on the outskirts. It looks like the kind of place you'd go to for a weekend trip. Antiquing and wine tasting, and farm-to-table vibes where you can "support the local economy" and pretend that Dollar Generals and Walmarts don't exist. Not bad. At all. I pull up the rental app I used to get my current place and search for the Dulaney zip code.

The first place I find is at least seven hundred less a month for an actual one bed with a full-sized window. God, that would be nice. The sliver I have now is barely enough to light the place and I always feel a little oppressed when I wake up, as if the ceiling is too close.

There's a spring festival on the first of the month, and the weekly farmer's market starts up in May. They have a June Pride parade and downtown stores are littered with LGBTQIA+ flags with the town emblem on them. There are local Facebook pages with people asking for advice or help and getting responses in the hundreds of others trying to aid. Dulaney screams "community" in a way that feels encouraging.

My first instinct is to run. Not away but toward and I don't know if I'm trying to outrun myself or the expectations that D.C. embodies.

"What's the job?" Sebastian asks, breaking the silence.

"Developing for an escape room company. They are wanting a more interactive and higher tech experience for their clients. Honestly, it sounds like they might need a collaborator rather than a developer but it's not expressly stated in the job title, just the description giving that impression."

An escape room in some town I've never even heard of before now. God, saying it out loud makes it sound like such a downgrade. This choice feels too big for just me to weigh in on.

"Let me see," Sebastian asks and I hand my phone, and the email thread I've shared with Mr. Dawson, over to him.

Sebastian mumbles as he speed reads the job description aloud and hearing it from someone else, it sounds like more creative freedom than I've had in my job, ever. They are definitely open to implementing ideas based on the developer's expertise. Collaborating instead of just doing what I'm told feels like a blast of fresh air after the over-air conditioned office I'm used to.

"They're offering a flat daily rate instead of hourly, which seems a little off, but the job is listed for the next nine months. They want 'Locke Box' ready to open for some kind of Christmas extravaganza—Dulaney's December Fest." I offer the information even though it's on the listing he's looking at, awkward with the silence.

Sebastian then passes the phone off to Farren to get her opinion on all this.

"It's not perfect but it could be a good refresh. There's nothing saying you can't leave if it doesn't suit you. Sebastian can keep an eye out for other opportunities if this one doesn't work out, but personally"—Farren looks at Sebastian with what I can only describe as concern—"if you're anywhere near where Sebastian was a few months ago, you need out. Sooner than later. They don't consider you as a person, just your output and impact on the bottom line. They don't take care of their employees at all. You don't deserve that, Rachel. Give yourself a chance at something else."

"What do I tell my parents?" It sounds stupid to say. I'm twenty-nine years old for god's sake.

"You tell them whatever you feel comfortable telling them."

*Even if that's nothing at all?* I just nod.

"You owe it to yourself to try. We can help you sublet your place if you get it."

Phone back in my hand, I close out the email app and reopen the search on Dulaney. I'm lost in between rows of Colonial brick and trees arching over roads to keep out the sun. I'm mentally sitting on my parents' floral couch like when I had to wait for them to go over my report card and hope I didn't mess up somewhere along the line. Torn.

"You're doing the right thing," Sebastian says, as if he can read my mind—or maybe just my face.

"It's kind of—immense."

Sebastian nods. "It's always scary going from what's comfortable to what's good."

When we say goodbye, I thank them. Farren pats me on the shoulder as if she wants to hug me but knows I'm not a hugger. All the way home I ruminate on Sebastian's statement because it never occurred to me that those things weren't interchangeable.

Comfortable. Stable. Stalwart. Pillars I built my house on. I didn't even let myself consider things that wouldn't contribute to the soundness of my life. Even the majority of people I date are good on paper and terrible on my heart. I'm sure there are still visible cracks where I caulked over the holes left by Riley's duplicity last year—a house I thought was built to last.

Sturdy. I'm sturdy and dependable. And totally forlorn. My willingness to "keep my chin up" and push through and hope things improve clearly isn't working. I'm being overlooked and taken advantage of for my efforts. It's time to change that. Starting with printing the resignation I drafted.

I can't stand to keep working there.

Not after what Andrew said and Keith did at the bar.

I'm choosing what's good.

I'VE NEVER BELIEVED IN LOVE AT FIRST SIGHT. ANYTHING AMOUNTING to fanciful can't be trusted. I might've stayed closer to my convictions if it were a person rather than a place, but it's hard to dismiss my immediate reaction to Dulaney. The U-Haul I'm renting coughs up some fumes as I idle at the stoplight but the sweet scent of early blooms carries on the wind and cuts through the smoke.

The apartment I found is perfect and it took some finagling but I was able to get them to agree to letting me move in immediately. It's premature, I know. I haven't even gotten through the interview yet, let alone been offered the job. But I couldn't sleep on Saturday and—

*Stupid. This is the stupidest, most reckless thing you've ever done.* The voice in my mind is pissed at this turn of events. She was particularly nasty when I dropped my resignation on Andrew's desk first-thing on Monday, effective immediately, and walked out to him sputtering behind me and thrown for a loop before 9 a.m. But I ignored her then, just as I will now. *Choosing what's good.* I remind myself. *Not what's comfortable.*

After quitting, I grabbed a coffee and headed to the Home Depot in Brentwood for a shitload of boxes, and then the U-Haul on the other side of the tracks. Sebastian and Farren agreed to my hasty text message asking them to help me find a subletter. And I spent the next two days feverishly packing up the last ten years of my life from my tiny dorm to my shoebox basement apartment. It takes less time than I expected, something that helps and hurts.

Now, I turn onto Church Street and down the side alley the owners of the building told me about. Feeling far too closed-in by the brick walls on either side with a truck I barely know how to drive, nerves skitter under my skin. Ten years with the Metro have spoiled me and the only time I really drive has been when I'm in Delaware with my parents. Each turn is hairy, every time I have to stop the truck too suddenly I cringe at the sound of my life rattling around in the back. The dress bag with my outfit for this afternoon's interview hangs off the "oh shit" handle on the passenger side and it sways every time I take a turn.

And then I'm in front of the building, hazards blinking. Mr. Collins meets me out front, a kind older gentleman who smells vaguely of pipe tobacco and strong coffee. Handing me an old metal key, I follow him as he explains the eccentricities of the place.

The brick leans more brown than red. Three stories, the middle with a huge bay window that begs to be a reading seat or a spot to people watch. The third floor lives under the charcoal roof tiles, but the windows are full-sized. The ground floor is a cute tea shop that houses rows and rows of flavors and various kinds of sugars. It looks cheery and light through the glass doors. Mr. Collins owns it and the apartment above it.

"There's a spot for a car around back that's included in the monthly rent. Water is also included, as we discussed. You'll be responsible for your own electric and internet." All run of the mill, all things I know.

"The door sticks when it rains, so you'll have to kick the bottom here." He points down at a permanent scuff on the bottom corner, an indentation into the otherwise-beautiful robin's egg blue door.

The hinges squeak when he swings it open and the landing smells a little musty, as if it hasn't taken a proper breath in months, and truth be told, neither have I. We climb the narrow wooden steps and I make a mental note to be careful on a night when I go out for drinks. Taking a spill down these will be nasty. He encourages me to slip my key into the slot and there's something very satisfying about turning a heavy metal key into an antique keyhole. The door has a handle, not a knob—burnished brass that's cool in my hand when I push my way in.

There are coat hooks on the wall beside the door, and a small closet with the water heater in it. If Sebastian and Farren's floors look old then these are ancient. Broad hardwood from old-growth trees is covered by a runner down the entrance passage and one of the planks creaks underfoot as I step fully into the space.

There's an old oil radiator beneath one of the windows in the living room. The room is separated from the passage and kitchen by a stately arch, the rich wood a similar shade to the floorboards. The walls are sage with wainscoting, the window trim white, and I'm completely in love. This house has what Ángel would call "character" and I get it. The space smells like old books, wood oil and dust.

"The upper level is mostly used for store overflow and storage for things we don't have room for in the shop, but feel free to stow whatever you want in there," Mr. Collins says and he continues down the passage.

I can do nothing but follow and try not to run my fingers along the wainscoting as I walk. He points out a bathroom with a clawfoot tub/shower combination with a curtain going all the way around.

"You'll have to give it a few minutes to heat up when you get the shower started. Don't be alarmed if you hear the pipes groan when you do, they're temperamental." He talks about the place like it's a person.

The woodland-themed wallpaper is a slew of dark greens and golds, and I'm not sure I've seen a bathroom with wallpaper instead of tile. The taps are split between hot and cold, metal handles with little white tabs on top that once would have denoted which was which but have since faded.

Mr. Collins continues on, pushing through another squeaky door and I'll have to get some WD-40 for all these unhappy hinges. The bedroom has two large windows that look out over the back yard, a brass queen-size bed frame with no mattress, and soft blue toile wallpaper.

"There's another bedroom just across the hall that the previous tenant was using as an office space, but this is the master. If you think of anything you need, just come down to the shop. We're open most days, except alternating Sundays and if there's some kind of emergency."

I stick my hand out to shake his and his skin is papery and dry in my grasp, some strength still there even though he's got to be at least seventy and should be retired by now.

"Thank you for being so accommodating. I know this was last minute but when I saw the listing I knew."

His smile is understanding, blue eyes crinkled in the corners with the movement. "She's a beauty. If it weren't for all the stairs we probably would've moved in here when we downsized, but my Tess has arthritis in her knees and I'm not getting any younger either."

We drop our hands. "Well, thank you again."

"I'd offer to help you carry stuff up but I'd be no use to you."

"It's no bother. I have some guys coming to help me carry the things inside. The unpacking will be my worry but at least I won't hurt myself trying to cart everything up these stairs." God, I can only imagine how miserable it would be trying to shove my mattress or couch up.

Mr. Collins heads down, his knobby knuckles standing out stark against his skin as he clutches the bannister on the way down. Pulling out my phone I check the progress of the U-Haul guys who are going to help me and they're out front within fifteen minutes.

Standing in the middle of the living room as they make quick work of what took me hours, I direct them like a flight traffic controller from my spot in the middle of nowhere and out of the way.

Boxes with scribbles on each side are stacked in their respective rooms and part of me—the pragmatic part—says I should wait before I unpack them. No point getting comfortable if it's all for nothing. The lack of a backup plan makes my stomach feel like a black hole but if I'm going to go so far out of my comfort zone—so removed from what my parents expect of me—I might as well go all in. Can't focus on anything but the positives right now.

Shucking my moving clothes, I wait a few moments for the shower to heat up and scrub the day from my skin. No hairdryer means I have to French braid my damp hair to keep it under control. The dress is goldenrod yellow, bordering on burnished, and I know it's bold but it plays well with my black hair and brown eyes. It's a warm shade but not as aggressive as red. I pair it with a cream blazer to bolster against the early spring chill.

My usual black dress seemed too somber for an escape room interview.

Fastening my smartwatch to my wrist, I take a deep breath before I slip some plain pearl earrings on, and carefully apply makeup around my dark brown eyes that's meant to look like it's barely there. The semi-steamy bathroom mirror says I look okay. The doubt in my mind says this was a silly idea. I didn't even take the time to google this person. From the name and the general tone of the listing, I'm picturing late forties—someone who's saved up money and is tired of their day-to-day in an office—graying, maybe a little nerdy-looking, not that it's a bad thing to be but my mind has a certain view of the kind of person that would start a business around a concept like an escape room and "jock" isn't it.

We're meeting at a coffee shop a block from here and my heart thunders every step of the way. Waiting for the green walk symbol, I clutch my bag against my body as if it'll protect me from a bad outcome, and my heels eat up the tar with broad steps to cross quickly. Mr. Dawson—*Bryce*—said he'd be sitting in the window with a denim shirt on.

Am I dressed too formally? I didn't exactly have a backup plan and half my closet needs to be ironed after the haste with which I shoved it into bags and boxes.

I round the corner and Bean-y Baby—a nineties-themed coffee shop—is right there. In its large boxed window, a man sits at a hightop table facing the door, his back to me.

His hair is light brown, too dark to be considered sandy but not quite what I'd call brunette, and it's just a little on the side of too long. If I'm right and this is Bryce, then he has some scruff going on his face and a hand wrapped around a ceramic coffee mug—no to-go cup here. I can't make out much more, so I steel myself with a hefty breath and hurry into the building.

The bell above the door tinks as I enter and Bryce's gaze shoots up to catch on mine.

*Fuck.*

Molten honey. The natural highlights in his hair and the flecks in his brown eyes are molten honey behind his roundish tortoise glasses. The teenaged me that was into history and archeology can't help but make the comparison to Indiana in his buttoned up scenes. What might he look like a little scuffed up? My feet carry me toward the table and I have my hand out to shake his out of habit more than thought. His eyes are shadowed with what I have to guess are sleepless nights and his mouth pulls down at the corners, just slightly, as if he's forgotten how to smile.

Bryce stands and I look up. And up some more. I'm not tall by any means but my heels make up the difference most of the time. Today is not one of those. His hand swallows mine, so large and strong and warm from being wrapped around the cup of coffee. And it heats more than just my hand.

*Double fuck.*

"Rachel?" His voice is a little rough around the edges as if he's not spoken much for the day.

"Bryce?" I want to kick myself for how breathless it sounds.

He swallows and I realize we're still touching. My eyes catch on our hands, the difference in sizes and shades. His have freckles, similar ones dotting the bridge of his nose. Denim gathers at his elbow, the shirt folded up over his forearms. More sprinkles of color, more freckles, and I can't help but wonder if he's covered in them.

*For god's sake, girl. Get a grip. If this goes well, he'll be your* boss. *The last thing you can afford is to screw this up because you haven't gotten laid properly in months. That bad rebound after Riley barely counts it was over so quickly.*

Slipping my hand from his, it feels even colder than it did outside with the bite of the early spring wind whipping against it. Bryce slides out the chair for me and I hop up onto the seat, wobbling a little, my feet off the ground. He tucks me in before I can protest.

"I—coffee." Is all I manage as I attempt to shuffle back out but it's awkward with this style of table and chairs. Whoever thought that bar-style seating for anything other than a freaking bar was a good idea, was a fool. I need to get away from him for a minute. I need to get my stupid breathing under control.

He blinks a few times before he stays me with a hand. "Don't stress about it. I'll grab some for you. How do you take it?"

"Americano is fine."

*You hate Americano. What the hell are you doing? It's going to make you jittery and you're already nervous.*

But it's the simplest thing I could think of and after days of running myself ragged, the caffeine is welcome.

His soft lips purse into something I can't place since I don't know him at all to know what it might mean, but he nods and ambles away. All long limbs and big strides, and strong forearms. And almost my fucking boss.

*Don't mix business with pleasure.*

Hands that big . . . would definitely be a pleasure.

*Shut up!*

Bryce is back, the mug looking tiny in his grasp and when he folds himself into the chair, his knees bump against mine under the table. Bryce jerks like I've shocked him even though I'm just sitting here, trying to pull myself together.

"So, escape rooms?" It's awkward but the best I can manage when my mind is misbehaving.

Clearing his throat, he nods, and his left hand wraps around his mug, lifting it for a sip before he answers.

White gold glints on his ring finger and my stomach drops to my feet.

Married. Of course. I should have checked before I let myself thirst like a fool.

*Unfairly hot in a disheveled way. Your boss—maybe? Married. Triple fuck.*

"Yeah, it's a market that's been on the rise for a while. Dulaney is a great town but it's lacking in that regard. The closest to this kind of entertainment is laser tag out by the old mall, but that's nowhere close to what I'm hoping to pull off." It's like a switch has been flicked on.

Bryce changes from kind of tired-looking and worn to awake, gesturing with those hands I'll be thinking about for a while.

"I've been to a few and they always feel kind of formulaic. Usually confined to one room, with the objective of finding a way out of the room . . . which I mean, *escape* rooms—it's kind of in the name, but I don't know. It gets tired after a while," he says.

I take a sip of the scalding coffee, bitter and watery, and not what I wanted but in keeping with my D.C. image. No one takes you seriously when you drink hot chocolate at a meeting. Coffee is a necessary evil. Though maybe I'll be able to ease into myself here. Bryce's denim shirt is kind of casual, right? My blazer is out of place here, surrounded by people in jeans and cardigans, and posters of the Backstreet Boys and Alanis Morissette. It's softer in Dulaney. Maybe *I* can be softer here too.

"What did you have in mind to shake things up?" I ask, actually interested in this now that we've gotten talking.

"Part of what I'm hoping to do is for all the rooms to have multiple spaces to unlock, not just escaping the main room. I'd also like to incorporate more of a goal-oriented outcome, an achievement beyond just being let out of the room at the end of it. There are enough escape rooms out there that stick with the original premise."

I think back to the escape room "team-building" exercise Andrew made us go to earlier this year and I can concede that he's right. It felt futile, too many overly loud voices arguing. One fucking genius swept the room and gathered all the clues and locked items into the middle of the room, completely negating the exploratory aspect of it in favor of winning "quickest time" to escape.

"Where does the development come in? Why are you hiring, I guess is what I'm asking?"

His plush lips tuck into an unhappy line for a moment and he sips his coffee before he responds.

"Honestly, this project is still in its infancy and I might have been hasty in posting that listing, but I thought it would keep me accountable if I knew I was paying someone to help this happen. Mostly, I'd like interactive aspects that I could use to customize the experience based on how it's going. I want magic mirrors, and hidden messages, and an app or program that I can use on my end to mess with the lighting and ambiance depending on the group and their wants."

It does sound like a challenge that could be pretty fun to work on, but the lack of a plan is a little alarming.

"Am I right in assuming that you're looking for a collaborator rather than just a straight-up app or software developer?" Better to get the expectations out before it goes too far.

He winces and then nods. "I'm not trying to mislead anyone with the posting, but this job is definitely more than just regular development. Don't get me wrong, I *need* a good developer, but at this point it's just me and the business part of my brain. I could use a creative touch and someone to bounce ideas off of."

God, I'm about to do it again. I'm about to say yes to a project that'll ask far too much of me and I'll excuse it under flattery at being considered so capable that I can juggle it all.

"Do you have experience in the escape room scene?" I ask.

How has this become an almost reverse interview? I'm not complaining but it does feel a little strange for the shoe to be on the other foot when I was the one that came here nervous out of my mind and trying to plan for every outcome or question. Somehow me asking the questions wasn't on my bingo card.

"Not at all." It sounds almost morose and I'm surprised to see so much doubt and hurt on his face.

"What made you want to get into it?" I pitch my voice kinder, less like an interviewer and more like an actual person asking a genuine question.

"I just got out of a long-time job in the corporate sector. It was exhausting working in that space and having every day feel the same. Mostly, I wanted a fresh start and it was a half-baked, almost manic idea that came to me when I was desperate enough to take a risk."

Good god. Are we the same person? I can't ask that of course. It's unprofessional but—I feel that answer in my bones. Instead I just nod.

"I understand that. I'm just recently out of the corporate space as well—contractor—and I've been looking for something a little less"—*filled with assholes,* my brain quips—"spiritless, I suppose?"

He lifts his coffee mug and it takes me a second to realize he wants me to clink mine against his, cheering our mutual disdain for soul-sucking, cog-in-a-wheel, capitalistic oblivion that our cubicles enforce.

"So, do you have any questions for me?" I lean over and pull my resume out of my bag as I ask, since he has nothing in front of him, not even a notebook. What the hell kind of interview is this anyway?

Hands swallowing the paper, Bryce only gives it a cursory glance before he trains those whiskey and honey eyes on me again.

"I've never done this—interviewed someone. It's pretty obvious, right?" It's said with a wry smile, one that doesn't reach the eyes and tells me he's self-deprecating without the humor.

"I think you're doing an okay job so far. It doesn't always have to be done a particular way." Why am I being so nice to this man? It's not just that I want the job. Rachel from D.C., Rachel the ballbuster, would've made a snide inner comment about how she had to be prepared. It's only fair that the potential employer should have prepared as well.

Rather, I watch as he swirls the dark liquid in his cup around, his eyes transfixed on the little whirlwind within it. "You're kind."

It's a statement from him. Not a "thank you" or a question, or anything other than a passing remark that sings through me. No one has ever called me kind before. I'm too hard for that, too reserved and judgemental, and driven. Except, I feel a little fragile myself and I'm only extending a courtesy I wish would come my way.

Maybe I wouldn't be this detached if I wasn't forced to be by the landscape of my industry.

My peers already consider me lesser for my sex. I've tucked

away the too-feminine, too-forgiving parts of myself to prevent them from getting crushed under Italian dress shoes that cost more than a month's salary.

"Bryce," I say and the taste of it on my tongue feels foreign. Like a new word I've learned but haven't quite translated properly into my careful little boxes. "I get it. I need out. The job I had was going to be the death of me if I kept at it, and even after all the years I gave them, it feels like I have little to nothing to show for it."

He watches me, a studious quality to his eyes made all the more intense by the glasses perched on the bridge of his nose. Pushing them up as an afterthought, he clears his throat before he speaks.

"I can't pay what you were making in D.C." He says it as if I didn't already read the job listing, but before I respond with that he carries on. "This isn't a straight-forward position. It requires many hats. We'll be researching other escape rooms, noting what works and what doesn't. I'll likely need to do remodeling on whichever space I procure—you won't be expected to do that but I want you to know the scope. I'm building a business from scratch and I'm not sure how to make it worthwhile for whoever comes to work for me."

If it is as involved as he says, then the daily rate makes more sense than an hourly programming or developing fee.

"So you're looking for a developer, a research assistant, a sounding board, a collaborator . . . basically a creative partner with a background in developing?" Many hats, like he said.

"It's an unfair ask, so if you don't want it I totally get it."

If I don't want it?

"Wait, does that mean I got the job?"

Bryce looks at me like I'm the silly one for sounding surprised. "Yeah?"

"You didn't ask me anything about my previous job experience, or my goals, or what I'd bring to this endeavor." It comes out involuntarily and I could kick myself for trying to give him reasons to walk back on his offer. But I feel like a kid that studied only to be told there was never any test to prepare for. Dressed up with nowhere to go.

"Your resume was extensive and I reached out to your reference who had nothing but good things to say about the quality of your work. You were five minutes early. You're professional, and you care enough about the project to ask questions about it rather than just trying to butter me up with qualifications that matter less than a willingness to work."

Well.

When he puts it like that.

"I—I want to say yes." But I'm scared to and I'm not sure why. The task is going to be daunting but that's never kept me from trying before. Maybe because for the first time in a long time I am out of my depth and not sure I can pull it off.

"What's stopping you? I'm willing to do what I can to get you on board, within reason of course. This is something I'd like to get underway as soon as possible if I'm going to make the deadline."

"Insurance, for one. It wasn't mentioned—there was no benefits section on the posting—and that's something I'd be uncomfortable going without." Especially living in a strange town and working with a strange man doing all sorts of unlisted activities that didn't make it onto the job description. I cannot afford uninsured trips in the wee-wah wagon—not that I can afford *insured* trips either but . . .

Bryce pulls out his phone, typing something into what I assume are his notes.

"That's a good point. I hadn't even thought of it for myself but it's a necessity for sure. What else?"

"A daily max of hours. The time was vague." After years of

eight hours being the minimum, not the regular, I can't imagine doing that to myself anymore—especially not at a flat rate.

"Eight hours maximum, I swear. Some days might be less, depending on what we have going on but you'll still get your full daily fee regardless. Plus no Mondays or Sundays, unless there's an emergency or clear need. If your job was anything like my previous one, then let me reassure you the last thing I want to do is overwork you."

He's careful in how he phrases it and I know by the way he says it that he'll be overworking whether I do or not.

*It's his business. His problem.*

Quirking one of his brows up as if to encourage me to keep going, I can't help but stare at how his hands envelop the phone he's been typing into.

"I'd like a share. Nothing huge, but if I'm going to be collaborating and contributing creatively as much as you say, I'd like to feel that." It's a huge ask and could be make or break, but I'd be mad if I asked for anything less than what I deserved for hard work provided.

His chest rises with a big breath and shudders on the exhale as he thinks it over.

"You don't have to accept my terms." I steel myself for the rejection. "I'm sure there are others out there just as qualified without as many asks, but I'm not going to take less than I'm worth."

His hand wipes over his scruff as he considers and then he sighs, mind apparently made up.

"Do you want to know why you? I mean, I mentioned knowing your qualifications but it's more than that." His voice is quiet, as if divulging a secret he'd rather not.

Leaning forward on my elbows to absorb what he's about to say, I wait on tenterhooks.

"Your cover letter. I—there was such a—"

*Desperation? Bitterness?* My snarky little mind-gremlin remarks and I hate that she's right. It was those things. I've never felt more like Meredith Grey doing that whole "Pick me. Choose me," thing since I sent out my first applications in college.

"—hunger to it." Bryce doesn't sound put off, and I like the way he phrased that.

I am hungry. For praise. For validation. For being someone's first choice when it comes to work.

*And other things?*

Married. He's married and I'm not looking to get into a relationship now. There's too many pieces in the air; if I started dating on top of all of it I would lose my focus. If I have any hope of this being a way to prove to myself, and others like Andrew, that I have what it takes to lead a project from the ground up—then I need to stay on track.

"It resonated with me. This isn't just a trivial project for me. I have . . . people that have doubted my ability to tackle something like this. I've been accused of being too meek and *compliant.*" Bryce spits the word like it's poison and I can't fathom that being true.

He might not be the most forceful person I've met but there's a quiet way he holds himself that feels capable. Solid. Steady and dependable and so much like how I try to come across that I wonder if my inner doubt is what people see instead.

"I aim to prove them wrong. This isn't a joke to me. I'm sinking every penny of my money into this and I plan for it to succeed. So I need someone as hungry as I am to make that happen."

Something I can relate to, considering I've thrown a bunch of money into moving before I even knew I had the job. So, I stop pretending this isn't what I want and stick my hand out across the table.

Bryce blinks at it for a second before he realizes what I'm

saying with that gesture. His large hand folds around mine again, and we shake on it. Lips quirked into the beginnings of a smile, those golden flecks in his eyes almost seem to sparkle.

"When can you start? Do you plan to commute or do you need help finding someplace nearby? I might be able to put some feelers out for you." His words come out in a rush, excitement an undercurrent to the haste.

My chuckle stops Bryce for a moment and he sits back as if he's realized he's overstepping—and with the tug between us notices he's still touching me. Our fingers release and his hands knit together on the table top as he schools his expression back to the neutral-if-sad one from when I first clapped eyes on him.

"No need. I've got it handled. Is tomorrow too soon to start?" No point mentioning how overeager I am that I've already got an apartment for a job that wasn't mine at the time.

"Would Saturday work for you? I need some time to put things together—a contract and that sort of thing. I also need to reach out to a realtor to find the right space and viewing venues on a Saturday when we can get a good idea of weekend foot traffic would probably be best." His smile is careful but devastating because I can tell just how much it would change his face if it was a full-on grin. Potential is always painful. Unfulfilled usually, and a word that says "not good enough." Although I hate to think it and lean into the stereotype of being unsatisfied with what he's given, I want a real one of those. A smile that goes all the way and not just a mirage of what it could be.

Why, I couldn't say—or am not willing to.

One thing's for sure. When I get back to the apartment I have two phone calls to make. First, Sebastian and Farren to thank them and update them, and figure out if my apartment has been leased so that's one less bill I have to worry about this month. And then Ángel.

Who is going to flip his lid when he finds out.

"Saturday is great. Would you like my phone number?" I ask, and then clarify, "Just to coordinate."

He slides his phone across the table with the "new contact" screen open so I do the same and it feels weirdly intimate to give someone my unlocked phone. Typing my name, number, and email into his phone, a message comes through on the little notification preview and I'm quick to hand it back over before I can read further than:

> **MOM**
>
> How did it go?
>
> Is she nice?
>
> I hope you—

My cheeks flame a little and I tuck my chin down as if I'm examining his contact in my phonebook.

But he doesn't notice because he's moving to stand, his phone dropped in his pocket. Our coffees are done and so is the interview now that we've reached an agreement. Bryce walks over to my side of the table and holds out a hand for me to take while dipping down off the bar stool.

It makes me think of that stupid scene in Beauty and the Beast, though that could just be because it's such an old-fashioned thing to do that it reminds me more of a fairytale than reality.

Whoever his wife is, she's lucky to have someone with good manners. The last time I went on a date they slammed the car door before I was fully inside and part of my dress got caught in it, flapping along for the entire drive. And then they rushed ahead of me into the restaurant, not even glancing back to see whether or not I was following.

Bryce and I stand like that for a second, my hand in his and my feet a little unsteady now that I'm back on solid ground.

"I'll see you Saturday," I croak and he drops my hand like it's burned him.

"Saturday." He agrees and then strides from the coffee shop.

And when he walks by the window, his mind on something else entirely and his gaze locked on the path ahead, he flexes his hand.

*That was so hot.*

Oh, I am in trouble.

*Fuck. Fuck. Fuck me.*

*And I kind of wish he wasn't married so he would.*

# CHAPTER 4

My phone buzzes in my pocket as I walk back to the parking garage, reminding me that I've ignored my mother's text message. One I hope Rachel didn't see.

Scratch that. *Messages*. I thumb through them as Dulaney passes me by, my mind on so much more than just downtown and all its memories.

MOM

How did it go?

What is she like?

Is she nice?

I hope you weren't too nervous.

We love you.

Please pick up a gallon of milk and some toilet
paper at the grocery store on the way home.
Your father got sidetracked and forgot when he
went out yesterday.

My mother's little barrage of messages swirl in my mind and I
don't know what to say. Circling the block, driving aimlessly
through downtown, I can't quite go home yet. Not while I'm so
keyed up and unsure of myself.

That was weird, right? That *interview* that was barely one at all
was the last thing I expected when she walked through the door
in her business garb with her tidy braid and her heels clicking
against the floor.

The first thing I saw and thought was that she was like
Stephanie. Polished. Professional. Ambitious. Should I really be
surprised that I found myself drawn to another person that is
more like who I want to be than who I actually am?

But then she struggled to hop up onto the chair in her heels
and she gave me such a raw once-over that I realized she might
have a veneer but it isn't guile. She bit her bottom lip in thought
before she launched into another question and even though it was
hard for me to force myself to meet her gaze the whole time—my
own discomfort aside—I couldn't help comparing her rich dark
brown eyes to the city roast Arabica beans Gerard keeps behind
the counter to make the shop smell inviting.

What is she like?

Pretty. Rachel Mackey is far more attractive than I was ready
for. She is quick and engaging and has the tiniest hint of a dimple
in her right cheek that never quite fully made its way out in her
half-smiles. The way she looked up at me, dark eyes and dark
hair, and closer than I've been to anyone in months, practically
sent me running as soon as I was sure that she'd be a good fit for

the job. She's stunning and that's not something I can focus on right now—and definitely not something I plan on divulging to my mother.

The last thing I can afford is to crush on my employee. I might as well throw my money out the car window while I drive through Dulaney if I'm going to let that stand.

I'm on my second drive up Main when I actually take stock of some location options. The stately Old National Bank-turned-Borders is empty and has been since they went bankrupt. Two blocks down, Dulaney's allegedly haunted old movie theater has shuttered and the marquee is yellowed and broken with only an "F" and "U" remaining. And a few blocks away, on the edges of the downtown area—further from the foot traffic than I'd like—is the old plant my grandfather worked at, sanding and sawing furniture he never got to bring home, working his hands into a rough surface I loved and hated to shake hands with on Sundays.

It's a strange juxtaposition, the old and the new trying to coexist in a place that hasn't quite found its footing in the current era. They're trying. The flags and the festivals, and the locals revitalizing this part of town but those empty locations—forgotten for a while—say that we aren't quite there. Taking pictures of every location with a "To Lease" sign out front, I finish my meandering.

Eventually I gather my wits enough to head over to the grocery store closest to our development and when I get home with my mom's requested goods she's in the kitchen finishing up on a pan of lasagna that's way too much food for just the three of us.

"Thanks for picking those up." She hugs me with her oven mitts still on and doesn't even wait for me to respond before she launches into something else.

"So . . . tell me about this girl."

"She's not a girl, that's demeaning to her and the work she's put into her career." It's blunter than I intended but something about the way my mom phrases it—the same way she would've asked if I'd just gotten back from a date—rubs me the wrong way. Maybe not because of how she'll perceive Rachel but instead how she'll perceive me and my reaction to her.

It takes such a long time to untangle my mind. I'd rather not have to do it in the moment in front of my mom.

"Well . . . yes. Still, how was it?"

She's not going to drop it and I hate the way I understand it. Once she's started on something, no matter how small and benign, it sticks in her mind like a burr—same way it does for me. Breathing through the choice between keeping my thoughts close so I have the chance to tuck them in their proper boxes or getting my mom off my back and out of her loop . . . I give in.

"I offered her the position. She seems very nice and took genuine interest in the idea. I'll need your help with some of the contract stuff because she raised a lot of good points and I'd appreciate feedback from both you and dad before I put it all in writing. We're meeting up again on the weekend so she can sign and to take a look at some options for spaces."

If she can sense my slight agitation, she makes no show of it. Then again, my mother and I are so alike when it comes to emotions—hard to express, intense but private unless we state otherwise.

"That's good. You know we'd be happy to help however we can. Whatever makes you happy is what matters to us." She gives me a small smile before she turns her head toward the living room where my dad's likely watching some How It's Made show. "Frank! Dinner's ready."

We settle around the kitchen table, pasta slightly too hot for comfortable consumption steaming on our forks and red sauce dripping when we're too slow to catch the bites in our mouths.

"Bryce says he needs help with some business stuff." My mom introduces the topic and I'm grateful.

"I offered the position but she had some asks—namely insurance, set maximum work hours, and a stake."

My father sucks a whistle into his mouth, "Smart. Definitely the right stuff to ask for. You gonna do it?"

"I told her I'd think about it and draw up a contract for her to sign this weekend. I'd like to say yes. I agree. Those are good things to ask for. I'm just a little upset that I didn't think about them first. In fact, I felt pretty unprepared for the interview on the whole. Being on the other side of this is stranger than I expected."

"You can't plan for everything, bud. No matter how much you want to. Sometimes there might just be something you missed, and that's okay." Frank Dawson is the kind of man that lives open and loud. Not a single emotion can hide on that face, including the kind smile he gives me now as he pats the top of my hand in commiseration.

"I want this to work."

"And it will. Your dad and I are here to help. Now, I'll draft up the contract and you and your dad can go over some potential locations. He might know someone in town that can help."

"Thank you, both." I've missed this—missed them. So much of what I had with Steph was private, and I liked it that way, but it made for lonely times when things became strained between us. Having the people who know me best to support me isn't something to scoff at.

I need unbiased outsiders to steady me when I get distracted. I need people who didn't feel how soft yet strong Rachel's grip was or the way she smelled like something understated and herbal, soothing instead of overly sweet. It may have only been an hour or so with Rachel Mackey, but she's done enough unbalancing to make me fixate on the wrong things. I need my parents to get me back on track.

It shouldn't matter how she smells, or looks, or how her voice is warm and even. Her merits and resume should speak for themselves, but I can't lie and say I'm not intrigued. She doesn't fit into the premade boxes I have, and only a few others in my life—people I've had years to become accustomed to—defy the parameters I have in place to understand people.

Stephanie fit comfortably in her box that came with its checklist of ways I had to please her, and still it wasn't enough. Just how the hell am I supposed to cope with someone I have no precedence for?

SATURDAY ARRIVES IN A BLAZE OF SPRING SUNSHINE CUTTING through the garage apartment window and the sound of my father mowing. Despite the nerves eating up my stomach, I managed a couple of hours sleep, and I step into a hot shower to perk me up enough to get through dressing.

Henley and jeans this time. The second meeting we'll be having where I'm not in my usual scratchy button ups and slacks. I don't know what it says about me as a business owner but the fabric is soft, long sleeves to stave off the still-chilly breeze, but thin enough for when the sun bakes the indoors. Despite the futility of it, I give myself a once-over in the bathroom mirror before I leave.

A little too shaggy for the office. My hair is longer than I usually keep it and the scruff I've kept at varying lengths over the last nine months has slowly become familiar. Paired with my outfit, I look—relaxed. Even though that word doesn't really feel like it suits me. Quiet, yes. Careful, usually. Relaxed, not within my mind.

Fastening my boots, I do my regular double knot. I should have told her to forgo the heels this time, in case we have any uneven flooring or way too many steps, but even if I'd thought about it sooner—we've less than an hour until we meet up at the old bank—I doubt I'd have gone through with it. Who am I to tell her how to dress? Why should it matter to me at all?

"You heading out? All ready?" My dad calls from his spot in the backyard as he watches me get into the car, wiping his forearm against the sweat gathered on his brow.

"As I'll ever be."

The ride downtown seems to take forever and I hit every red light on the way there. By the time I'm parked with the meter paid and outside the steps of the Old National, Rachel is already there.

And chatting up a storm with Jim—the real estate agent I've reached out to for help—one of my dad's not-quite-friends-but-friendly-acquaintances people.

"Ah, Bryce!" He steps forward and gives my hand an enthusiastic shake. "I was just telling Miss Mackey here that we've got an exciting lineup. I've got you scheduled for the three you mentioned and if those don't work for you, I can set up some others for another day. There are two options I know of on my end. It'll be a packed morning but your dad emphasized how important it is to get a jump start on this, so I hope you both are ready."

Rachel gives him a smile, one that has the tiniest flash of dimple, but not all the way there yet. When she turns that smile to me I almost choke.

She's not in heels. She's not in anything stuck up at all.

Jim swings the heavy doors inward and she follows close behind in loafers, her shapely legs clad in blue jeans, and a button down loosely tucked into them. It should look semi-professional but something about the oversized shirt on her petite body, the collar slightly askew and the buttons around her throat undone that is a little too—rumpled for me to get my mind off.

And boy is my mind having a field day wondering what she'd look like in one of *my* shirts.

"It'll need a lot of work but there's some offices off to the side, two conference rooms upstairs, and the vault is a pretty fun touch!" Jim's voice bounces through the cavernous space, the super high ceilings and emptiness stretching and throwing his words around.

The space could be beautiful. Marble and heavy steel and possibilities. But there's ugly eighties industrial carpeting curling up off the floor, yellow glue tacked underneath it and covering whatever tile or wood lay beneath. The offices and conference spaces are separated by glass and cubicle-type walls. None of this is conducive to creating a "locked-in" feel and it would be a bitch to keep clean, not to mention heated in the winter.

"What do you think?" Jim asks and Rachel looks up at me, all big bright eyes and questions behind them.

"It's lovely but I'm not sure it's the right space. I don't mind the double levels but it does make it much harder to see multiple rooms happening at once. I think I'd prefer something a little closer with definite separate rooms or the capability to easily make them." I say to both of them and she nods, as if mentally notating what I'm saying.

Jim walks us the two blocks to the old movie theater, chatting to Rachel about the history of the town and she soaks it all up.

"Dulaney was settled in the 1700's by a family from Ireland. Since then it's been home to slavery, war, ghost stories, and so many German immigrants that it has a sister-city back in Bavaria. A lot of families have been here a long time and you'll hear a lot of people with the same names as our streets. We had a big flood in the nineties that damaged a lot of downtown. Since then it's been bits and spurts of progress. We're finally getting to a point where people are starting to move back and revitalize the town."

Jim looks back over his shoulder at me and gives me an approving nod. "People like Bryce here, for instance. I can tell you, my grandkids will absolutely love this place, especially since the ice rink closed down ten years ago. It'll be good to keep people entertained and out of trouble."

As if to emphasize the words "closed down", we round the corner to the theater and Jim gets us inside. There's little light here, the opposite of the bank, and so dusty that it sticks at the back of my throat. I clear it once, twice, and give up.

The theater isn't a bad option at all. There are well defined rooms where each screen used to be set up. Even though the ceilings are still quite high, and the chairs will all need ripping up—along with the carpet—*god*, so much carpet. The walls are covered in graffiti and there's a lot of random trash littering the place. But there's a long passage up above between the projector rooms, which I didn't know as a kid, that will serve us well. I thought each little window in the back was its own room. Instead it's a long hallway with little nooks for each, no bigger than a bathroom or coat closet.

Throughout our little trek Rachel thinks to ask Jim how many outlets are in the room, and how long the place has stood empty. Jim recommends a good inspector and makes an offhand comment about the electric being older than dirt and off for years.

Overwhelm sneaks up on me. Between the stuffy rooms, the dust clinging to my skin and throat, and the dark I have to squint through to get an idea of what I'm looking at, it's beginning to grate. This might be a good option but I'm ready to quit it now. I make a show of looking down at my smartwatch.

"Hey, Jim. I like this place better than the bank but I have Rachel in a bit of a time crunch and I'd love to be able to narrow it down some more."

She looks up at me, her face half shadowed, mouth open to contradict what I'm saying but something akin to understanding flashes across her face and she just nods instead.

"You got it. I'll just lock up but you guys feel free to head on over to the mill in the meantime. I'll meet you there."

We step back out on the curb. Jim's parked on the opposite side of the block from me and is fussing with the heavy chains someone's added in addition to the regular locks—no doubt thanks to the graffiti. Rachel stands out on the corner and soaks up the street around her, just starting to brim with people walking their dogs and browsing the shops that have opened since our quest began.

"I'll meet you over there?" I ask and her attention snaps back to me.

Biting down on her bottom lip she takes a deep breath before speaking. "It might take me a minute to get there."

"I get it. The area is still new to you and it can be hard to navigate the one-way streets downtown."

"Actually, it's more the fact that I'll be walking." She hoists her bag a little higher onto her shoulder as if preparing to do just that.

"Walking?" I ask.

"Yeah. I don't own a car." It's a little sheepish but not ashamed.

"Oh."

*Oh.*

Really? That's the best I can manage? But there are too many questions sparked by that one sentence and I'm not sure which to go with. Luckily the rational part of my brain wins out over the curious one.

"You're welcome to drive with me. I'm parked just down the street." I point, as if it were necessary.

"I'd appreciate that. Thank you. I'd hate to slow you and Jim down. Since we're on a time crunch and all." It's said tongue-in-cheek, as if she's uncovered my secret and wants in on it. Her smirk is there then gone when I don't immediately respond, my mind whirling trying to figure out how much of it is teasing.

Rachel looks up at me expectantly, so much shorter than my six four now that she's in flats, and I realize that despite my pointing she has no idea which car is actually mine nor does she have a means to get in without me.

My strides eat up the difference but she keeps up, her hair bobbing along in its ponytail as she walks alongside me. My dad's voice is in my ear when we get to the car and I open the passenger door for her.

"Thank you." This time the dimple creases her cheek and I find myself giving her an answering smile of my own.

The radio hums quietly as we chug down Main toward the outer parts of downtown.

"Hey, I know we don't know each other very well, and it might be presumptuous to say this to my new boss on day one of working but . . . I'm here to help. Let me know if I can. I don't want to overstep or anything so if my questions with Jim were pissing you off I'd rather you let me know outright." She's turned to face me, and I can practically feel her eyes on the side of my head.

"No. No! That's not it at all." I steal a glance at her at a red light, hoping she can see the sincerity on my face, and pretending I'm not trying to pick out the shades of warm earth in her eyes. "I'm—not very good at this stuff. I've never been anyone's boss and I've never run a company, and I'm worried I'm in over my head."

Rachel is puzzling me over, the same way I'd like to do to her. "So, you weren't mad that I was kind of getting into the thick of it there? I'm not trying to be bossy or overbearing."

Part of me wants to ask why there's a tinge of worry, a negative turn to her words as if she's been accused of them before and is waiting for some kind of inevitable.

"Not at all. Please, ask whatever you can think of. I value your input. The only reason I wanted to leave was because it was starting to get to me. I don't do very well in the dark. Plus with the dust . . . it just felt like the place was looming, shrinking around me." I'm not usually this honest, and never with people who don't know me and how I can be, but the last thing I want is her thinking she's done something wrong.

My hands tighten on the steering wheel, leather creaking a little as they do and I remind myself to do that deep breathing exercise they had us practice at the company's one-month-stint of office-wide morning yoga sessions.

"Oh." Is all she says before she clears her throat, likely weighing her words. "I'm that way with temperature. If I get too hot, it's over. I can't focus on anything else. I'll never live in Florida, I can promise you. That's not even accounting for the alligators and the snakes." She shivers with disgust and I can't help the chuckle that escapes at the sight.

And it's just that simple. In a few sentences Rachel Mackey has turned me inside out and right way round, dusting off the shoulders and I'm ready to go again. When I look over at her—not at a stoplight but a rather risky stolen glance after changing lanes—she's looking out the window and drinking in the sight of the old Civil War markers along Main, each picture describing an event. My freakout is over, washed away by understanding and letting go.

"I have to ask. Why Locke Box?"

"It's my middle name. Bryce *Locke* Dawson. Not quite sure what my parents were thinking but it serves my purpose well enough now."

"Meant to be, for sure." Our eyes meet at the next red light, the last one before the mill, and something weird curls inside me at her words and the conviction behind them.

Maybe she's right. Maybe this *can* work, if I let it.

My rumination is cut short when we pull up the gravel drive toward the mill. Our arrival is a rush of tires, the click and zip of the seatbelts set free, and shoes on shifting ground. This time when Jim lets us inside, Rachel lets her questions run wild.

I follow behind them, acclimatizing myself to the sawdust smell from outside, before it can get too overwhelming. The floors are concrete and the brick building stands tall around us. Small square windows take up most of the upper parts of the walls and I swear I can still smell the machinery even though it's been gone for years.

My grandfather brought me here on a tour when I was a kid and somehow the impression of it stuck—the work benches, the loud grinding of the saws against wood. My eyes are covered with protective glasses and too-big ear covers held against my head with my hands. I must have been seven or eight.

I miss him.

"So, what do you think, Bryce?" Rachel asks, pulling me from my memory.

It's not right. No matter how much I want it to be. No matter how much it makes me think of family and tradition, and Dulaney.

"It's a stunning space but it would probably be better suited to an event venue or brewery than an escape room."

Jim slaps me on the shoulder as we head back out. "Oh ho, you are speaking my language. You ever decide to open up a brewery and I will be your first customer."

I huff out a laugh at his enthusiasm and I realize I've missed this too; not just my grandfather but Dulaney and the people that make it feel like home no matter how long I've been away.

"I don't know. Letting you in would also mean I'd have to be the one to kick you out if you got too rowdy and if I recall a certain barbeque during mine and your son's senior year of high school, you definitely know how to rile up a crowd."

Jim's face is confused for a moment as he rifles through the years and when he comes upon the memory I'm referencing—the day our high school won the championship and he decided to play DJ and dancer, complete with an AC/DC air guitar and leg kick—he bursts out into guffaws.

"What a blast from the past that is. You're right though, better stick to this escaping thing. From what *I* remember you were always messing around with stuff like that. I just hope you've gotten better at it."

My cheeks flame at the reminder and Rachel's expression is careful as she absorbs all she can from our interaction.

"Here's hoping. Thanks for helping us out today. I'll be in touch with you soon on whether or not we need to view those other two properties you mentioned."

And then Jim's out of there and it's just me and Rachel and the ghosts of my past.

"Lunch?" she asks, walking toward my car, and only then do I feel the hunger gnawing at my stomach and remember I skipped breakfast as well.

"Lunch sounds great. You let me know where you're staying and I'll drop you off afterwards as well."

"There's actually a Japanese place right across from my apartment I've been interested in trying. I'm over on Hoffman."

We drive in quiet, me lost in thought and Rachel entranced by Dulaney in a way that I have forgotten to appreciate. Once or twice she asks me about a particular building—the local canning plant where they make everything from jams right through to soups and pickled vegetables. A hollowed out shell of stone that used to house a few small businesses—like the tailor that helped me with a tux for prom when nothing suited my tall and broad frame—that burned down a couple of years ago. There's a plaque out front with plans to turn it into a community garden.

I pull out onto the street, lucky to find a spot near the restaurant, and back into the parallel parking. Not even thinking about the fact that I've got my arm across the back of her seat and I've turned myself to look out of the rear window, until I hear a small snick in her breathing, as if it stopped for a moment and she had to remind herself to start again.

"I'll—uh. I'll go get us a table while you pay the meter." Rachel is out as soon as the car's no longer in motion and I can't even begin to unravel what just happened.

Pulling out my phone, I buy us two hours on the parking app. It's overkill but I'd rather not take a chance on getting towed. When I get inside and up the stairs to the second level, Rachel is sitting in a small booth by the window, staring out at the street we just came from.

As if she can sense my approach—despite the steady din of the restaurant—her ponytail whips over her shoulder as she turns her head to face me. And somehow, with no particular reason I can put my finger on, I know I am in a world of trouble.

I'm a mess of grief, anger and determination, and somehow—impossibly and inconveniently—there's a stirring of something I haven't felt for a long time. One I'm not ready to name. Something that I can't afford to entertain right now.

I slide into the booth opposite her and she tugs the table closer to her to accommodate my legs, a small smile on her face like it's nothing . . . as if she'd done it out of reflex alone and not consideration.

Rachel flicks through her menu, handing me one to peruse on my own, but I'm stuck. On silky black hair, and big brown eyes, and the uncomfortable feeling of being seen—and liking it.

# CHAPTER  5

Why does he have to be so . . . so . . . Ugh.

It's impossible to focus. All morning has been me trying my best to be professional, to ask the right questions and toe the proper line. I have to make a good impression. I can't afford to mess this up. My rent's been paid for the month and Farren texted me that they might have a subletter, but I'm hanging on by my fingertips when it comes to cash flow and this job is the only thing standing between me and having to slink back home—a disappointment.

It's for that very reason that I am incredibly pissed at my inner comments throughout the location scouting experience. Because, despite her usual propensity for snarkiness and pulling me back on track through deprecation, my inner voice has latched onto something else to focus on.

Namely, Bryce Locke Dawson—my cute, definitely kind of shy and surprisingly vulnerable boss. So different from the picky, arrogant assholes in D.C. walking around like their biology alone is something I should bow down to. Bryce's got that fucking Hallmark Christmas movie hero vibe and despite how awful I pretend those movies are, I still swoon when Mr. Small Town shows up in his laid back outfits after all the stuffy suits.

*That henley, man . . . Whoa. You know, those romance writers have it right. It's definitely a main character type of outfit. Between Hallmark movies and my secret romance stash on my kindle, he's definitely swoonworthy.*

Stop. No. We are not doing this right now.

I grip my menu tighter, my eyes blurring on words, skimming all the way from gyoza to the lunch bento without seeing a single descriptive ingredient. How can I when my mind keeps getting tripped up on that moment in the car? Bryce rested his arm on my seat, backing into the parking spot with no help from a fancy little back camera. Just gripped the headrest in his big hand, the heat off his body close enough to feel, and a whiff of either his body wash or cologne sending my head spinning.

*Boss, boss, boss,* I chant to myself.

*Married. Married. Married.*

I am not this kind of woman. I don't step in places where I don't belong. Every Friday at the bar I am careful to check for rings, to talk and gauge, and make sure that my momentary lapse —my stupid need for companionship—doesn't ruin it for someone else. Maybe he's hot to me *because* I know he's unavailable and therefore I can't and won't pursue anything—a form of self preservation to protect me from getting hurt.

It's been a long time since I let myself be vulnerable in front of another person, and the response made it so I don't really want to do it again. My ex-girlfriend Riley was understanding, until she wasn't. What we were worked, until it didn't. Riley had no qualms about blowing up our relationship and someone else's by cheating because my weakness scared her. So, I go out on Friday nights, and I find something meaningless to tide me over until it stretches too long or I get too tired of pretending.

I'll have to find a pub or a bar to socialize nearby. I'm lucky that Ángel wasn't working and expecting me at the bar this weekend but I'll have to actually call him and let him know that I'm officially no longer in D.C. and our tradition will have to be on hiatus until I get back. I've been too scared to tell him. Like that will finally make it all real even when the job and the apartment don't.

*If you go back.*

What? Of course I'm going back. This is a temporary position, once I'm more financially secure and I've had a chance to find my footing in the freelance community—or something more permanent again—I'll be back.

*Where you started?*

I so do not have time for this. I'm trying to focus on the present and the moment I find myself in—the space I find myself in. So much has changed in a week, it's astounding to me.

Bryce's leg is bouncing under the table and I don't think he even notices how it's making the little floral arrangement on the table rock. Is he nervous too or is it a regular thing for him? I find myself wanting to figure out how he thinks, what's going on behind those gold-flecked eyes and too-serious expressions.

He's not . . . grumpy, exactly. But he has an air to him that says something is weighing on him. Bryce was kind enough to set me at ease when I worried that I was overstepping, driving the situation and the conversation with Jim. It's refreshing to know that I'm not "in the way" or that my initiative isn't intimidating him. It's few and far between that I've met people—men especially—who are willing to admit they don't know what they're doing and need help.

I didn't miss the way his lips parted in surprise when I didn't make a big deal of his opening up to me. But I'd want the same.

I'd want it to just be normal. It's hard enough telling the truth when you're afraid of what it says about you without the other person making you feel self-conscious. Today was—exciting. Each building had its own character and imagining how things could look in the space we were in was a challenge I hadn't considered and far more fun than I thought it would be.

Being outside of a cubicle, away from gray walls, squeaky rolling chairs and the constant clack of fingers on keyboards was so refreshing I'm worried I might not be able to return to it if this keeps going well.

*Don't celebrate early. There's plenty that can still go wrong.*

My stomach grumbles, pulling me from my head. Fuck. I need to focus.

Settling on the first thing that sounds good, I place my order with our waiter, and Bryce follows suit. His voice is a low rumble against the torrent of my thoughts, soothing.

*Stop.*

I switch tactics.

"So, how do you think today went?" I ask, desperate to center myself in this conversation and avoid more thoughts. Plus, I am curious about his opinion. He didn't really share it while we were on location.

"Not awful. It's going to be a lot of work and I think I didn't realize until today just how much is going to be required. Obviously, I could go for a strip mall or something else that's a quick fix of flimsy walls. But I want character. I want downtown, charm, and history."

I get it. My eyes have been glued on every inch of Dulaney I've been able to see. Downtown is especially interesting because you can tell when certain parts were built. Some homes and businesses have a solidly colonial feel to them but there are a good share of Victorian style buildings as well. Turrets and trim, and colorful accents that seem at odds with the stoic and serious white or brick squares with shutters on each window and a door in the middle. Gingerbread houses and George Washington.

D.C. had its own flair and influences from all over the world, but in Dulaney those influences feel . . . closer and more intimate. "I think you're off to a good start. Once you've decided on a building we can brainstorm some room themes and puzzle ideas for me to work on while things get fixed up."

His sigh is unmistakable and I get the feeling that he's trying hard to hide how overwhelmed he is. I get it. I would feel the exact same way if the roles were reversed.

"Speaking of working together. I've got a contract for you in the car. I meant to give it to you earlier but I was caught up in location scouting. It includes your asks on health care, maximum hours, and that share you mentioned. My mo—managerial person who's been advising me drew it up. Please take a look at your leisure. If you see anything you don't like or want changed, let me know. You can text me when it's done or just give it to me the next time we get together for work."

Bryce props his chin up on his fist, elbow on the table, and again I hear my mom's insistence on proper manners and elbows *off* the table rear its head. She's drowned out fairly quickly by the grating voice in my head that's latched onto the image of his shirt sleeve pushed up to the crook of his elbow, his forearm out for all to see.

God, I need to calm down. This isn't the Victorian Era and I'm not some scoundrel panting over a flash of ankle. He's my boss. He's also like three feet away and staring directly at him is getting a little overwhelming. "That sounds great! I uh—I'll be right back." I scoot out from the booth and turn back to face him. Why, I don't know.

He's got a question on his face so I blurt, "Ladies room," before scurrying off to some area behind Bryce even though I have no idea where it is in the first place.

Rounding the corner, I target the first employee I see and they very kindly point me in the right direction. Staring at myself in the restroom mirror—my eyes wide and cheeks flushed, my hair a little windblown from our walking—I can see the underlying fear and excitement in my eyes. I want this to work. I *need* this to work. With student loan bills, my parents' ever-looming expectations, and my desire to prove I'm more than just a fucking skirt at a keyboard, I can't afford for it not to.

My phone buzzes in my hand, a text message from my parents popping up and dread replacing the excitement in my reflection.

MOM

Hope you are well.

Your father and I are having a good time at Bethany beach before all the tourists arrive for the season.

How is work going?

Theoretically, I know this is sweet and she's checking in on me but it never escapes my notice that my mom doesn't ask me about my well-being, only about my job. Before that it was questions about school, no boys (or girls) and nothing too deep. It's always like that, like she's scared that if the question does come up and the answer isn't what she expects, she won't know where to go.

Everything with Sarah Mackey is carefully crafted. Despite an average, just-below-the-comfort-of-middle-class upbringing, my mother has worked hard to give the appearance of more. Saying the right thing—being measured in how she does it—dressing the right way . . . my mother's always tried to present herself well to get into people's good graces.

Not that there's anything *wrong* with that, but it does make it hard to confide in someone who is more concerned with how things look than how they actually are below the surface. As long as I look okay, as long as my job sounds good, that's enough for her.

I suck in a deep breath, half to quell my overreaction to Bryce's freckled forearms and half to steel myself into giving the proper response.

> Glad to hear you all are enjoying yourselves.
>
> Have some boardwalk fries for me!
>
> Work is going well, just busy as usual. Very much same old, same old.
>
> Thank you for checking in. Hope you guys enjoy the rest of your stay.

I hesitate between calling it a visit. Then a stay. Then a break. Then a vacation. Typing and erasing, the three little dots making my message likely seem far longer on her end than it is in actuality. There's no way I can tell her that I quit my "dream job" just when it looked to her like I was going to start moving up. There's even less of a chance that I can admit I've "thrown it all away" on a position that isn't permanent and doesn't pay nearly as well as the previous one.

Another big sigh works its way out of my lungs and I pat some cold water onto my cheeks to ground myself. I've responded. We both know the other is alive and *apparently* well. If she sends anything back I can reply later. There's no point working myself up over this while Bryce waits for me back at the table.

Making my way back to my seat, I notice Bryce talking to someone and I inch closer, but not all the way back to the table. I don't want to interrupt.

"—surprised to see you out with someone. She's stunning. Didn't know you had it in you, Dawson, you sly dog."

"It's not like that, Nate." Bryce's words are clipped, like he's annoyed or embarrassed and my face flames at his tone.

"I get it. I wasn't expecting to see you out with someone that wasn't Steph... someone that looks nothing like her. I'm not trying to imply anything or make you uncomfortable. Last I heard, you guys"—whatever Nate sees on Bryce's face has him pausing before he shifts gears—"It's just good to see you, though. Logan mentioned you were back in town for a while. We should get drinks sometime. I'm here if you want to talk." The offer from Nate seems genuine but there's practically a radioactive wave of discomfort coming off of Bryce. His shoulders are tensed, his hands fisted on the tops of his knees, out of sight of his friend.

"I—again. Today with Rachel, it's—it's business. Besides, Steph doesn't . . . she's not . . . her and I aren't—" Bryce full on stammers, tripping over the name, and I can only imagine that Steph is his wife and the idea of anyone getting the wrong idea about him is terrifying to him.

Nate holds up a hand to stay him, as if to say it's okay that he can't put it into words.

"Say no more. Just let me know when you want to hang out and we'll make a plan. It's good seeing you." Nate smiles at Bryce and then heads back to his own table. I take it as my cue to return.

Sliding into the booth I can only hope that my cheeks aren't as hot as they feel and that Bryce doesn't suspect I've just been eavesdropping on him and his friend. Thankfully he's too wrapped up in his own thoughts, and our food arrives shortly afterward. Despite my overactive mind and his apparent internal rumination, it doesn't feel awkward, just lacking.

I *want* him to speak, I realize. Although the silence is just a tepid, neutral thing between us, I wish he'd disrupt it or at the very least my thoughts so that I'm not mentally trying to picture what his wife looks like.

Blonde, maybe?

Our plates cleared and taken away, the waiter drops the check in front of Bryce and he pays before I can protest.

"Working lunch," he says, waving me off with a tight-lipped smile, as if even that much of the facial movement is too much.

"I'm not going to complain too loudly. Thank you." I follow him out to the car and he hands me the stack of papers that's lying on the backseat.

"I'll see you next week?" I ask, and his eyes focus on me long enough for him to nod.

"I'll email you, but it'll likely be Tuesday, depending on my chat with Jim and going over the budget now that I've seen how much work some of these places will need."

"Sounds good, thanks." Stilted. My words feel like I'm trying too hard, as if me saying the right words the right way will pull him out of whatever's occupying his mind and making him frown like that.

"Right. I'll wait here until you get inside safely."

I want to scoff at his offer, point out that it's full daylight and my place is literally just across the street, but I don't. It's genuine, and something inside of me kind of . . . settles. No one has ever offered something so kind, so quietly caring. It's just the decent thing to do and Bryce, yet again, has done it without even seeming to notice or try.

Half-walking, half-jogging to make the break between cars, I jaywalk across the street, not keen to go down a block for a crosswalk. Pushing into the entryway for the apartment, I turn to wave at Bryce.

He's standing, watching. His forearm rests on the top of his open car door and his expression is inscrutable from across the road, but he gives a little answering wave and then folds his body into his car. Within moments he's pulled out of the spot and down the street, and I watch until the car fades from view, unsure why I do.

Maybe to extend him the same courtesy?

Maybe just to prolong this moment because all that's waiting for me upstairs is unpacking and more unpacking. Ugh. Gotta get it over with sooner or later. I trudge up the narrow stairs, slot my old key into the door and step inside my apartment.

Boxes upon boxes, some unpacked and broken down, most still taped up or hanging half open because I needed something but didn't want to bother with the lot, wait for me.

I suck in a deep breath and stretch my neck to either side, feeling the pull and pumping myself up for the task. Setting a two-hour timer, I get to work in the living room and try to ignore the waiting text message from my mom and the puzzle that is Bryce Dawson.

"OKAY, WHO DIED?" ÁNGEL ASKS ON THE OTHER END OF THE CALL before I can even get a greeting out.

My breath huffs out on an incredulous laugh. "No one. Why is someone dying?"

"I don't know, why are you calling me at six p.m. on a Saturday night? Why are you calling at all? We communicate through snarky bar visits and memes. This is a new development for me, so excuse the skepticism and concern."

Dropping back onto my bed, I stare at the ceiling, watching the sunlight retreat out of the room, tugging the shadows along with it so they take up the space where the day has been.

"No one is dead. I wasn't aware that calling you would elicit such a strong response. I thought we were friends, and friends sometimes do this thing called talking. Mobile devices make it easier when people aren't in the same room, that's all this is."

Ángel's "Hmm" stretches through the air waves, as if he

knows this is bullshit—which it is—but he could at least play along for a bit before he calls me out on it.

"Okay, you caught me." I sigh.

"Please tell me it's Keith that's dead."

"Nope. Well, not as far as I know since I no longer work at Lakin-Cole or live in D.C. for that matter."

There's shuffling on the other end of the line, like Ángel's dropped the phone and scrambled to grab it. When he responds it's much closer and louder. Off of speaker, perhaps?

"*Rachel*," Ángel says my name like it's a warning, "spill."

I regale him with the whirlwind that was my quitting and moving, and the encouraging visit with Sebastian and Farren. Throughout it all, Ángel makes noises at the appropriate times, just listening. I'm so grateful to him. Even though he's fantastic at listening—an occupational hazard, he's told me. A lot of people will spill their guts when they're drunk, and the bartender is usually the closest friendly face—and one that can't leave. A captive audience for their misery. It's not until Bryce comes up that Ángel actually gets animated.

"*Bryce*, huh? Tell me about this guy. Old? Bald? Conspiracy theorist?" There's a bright quality to his voice and I know he's eager for information. So, I'll give him the barest.

"Not old. Not bald. Plus, you know me better than that. I might have been desperate for a job but I'm not stupid. There's no way I would have agreed to taking this position if he'd been a conspiracy theorist, or had bad vibes."

"Oooh, so he's got good vibes *and* he's hot?" The humor in his voice is hard to miss and I hate that he knows me so well.

"When did I say he was hot? I *never* said he was hot."

I can hear the pause on the other end of the line, feel the raised eyebrow and the unsaid "seriously?" and Ángel doesn't let it drop, despite my trying to play it off.

"I've watched pick-up line after pick-up line, one disastrous date after another. I've dissected each person you met at the bar, and we've talked at length about how *this one* had a soft hand-shake and clammy hands. Or *that one* was twenty years older than you and smelled like his wife left him and took the washing machine so he covered up his bathroom sink wash job with strong cologne."

He's not wrong, but I'm not quite sure where he's going with this and I'm not willing to ask and dig the hole further.

"The fact that you've told me nothing about this guy speaks volumes. So, are you going to tell me or do I need to play twenty questions like this is some stupid high school thing?"

Rolling onto my side, I stare out at the lights inside neighboring buildings that have flickered on. I should close the blinds. Heck, I should hang the curtains I have sitting in boxes. I should change out of my sweaty work clothes and take a stinging shower but the bed had felt so good after unpacking that I couldn't resist.

"*Fine*. He's . . . hot." It's an understatement but I'm not sure how to sum it up in a way that would capture the reality of the situation.

"Hot, how?"

"It doesn't matter." Sitting up, I try to coax myself up to go and shower. It'll be a good excuse to get off the phone anyway.

"Rachel . . ." That warning again. I hate that it works and I am so glad that I have him to talk to.

"Tall, like really tall, and broad to boot. Thirty-ish. Brown eyes and hair with natural golden highlights to it that stylists would kill to emulate. Big hands. Chivalrous." I keep the information to a minimum, reluctant to part with it and unsure why.

"Yeah?" He's excited for me, I can tell.

"He's my boss." I try to quell it, for both of our sakes.

"And?" Ángel drags it out, as if it's no big deal. Would he be this cavalier if he was attracted to his boss? Probably.

"And he's married."

There's a beat, the word settling between us.

"*Fuck.*" It's so disappointed I laugh out loud.

"Right. Anyway, I need to stay focused. But I wanted to update you so you know why I'm not at the bar on Friday and likely won't be for a while unless I find a car or some other way into the city."

"You know, I've always wanted to see . . . Dunville? Nothing more appealing to a city guy like me than a cute town in Maryland—get a break from it all."

"*Sure*, you have. It's *Dulaney,* by the way." We both laugh at his misstep, whether it was purposeful or not, it's gone a long way to help me feel more settled in my choice to stay here for now.

My mom's message and my attraction to my boss has me feeling a little unmoored and knowing that Ángel is there, my life preserver when my mind threatens to drag me under—it's appreciated.

"I'm serious, though. I have a car and I'm happy to come up there and check on you. One of us has to make sure you keep it in your pants." It's such a fake scolding that I have to bite my cheek to stop from laughing, pretending to take him and his warning seriously.

"Yeah, and we both know that *one of us* is going to be me."

"I never claimed otherwise. Maybe he has some hot friends? If you can't have him, you might as well go for the next best thing."

"*Or* I could do the job I came here for and actually be professional."

"Where's the fun in that?"

"I'm not here for fun. I'm here for work," I remind him, and myself.

"The job listing said '*Stay for the fun*' so that's not accurate. You're not following the job description. You're actively sabotaging yourself by not doing what I say."

"Oh, shut up!" It's said without venom, but I'm clinging to my

morals with both hands, trying not to let his voice and that traitorous one in my mind get the upper hand.

"Text me your address and let me know when you want me to
come up. Even if you decide to stay professional I can, at the very
least, come join you for drinks or something one night so you
don't completely lose yourself in this job."

I want to argue and say that won't happen but . . . it likely will.
Without Ángel, and that first Friday Night Drinks all those years
ago, I would have buried myself in Lakin-Cole the same way
Sebastian had, without a bad influence to keep me corrupted and
sane.

"I will. Thanks, Ángel. And you better get used to me calling
you."

"Nope. It's gross and unnatural."

"Love you too. I'll see you soon." I hope he can hear my eye
roll through the phone.

"You sure you're not sick or something?"

"Positive."

"Oh no! Not a positive. Maybe there's a treatment for it. I've
heard they've made great strides in detecting body snatchi—"

"—*Goodnight*, Ángel." I hang up to the sound of him laughing
and my smile stays on my face, a wisp of gratitude.

Waiting for the creaking pipes to heat, I trace my fingertips
over the water droplets until they're satisfactorily warm and step
under the spray. Scrubbing the day from my body, I can't help the
little curl in my stomach—the one that's keen to see where this
goes, actually excited at the prospect of work.

When I step out, hair wrapped up in a towel with another
encircling my body, I glance at the contract and nearly choke on
my own saliva.

It's not just a stake.

Bryce is offering twenty percent of the business if we make this
a success, with no investment expectation from me.

*I value your input*, he'd said. It had sounded like a platitude at the time, similar to Andrew's words when trying to assuage me. Unlike Andrew though, Bryce put his money where his mouth is —literally.

And I'm so shocked by the offer that I don't even hear my inner voice's quip about Bryce's mouth and where it should be.

# CHAPTER  6

*Out with someone that wasn't Steph . . .*

*Wasn't Steph . . .*

*Steph.*

Nate's words follow me all the way home, in every heartbeat and clicking of my blinker as I drive through Dulaney on autopilot with my world dropped out from under me again. I made it a few days without thinking of her. At least not in any way that hasn't been pushing me forward with the new endeavor. Whenever it starts hurting, I remind myself how I plan to deal with it.

The hyperfocus on the new business has been taking up every inch of my brain space until it's become all I can see. It's been years since I've felt this single-minded and intent on something to this degree. I was, and am, more than happy to have it continue that way because at least then I'm not drowning. I don't know why I thought I'd be able to avoid her here. Even though my life with Steph was in Philadelphia, people here know of us, some have even met her on the few instances I made my way back here.

Nate is one of those people.

He knows. Everyone knows. The second Steph changed her name on socials to her first and middle, cutting off the Dawson and leaving it to rot, everyone knew. By the time she'd scrubbed me from the rest of it and unfriended or unfollowed the people tangential to my life, I'd already had an influx of messages checking on me.

*Are you okay? I saw Steph's Insta.*

No. No, I wasn't okay and I wouldn't have known jack about Steph's Insta unless they said something since I don't have one of my own. Concerned friends were how I realized my ex-wife had removed me from her online life and past with surgical precision, even going so far as to carefully crop me out of pictures I distinctly remember being in.

Logan let me stalk her socials through his phone on a particularly rough night around last Halloween. Steph dressed up as that character from *13 Going on 30* with the colorful dress and captioned it "Thirty, Flirty, and Thriving" with her pina colada'ed hand thrust up into the air like she was toasting with the whole damn world.

All of it comes rushing back now that the diversion of dusty movie theaters and a shiny, swishing ponytail isn't in front of me. Nate's other observation pierces the veil of my heartbreak at the reminder of touring the spots today.

*Someone that looks nothing like her at all.*

Rachel. Rachel with her hungry eyes, and bare face, and the way I can see her brain turning before she speaks. She's measured. Something about how she acted in her interview and the careful way she spoke to me today about not wanting to take over or step on my toes gives me the impression that she's had to learn how to do that—train herself to respond in a way that's expected of her, and that resonates with me. There's something deeper buried there and I wonder what type of woman waits beneath the constructed shell of professionalism and fear of failure.

Her facade isn't physical the way Steph's was. Steph covered up the cracks through her physical appearance—competence through optics. It's how she got me in the first place when she was in college. Looking for a tutor, simpering and gushing over my capability, even though deep down I knew she was just using me to help her do some of her assignments. Still, the young, insecure guy who'd only ever felt like a weirdo up until then didn't want to question it too hard.

And I grew into my overly large hands and feet, my lanky body finally filling out, which helped attract Steph too. She was convinced we'd be a "power couple," and I was just happy to be along for the ride. Steph made me feel seen at a time where being invisible was all I'd ever known. Now I know there are far better ways to be loved than to have to wait for someone's gaze on you to feel important. I only wish I'd learned the lesson before years of my life and my heart were given away.

Pulling into my parents' driveway, I take a deep breath to steady myself before I climb the steps up to the garage apartment without heading inside to talk to them. My mind is a mess right now. I need time to sort through the past and the present and a future I never envisioned but I'm determined to see through.

Afternoon fades into evening, my mom dropping dinner off outside my door as if she can sense I need space. My eyes are leaden, the promise of sleep teasing me after hours of mental planning. The list of tools and tasks grows and grows until I've got a notebook full of the next few months of my life.

Part of me cautions that I should schedule time in there to breathe . . . to let myself think, but that's a dangerous game and after nine whole months of thinking—of considering every angle of my failed marriage—I'm ready to put it behind me. Lifting my hand up, the moonlight from outside glints on the white gold on my ring finger, and I twist my wedding band around and around. It would be so easy to tug it off and toss it out. It's just there out of habit after all. So easy and yet . . .

I'll do it. Soon. I owe myself that final step, but damn my inability to admit absolute defeat. Taking it off means finally acknowledging that I knew we were over far before those papers were served. It's my own yoke of safety. Taking it off removes the last barrier I have between opening myself up to the possibility of hurt.

I fall asleep with smooth metal on my skin and when I dream, it's of a black, shiny ponytail and a small hand tucked inside of mine for the barest of moments. Not enough and not allowed, even in the depths of my subconscious.

I VISIT THE REMAINING TWO LOCATIONS WITH JIM ON SUNDAY AND although I feel terrible about it, I don't ask Rachel to come. Waking up multiple times last night with her at the edges of my mind has left me unsteady and I know if she joins us today I won't be able to focus at all. This was such a colossally bad idea. Rachel Mackey is my employee. I need to get myself under control so we can tackle the week ahead and every week after that.

The showing is lackluster without her. Jim tries his best but I'm in a foul mood and the locations he has for me do little to improve it.

"It's an old fabric factory. Small-scale but it's been untouched for a while," Jim explains as we walk through the squat and long room.

It's similar in feel to the mill location from yesterday but there's no lingering scent of sawdust in the air, just cold scrubbed concrete and windows comprised of small squares that are too grimy to see through. We'll have the same problem here as we do there. Building rooms from scratch, trying to soundproof them, it feels a little overwhelming.

The second, and last, location isn't any better. Despite it inhabiting all the charm and history I'd like, it's unsuitable. Too far from downtown, the Colonial Brownstone *is* stunning, but the doorways and passageways are too narrow, and the tiny steps up to the front door too steep. The spiral staircase is a nightmare on its own. There's no way this will be an accessible building without a lot of time and money. Something I am limited on. So, the choice is made, almost for me.

"Thanks for bringing me out here, Jim. I'm going to confer with Rachel and get back to you as soon as possible, but I think I have an idea of where I'm headed. I appreciate you taking the time to help us." I hold out my hand for the realtor to shake and Jim gives me a kind smile.

"I look forward to hearing from you, and I meant it. It's going to be great to have a place like this in town. I'm glad you found your way home."

The words hit me in the solar plexus and all I can do is give him a tight smile, my ability to speak momentarily failing me. Driving off shortly after, Jim leaves me standing on a residential sidewalk with too much buzzing in my brain. There's really only one person I can, and want to, talk to about this.

> Sorry to bother you on a Sunday.

> Do you have a minute to talk?

> I think I have a location in mind but want to run it by you.

> I'm near downtown if you'd like to meet
> somewhere.

I'm not sure why I've even phrased it like that. It's not as if she has any bearing on what place I let. Rachel will be dealing with what's happening inside of the building, not which one it is. Still, I meant it when I said her opinion mattered. The reply comes swift.

RACHEL
> Hey! I'm in the middle of something

Heart dropping into my shoes, the force of my disappointment is a shock to the system. Before I can even try to grab my words back through the ether she follows up with,

> If you don't mind meeting at my apartment, we
> can discuss here.

> I'm about five minutes out. Is that okay?

> Perfect. Door's unlocked!

> There's a parking space behind the building

That . . . doesn't seem safe. I would've thought a girl from D.C. knows better than to leave her house unlocked, but then again, I did say five minutes. Maybe the thing she's in the middle of is time sensitive and she can't drop whatever it is at a moment's notice when I arrive.

Thankful that I don't have to brave the Sunday post-church downtown parking situation, I head toward the robin's egg blue door I'd seen her disappear into yesterday. The shop beneath her apartment has their door ajar and the rich aromas of tea, herbal and heady, floats out onto the sidewalk. I allow myself one deep, calming breath, nodding at the old man behind the register, staring out the window at me before I head upstairs.

It turns out the thing she's in the middle of, the one that prevents her from locking her door, isn't time consuming so much as it is dangerous.

Rachel stands on the corner of a console, probably for her TV which sits haphazardly on the floor off to the side. Reaching over, screws in her mouth and an old screwdriver in her hand, she's trying to mount a curtain rod bracket without the proper equipment and is practically halfway to falling. There's too much weight on one foot, and she's balanced precariously.

Rising up onto her toes, her back foot stretched out behind her as she braces herself on the wall to reach further, I feel my heart stutter. The muscle in her calf flexes, clad in what I can only describe as if leggings were shorts, leaving most of her legs bare. Fear and anger that she'd do something this foolhardy fill me.

"Are you out of your mind?" It comes out harsher than I intend, already stepping in to try and help.

My body knows it was a mistake before my mind catches up and it's only for that reason that I'm close enough. Long legs eating up the distance between us in three lengthy strides, I'm near when she whips her head around, her body pivoting to give her a better view of who's just spoken.

Screws fall from between her lips as her mouth drops open in shock, clinking against wood as they tumble and hit. Rachel's spin causes her to lose her balance, her small hand reaching back and gripping the slightly textured drywall as if it'll provide a means of stopping gravity.

I've never seen someone fall in slow motion but somehow she manages it. Enough time for me to reach out my arms and catch her before she lands head first, or more likely on her side, from a few feet off the ground.

Rachel's breath leaves her chest in a little "oof" from the collision of her body dropping against mine. Face buried against my shoulder, her arms and legs tucked in slightly as if she'd tried to curl into a ball to lessen the impact of her fall, she's warm and soft in my arms.

My brain is still lagging behind my body, it takes me a full five seconds to convince my hands and arms to let her go so she can stand on her own. Her body sliding against mine as I deposit her onto the floor is wicked, and her cheeks are flushed a deep red.

When she looks up at me it takes a moment for her eyes to switch from glassy to something sharp.

"Am *I* out of my mind? What kind of person startles someone in the middle of a dangerous task?" The breathiness of the statement undercuts the incredulity and anger she tries to inject into it.

"So you admit it's dangerous?"

We're so close I can feel her heaving breath against my neck where she's staring up at me, her eyes trained on mine and I know I should take a step back but I can't. Not when she's in my space and smells earthy and fresh, citrus and sage, and something wholly her own that I can't put a name to.

Her mouth opens and closes as she tries to formulate an answer, the wall behind her and me in front, and her eyes wide with indecision. "I—I don't have a ladder."

"So you opted to potentially crack your skull rather than ask for help?" I don't know why I'm being so harsh. I've never spoken this way to anyone before but the fear of what almost happened has stoked something dormant inside of me. Coupled with the latent attraction and the fact that Rachel has been on my mind almost constantly since we met, it's the perfect storm for irrational reactions.

"I'm not good at asking." Her gaze drops, her eyes somewhere on the collar of my shirt, and she says it with dejection and a hefty dose of defensiveness.

"Next time, please try. I'd hate for you to get hurt, or struggle, when I'm right here. I know we're working together but I hope it's not too much of a stretch to consider us friends now."

Her brows draw down over those dark expressive eyes, as if she's measuring whether or not to speak. I've spent so much of my life trying to read and decipher the things people *don't* say. Body language, facial expression, and tone of voice. It's been a constant study to read between the lines and I still feel like I'll never quite get it right. I want to ask her to please just say what she's thinking. The suspense is killing me and the proximity doesn't help.

"I'm not sure your wife would appreciate me taking your time on a Sunday because I decided to hang some curtains."

It's like an electric shock. The words *"your wife"* clang inside my mind and I wonder what she knows.

"I don't—I'm not sure—How?" It's a mess of a sentence but somehow she understands what I'm trying to say.

"Ring. Left hand."

I lift up the hand in question, the ring on my third finger glinting muted, it's scuffed and a little worn after five years, and I haven't had the energy to polish it.

"Oh." I don't know what else to say. I haven't had the courage to take it off for any extended period of time yet. It's been there so long it feels like a part of me.

Rachel's eyes rove over my face, and she must see some kind of devastation there because she sucks in a shuddering breath and rushes to speak. "Oh my god, I'm so sorry. I didn't mean to bring —I'm sorry for your loss. I didn't know. I—"

I bark out a bitter chuckle, her concern shifting to confusion.

"Not dead. Divorced. Just haven't gotten around to taking it off. We finalized it earlier this month after being separated for nearly a year." It's the first time I've said that out loud.

Everyone around me already knows, so I haven't had to admit it verbally. But with Rachel, it feels real for the first time. The lonely months leading up to the end of my marriage, the late work nights and the cooling down between us . . . all of it right through my nine months living in an empty house and questioning what comes next. It finally feels like something other than a fever dream and I rock back on my heels at the revelation.

"Well." The word feels layered with meaning I can only guess at. Rachel places her hand smack in the middle of my chest to ease me backwards and steps out around me once she's made that space—her touch gone but burnt into my skin and my head buzzing with thoughts too wild to pin down. "Want some coffee or tea and we can talk about the location?"

Right. I forgot for a second why I'm here in the first place.

"Tea, please. Whatever you have. No milk or sugar."

"I have something herbal, I think. Just give me a moment and I'll be right back. Feel free to make yourself at home." She gestures at the space around us and I actually take stock of the room for the first time. Rachel slips into the kitchen and though I can still kind of see her, it's not as direct.

Thank goodness for that. My heart hasn't beat calmly since I set foot in this apartment and I might be able to get it under control if she's not in the same room. The living room is in various stages of unpacking, although it's mostly there. Just a couple of boxes stacked up in one corner. Rachel has a stunning green velvet sofa, and a deep set armchair that looks perfect for reading, facing the TV stand she just fell from.

Her hardwood floors are covered by a rug and she has a standing lamp between the couch and chair, further cementing the idea of a reading spot. Lastly, she has a dark brown—possibly mahogany—bookshelf with various titles. Some lay on their sides, others stacked and held in place with knicknacks to keep them from falling all the way over. Two boxes wait at the foot of the shelf and it takes everything I have not to go over and snoop.

My restraint is good because she reappears a moment later, two mugs in hand and gestures for me to sit. She's got a folder tucked under her arm and once I've taken my tea and sat down on what I'm always going to consider the reading chair from now on, she hands it to me.

"Signed contract. It all looked above board to me and I appreciate you being willing to consider those changes." Her smile is open but there's a tightness around it that makes me feel like she's holding something back.

"I appreciate you getting it back to me so quickly. So." I take a deep breath. "I won't take up much of your time. I just wanted to go ahead and let you know that I toured the last two spaces with Jim today, since I didn't have high hopes for them and my worries were founded. Neither were better than what we toured together and just looking at the budget and timeline I'm under, I think the movie theater might serve my purpose best?" I don't mean for it to sound like a question but I do want her opinion.

Several thoughts seem to flash across her face as I talk but she nods by the end of it.

"Although it was dark and dusty, it did seem to be the easiest to convert into something else."

"It's also the most accessible of the buildings and right downtown. It's just going to take some elbow grease."

She raises one of those dark brows at me and I jump in quickly with, "Mine. Not yours. What I'll need help with from you is brainstorming room ideas. Once we have a set few I'll ask you to take a look at what kind of equipment you'll need to outfit each room to suit the ambiance and other tech necessary to pull it off."

"What do you need from me now? I feel kind of useless not knowing what to do and I don't want to just sit on my hands. I need to earn my keep." Taking a sip of her drink, her throat bobs, both her hands wrapped around the mug like she needs something to do with them or she'll fidget.

"Besides figuring out renovation, which again is my problem, I would like to visit a few escape rooms over the next few weeks in the area to get a feel for what they're doing—what works and

doesn't and where there's a gap in the market for specific ideas—
that sort of thing. I'd appreciate it if you could come with me.
Once we have a plan for where we'd like to go, I'd appreciate it if
you could document our ideas, perhaps brainstorm some cool
ways to integrate those with the software and app."

Rachel nods. "So, when do you need me?"

Something traitorous inside my mind thinks of how soft and
warm she was pressed against me, long dormant stirrings coming
to life, and I have to take a sip of my own scalding tea—trying not
to wince—before I can speak. It's been so long since I've touched
or been touched by anyone other than my loved ones.

"Tuesday? I've already monopolized the day off I promised.
We could probably hit two or three rooms a week so we have time
to debrief without having them all blend together. It might be best
if I rope some other people in once we get closer to having something concrete so we can have a sounding board. You're welcome
to invite anyone along that you think might be able to help out.
I'll cover the costs."

"That sounds great, even if it feels a little bit like spying." She
waits for me to sputter before she laughs at me. "Don't worry. I'm
not above spying. I have a few friends that I think might be helpful. One is another developer and he's with a board game
designer so they'd be perfect. My best friend is blunt as hell, so
he'd be useful as well." Rachel smiles as she mentions them, a
softness to her, and I find I'm strangely nervous at the prospect of
meeting the people that are meaningful to her.

"I'll get in touch with them and see what works best. Maybe
the end of the month or the beginning of next? May still gives us a
good amount of time before the deadline," she says.

"That would be great. I'll probably drag my best friend Logan
and his wife along. He's a marketer and would be an asset when it
comes to what might sound most appealing and easiest to sell."
I'll just have to make sure Logan and Gabrielle are on their best

behavior. The last thing I need is them meddling where they don't belong.

"Perfect!"

"I'll . . . I'll pick you up Tuesday around ten?" It's halting and I wonder if I'll ever get good at talking to her, to anyone, and having it sound smooth.

"I'll be ready."

I down the rest of my drink, the herbal tea burning all the way down and rise, taking one last look at the space and her before I turn to leave.

"Bryce!" she calls out once my hand is on the door, ready to leave.

I twist around to look at her, a deep breath stuck between my ribs.

"Thanks for catching me." Rachel's smile is small but sweet, genuine.

"I'd say anytime but I really hope you don't make a habit out of almost killing yourself. I'll bring a ladder by. No more balancing acts, okay?" Our shared laugh spreads through me like sunlight and I'm a cat curled up in the beam. "I'll see you soon, Rachel."

"Soon," she agrees.

Somehow I make it back to my car, and then home, and then onto the internet for the first local spot I can find to nab whatever tickets they have left for Tuesday. It's not until later, with my tasks completed and my mind still abuzz with what happened at her apartment that I twist my ring off my finger and set it down onto my nightstand.

# CHAPTER  7

ROPING MY FRIENDS INTO THIS NEW ENDEAVOR WAS EASIER THAN I expected, or rather hoped, even though coordinating schedules for so many of us took the better part of the last month. We are solidly in May and the wait to see everyone and get their opinion has been difficult.

Heaven only knows how they'll react to actually meeting Bryce in person now that they've been getting hints and asking questions about him for a couple weeks. Sebastian and Farren are excited to help out with the job, especially given how they both understand what leaving Lakin-Cole is like. Ángel on the other hand . . . Well, I'm not quite sure he'll be able to keep his mouth shut. Everything from how my last job ended all the way through my relationship mishaps—he's a landmine with a sensitive trigger. Multiple parts of my life are poised to collide tonight.

Taking a fortifying breath, I smooth my hands down my shirt and try to ignore how clammy my palms are. Bryce is on his way and after a few weeks of car rides and tentative escape room experiences, I feel like I'm ready to lose my mind. We haven't gotten nearly enough done, and it's been surprisingly difficult to scope out rival companies when their dates and times are all booked up. But I suppose that's what we get for not planning as well as we could have. I'm still getting paid for the days I'm scheduled even though we haven't been able to accomplish as much as we'd like. Sketching out some ideas in secret has filled the rest of the time and I can only hope that Bryce doesn't get upset once I show them to him—given how premature they are.

Bryce has been apologetic, kind, and totally unaffected. The same can't be said for me.

My clothes smell like him, the tiniest bit, traces from working so closely all month. My mind is filled with small, inconsequential things that shouldn't matter but do. Like how he always opens doors for me, offering his hand when the terrain is uneven or there's a significant step up or down as if he knows that I can be just the slightest bit clumsy. I can't erase the way the brief impression of his hand against mine feels, especially not since he took off his wedding ring.

The tan line is still there, faint and fading daily, but somehow it feels significant that he removed it after our . . . mishap over my curtain fiasco. What a mess. He should've just let me fall on my ass. It would've saved me from knowing just how solid he is under those henleys and denim shirts. I need a stiff drink and a good orgasm, and since I'm *not* going to get involved with my boss, both of those things will have to fall to me.

My phone buzzes in my hand, Bryce's contact on the notification window.

**BRYCE**

I'm downstairs. Do you need help with anything before we head out?

He's taken to asking this every day, ever since he caught me and I lost my mind right along with my balance. It's sweet. It's unnecessary. It's unfairly hot given that he's just trying to do the right thing and I've taken him up on that offer already by letting him hang the curtain rods, his height making it a cake walk—*without* the need of a ladder.

*Don't think about that now. You're on the clock. Keep it in your pants.*

I'm all good, thanks! Be right down.

Spring is in full swing, cherry blossoms have come and gone and branches with bright green leaves line the street. Colorful blooms spring up in the window boxes and front beddings. Businesses and homes alike seem to have embraced the longer and warmer days happily now that the clocks are set to a new time and the dark of winter is a distant memory. Floral wreaths decorate front doors and I'm tempted to get one myself for the downstairs door. But it feels so . . . domestic. I've never been one to decorate seasonally, or at all really. Dulaney just makes me feel like I can be different—more involved in life when I'm not chained to a desk for the majority of it.

Bryce waits outside the car—because of course—he couldn't just sit inside and honk like a normal guy and make it easier for me to forget how devastatingly attractive he is as a person. Opening my door for me, he gives a smile that instantly has me flushing and I seriously need to get my shit together because I haven't blushed over a guy since I was in middle school.

The closer we get to D.C. the tighter the knot in my stomach twists. It's barely been two full months. I shouldn't be this filled with trepidation over returning to a city that's been my home since I was eighteen. Although it's probably for that very reason—the over-familiarity, the feeling of failure so bad I had to leave—

that has me crossing my arms across my abdomen as if I can physically restrain my feelings of unease.

"You okay?" Bryce asks, turning down the music that's been thrumming in the background, too low for me to fully hear the lyrics but enough to keep the silence from being all-consuming.

He steals a glance my way and I grit my teeth through the stress of him doing that when the beltway is a fucking nightmare and even a second of distraction could result in him rear-ending one of the fools ahead of us that can't drive to save their lives.

"Nervous, I guess." It's an understatement and I'm not sure how to put into words why I am.

It's a mix of not being back since I left Lakin-Cole and all the strain that I was under—stress I hadn't even noticed was slowly driving me to the brink until it was removed and I could breathe again. It's the knowledge that my parents have no idea that I've moved and besides my brief text messages with my mom I haven't bothered to reach out and tell them. It's blowing Ángel off and telling him I'm busy when in reality I just don't want to have to talk about my attraction to Bryce and have it be a real thing.

It's the fact that my friends will be joining me tonight and I have no idea how they'll react, whether they'll judge me for this choice or find me lacking somehow. Mostly though I'm worried that Bryce will see more of me, learn more about my background, and realize that I'm white-knuckling my way through life—not nearly as confident or capable as I make myself out to be.

"There's no need to be. Logan and Gabrielle are really nice. He's known me since we were in school, so if anyone has reason to be nervous it's me. He's likely to embarrass me and I'm not sure whether his pointing out that I have no idea what I'm doing will make you want to quit while you're ahead." His hands tighten on the steering wheel even though his voice is even—betraying the nerves under the surface.

Again, I'm surprised at his willingness to be honest and

vulnerable. When compared to Riley's half-truths and careful sentences that hid her deception, it's unnerving. When put up against the veneer at Lakin-Cole, dressed up in HR language to cover the misogyny and bias, it's almost unbelievable.

I sputter out a laugh before I respond. "It's not your friends I'm worried about. It's mine. My best friend especially can be a bit . . . nosy? I'm bracing myself for them to either embarrass me with stories no boss should hear, or for one of them to get all up in your business asking too many questions—likely of a personal nature."

We make eye contact again and the flip inside my stomach isn't just from the fear of a fender bender.

Pulling into a parking garage close to the escape room in Glover Park, not too far from Georgetown and my old university, I can't help but compare it with Dulaney.

Crossing the street causes a panic because D.C. drivers don't give a damn about pedestrians or cyclists, and the cyclists don't care about people crossing either. It doesn't escape my notice that Bryce walks on the street side of the sidewalks, and his hand twitches, arm slightly outstretched behind me but careful not to touch—as if he wants to guide me or be able to push me out of the way of one of said crazy drivers should the need arise.

I've always prided myself on being independent—strong and capable, and ready to take on whatever and fuck anyone that gets in my way—but something about that gesture . . . I feel cherished instead of condescended.

By the time we make it to the escape room my cheeks are flushed from more than just the walk. Our friends are already waiting in the lobby and the game master plasters on a huge smile when we finally join the group. I want to greet Ángel, and Sebastian and Farren, but the pink-haired, pierced employee launches into her spiel and the group's attention is focused forward again.

"Welcome, welcome! I was just explaining to the others that we don't actually lock you all in the room and you're welcome to use the bathroom whenever needed. Your room is all the way to the back of the hallway and to the right, the restroom is the door directly across from it. Now, are we ready to start?"

We give a series of nods and I take the time to peek at Logan and Gabrielle. He's not quite as tall as Bryce, though that's not an easy bar to reach. Curly brown hair that's short on the sides and a bit swoopy on top. He's round cheeked, as if he never quite lost his baby face, and his blue eyes sparkle when he looks over at his wife. Gabrielle is taller than me and Farren, with wild curls and a cheeky smile that contrasts stunningly with her dark skin. They steal a glance at us in the back and as soon as our eyes catch we're all quick to look away.

I've missed most of the presentation but this is my fourth of these things in the last two weeks alone and I could probably scent the metallic tang of a padlock a mile away. We file into the room one by one and once we're "locked in" we all look at each other with sheepish smiles. I wait a beat for Bryce but he's swallowing hard and so I take the initiative.

"Hi, I'm Rachel." I reach out my hand for Logan and Gabrielle who point at themselves and provide their names even though I already know.

"This is my boss, Bryce," I say to my friends and then I turn to look up at the man that's had my brain fuzzy all month, my gaze catching on him for just a moment too long to be casual before I turn back to my friends.

"And this is Ángel, Sebastian, and Farren." Ángel starts them off with a little wave, a smirk thrown my way that I'm going to elbow him for later, and Farren and Sebastian follow suit as I list out their names. "I know Sebastian through our former jobs, Farren is his partner—the game designer I told you about—and Ángel is my best friend."

Ángel is my worst-one-night-stand-turned-best-friend-and-wing-man and he smirks at my sappy title. We've never actually said it out loud, but it's true. Nobody in this room knows me better. Hell, nobody knows me better, in general. Sometimes I wish it had been us, but it never would have worked.

He's too snarky and flighty. I'm too outwardly buttoned up with fucked up interpersonal relationships from my parents through to my exes. Neither of us knows how to care for ourselves let alone someone else. He's seen my ugly and time took care of the rest. Whatever budding attraction may have existed all those years ago faded into something easy and far healthier for the both of us.

"Nice to meet you all," Bryce says beside me, his voice low and soft as if he's shy about being in a room where the people he doesn't know outnumber the ones he does.

I don't dare count myself among the people he knows, not when everything is so tentative. Maybe in time we'll be real friends. Maybe soon I'll be able to set aside these conflicting feelings and I'll see him and he'll see the real me—not just the practiced one.

"Right, you two are the experts, so put us to work!" Logan says, breaking the awkward silence and we split off into our respective little groups without thinking about it.

I'm not sure how to feel about the fact that Bryce has opted toward one corner with his friends and left the other to me and mine.

"Right, so when you said he was hot that was a massive fucking understatement," Ángel hisses loud enough for me, Sebastian and Farren to hear and she giggles when I poke Ángel in the ribs. Sebastian just watches us with an amused half-smile on his face and his arms crossed, the scene unfolding.

"Shut it. I am not discussing that right now. We have an objective to reach and the last thing I need is you sticking your nose into nothing."

"I don't see the ring, Rachel," Ángel says it innocently, but the mischief behind his eyes has me rolling mine.

"Divorced."

If we weren't conspiring, whispering in the corner, Ángel might have whooped out a victorious laugh.

"That doesn't change the fact that he's *my boss. I am* currently *on the clock,* and I have no idea if he's interested." I thank goodness that the game master has started up some spooky soundtrack for our investigative task inside this supposed haunted house, because I really don't want anyone on the other side of the room to know what I'm saying.

"Oh, he's interested." Sebastian pulls me out of my irritation at Ángel's audacity, his eyebrow raised as he looks behind me, presumably at Bryce.

I sputter at Sebastian, unsure what to say and his half-smile stretches into a full blown grin before he speaks with unrestrained glee, "Oh shit. You've got it bad. I've never seen you flustered . . . ever."

"I do not! I am not!" I say in a hushed, frantic voice. I know it's petulant, protesting far more than what's necessary, and Ángel just gives me a look that says I can try but I'm not fooling any of them. Despite keeping my text updates to them this past month as dry as possible, clearly I've given away too much.

"Let's get to the fucking task at hand before I lose my damn job." Grumbling, I start pulling open drawers looking for clues.

Our little group breaks up and soon we're combing the room for anything that might get us answers so we can get the hell out of here. Gabrielle finds a hidden message in the mirror once she fogs it up. Logan tugs on the bust of the main character of the room and we hear a loud crash, something falling down through the chimney.

This is one of the better rooms we've done with a lot of interaction besides just finding locks and twisting combinations into them. We comb over the map for a clue as to where our victim went and who he met, trying to work backwards through our murdered homeowner's last day to figure out who killed him and why.

The hour ticks by, every fifteen minutes punctuated by the ding of an analog clock above the door. Farren is first to integrate herself into Bryce's group, Ángel following close behind. Sebastian has the sense to stay near me, or perhaps he's still kind of wary of new people until he's had time to suss them out.

Maybe he just wants to watch Farren bend over to tug on a loose floorboard and admire her backside, who knows? As for me —I'm overheating. I'm desperately scouring the last will and testament of Lord Huckleby when all I want to do is watch Bryce.

How his brows knit over those warm eyes and the way he tugs a corner of his bottom lip between his teeth when he's concentrating too hard is distracting. I can smell his cologne all the way over here, not because it's strong, not because I have some stupid heightened sense of smell, but because I know exactly what the scent is. I could conjure it from memory if I tried.

How the fuck am I going to make it through the remaining months of my contract and stay unaffected?

"Mind if I take a look?" Bryce asks behind me, as if I've summoned him through thirst alone.

"Not at all. I'm trying to figure out who had the most to gain from his death." I don't turn, afraid to when I can feel the heat of him behind me and if I do, if I step back, I'll be too close in his personal space.

His hand reaches over my shoulder, his bicep next to my cheek and he takes hold of the parchment—right above my hand, his pinky touching my thumb. Bryce shuffles slightly closer, looking at the paper that's totally blurred in my vision, because he's against me now. Just barely. Just enough to make me forget how to swallow properly.

Those notes of his scent that teased me across the room totally invade my senses.

"It was his nephew," he says and I feel the words against my back, the rumble of them passing through me like I'm made of air and pulled taut as a drum.

"Look." Bryce leaves me holding the parchment and runs his finger along the line bequeathing the fortune to Huckleby's nephew, Henry.

And then he's gone, across the room before I can suck in a shuddering breath that doesn't carry his smell.

"Try 'Henry' on the letter lock!" Bryce says.

Ángel fumbles with the wooden rods, twisting them so the five letters align perfectly and then a book dips down from the bookshelf behind us, a soft clutter sounding behind it. I tug the book from the shelf and inside is a small (fake) dagger coated in blood (also fake) with the initials HH carved into the handle.

"Congratulations! You solved the murder of Lord Huckleby and found Henry's dagger before he could come back to catch you snooping, without any hints and within forty minutes. Good job, everyone!" A disembodied voice sounds over a speaker, startling us in the room.

A few moments later the host comes into the room with a camera and urges us to stand in front of the fireplace to take a group picture. Somehow I end up wedged in the middle, caught between Bryce on one side and my friends on the other. Bryce's arm wraps around my waist from behind, his other likely doing the same to whoever is on his other side, but it's scorching. The imprint of his large hand on my side feels like standing too close to a fire, not hot enough to burn but dangerous all the same if I take just one step nearer.

"Thank you so much!" Bryce thanks the host and we follow suit, filing out of the building and onto the sidewalk.

"You guys want to grab some dinner? There's a good Asian place near here," Farren offers and the group agrees.

I'm last to join them outside, off kilter, and Ángel notices.

Threading his arm through mine, locking elbows like we're Jack and Jill bounding up a fucking hill. "Come on, let's get you fed. You always function better when you have carbs in your system."

"I'm not sure food's going to fix this, Ángel."

He tuts in understanding, "You either need to get over it or be brave enough to take a risk."

"It's just an attraction. Nothing more..."

"If it was just attraction then crab rangoon would've been enough of a distraction to pull you out of this."

We walk down the block, Ángel and I trailing behind the group as I hear Farren faintly talk to Bryce and his friends about board games and hers that she designed.

Settling down to eat I somehow find myself next to Bryce again, and Ángel on my other side. Farren and Sebastian are not so subtle across from us and Logan and Gabrielle keep looking at me like I have something on my face, which Ángel has assured me I don't.

"So, how have the first couple months been?" Logan asks, his eyes kind on Bryce.

Bryce takes a bracing breath beside me, the side of his arm brushing against mine as his chest fills with air and he blows it out in a huff.

"That bad, huh?" Logan asks.

"We're a bit behind, I think. It took a while to close on the building, we haven't been able to check out very many escape rooms, and we haven't even started brainstorming room ideas even though we've been learning a lot about mechanics."

Logan grimaces at the stress in Bryce's voice and I can't lie and say I haven't seen those dark circles and sad brackets beside his mouth. Not as bad as the day I first met him but nowhere close to gone.

"You haven't started with ideas but . . ." I whisper beside him and Bryce twists to look down at me, a question in his eyes.

"I know things haven't exactly been going to plan for you so I started taking notes after every room we've been to—even though it hasn't been very many—but once I noticed deficiencies or things you seemed to particularly enjoy I made a point of writing them down. Since then I've been researching a few popular themes so you can have a familiar cornerstone, but I've also been writing down ideas to bring to you. I have a whole notebook for when you're ready." It flows out of me in a rush, my eyes never leaving his, and I feel heat creep up my neck.

It isn't just that he's good looking—which he is—but it's the way he doesn't make me feel like I need to be anything other than myself. I find the softness creeping out—the vulnerability and hope I don't let many see. Bryce gives me the silence to work through my thoughts, the grace to let me speak my mind when I'm ready, and the knowledge that he sees me as a person first, not just a bottom line.

I really shouldn't be this affected by common decency but the bar has been pretty low, especially recently given Andrew and Keith's treatment. Coupled with the blazing shitshow of Riley cheating on me with someone else—also in a relationship, thus blowing up two in one go—it's been hard to believe the best in people. Bryce has made no move, he hasn't even indicated that he's interested. Not that it should matter. I'm trying to stay professional here and he's clearly not over his ex if he was still wearing a wedding ring almost a year later. Though there was no denying the curl in my stomach the next time I saw him after asking about it and it being gone.

Despite how much I'm attracted to him, I don't and I won't push. Bryce has enough on his plate as it is, he doesn't need to add firing an employee because they were interested in something that wasn't reciprocated and is wholly unethical.

"You . . ."

"You told me to pay attention, to take initiative, so I did. I hope you don't mind." I hate how small my voice sounds, how breathless. I feel like I'm back in school, pushing my way through classes to hit that top spot and be told I've done well. I've earned my place. It was so much easier to achieve back then.

"Mind? God, Rachel. You're a lifesaver. I've been so stressed about starting this up, and the admin that came with it that I was unprepared for. This is wonderful, you're w—" Bryce catches himself and I hold my breath waiting for what he was about to say but he clears his throat. "You're helping me out more than you know and I'm sorry it's been such a mess. I know coming from a big company to my . . . less-than-put-together business is a downgrade."

Ángel scoffs next to me and I finally tear my gaze away to give him a dirty look.

"What?" Ángel defends. "It's so not a downgrade. They treated her like trash, especially Keith and that two-faced ex-boss of yours." Ángel gestures to Sebastian as if he expects him to back up his claims.

"What did they do?" Sebastian asks with a slight edge to his voice instead and Farren pulls a face that lets me know she never did tell him after I left that night.

"After the debacle with confronting Andrew and his sexist bullshit, they forced her to go out and celebrate the promotion that should have rightfully been hers—I still think you should look into filing some discrimination thing"—Ángel pauses his answer to Sebastian to scold me before he carries on with my old colleague—"Keith had his drunk paws all over her in the bar, insulted and hit on her, practically told her that if they messed around it would be fine cause he's her boss now and nobody needed to know."

"*Ángel*," I grit out between my teeth, ungrateful for his airing my dirty laundry in front of my new boss and his friends, and Sebastian for that matter even though that's not as bad. He knows it was shitty there. I'm just not pleased that Ángel took it upon himself to tell the rest of the table as well.

"What the fuck?" It comes from Gabrielle and the whole table turns to look at the woman who up until now has been fairly reserved unless spoken to directly. Logan barks out a laugh beside her and it kind of dispels the tension for the whole table.

"I could apologize for my language, but I won't. That's so not okay." Gabrielle on the brink of anger does not look like the type of woman you should cross and I will make sure I never do.

"Right?" Ángel emphasizes beside me and I give him that elbow to the stomach that I've been thinking about way too many times tonight. His breath huffs out of him in a little grunt and I ignore it to look at Bryce.

His expression is shuttered and I don't know why it bothers me but it does.

"It's *not* a downgrade. Not being chained to a desk, getting to see Dulaney and go to escape rooms, and brainstorming themes and how they can be incorporated into a design is not a downgrade. It's more creative freedom that I've had in years and I'm grateful you hired me." I hope he hears the sincerity in my voice. Even if Lakin-Cole and its employees hadn't treated me like this I'd still be grateful.

Bryce's lips are pressed into an unhappy line, the biggest sign of discomfort I've seen on him today. His body is tense, shoulders slightly raised as if he's holding himself as still as he can without his agitation escaping. *Not* that I've been watching for that sort of thing since I've noticed physical tells are the easiest way to know what he's thinking—not at all. I give him a small smile and his lips soften a little, a slight curl at the corner of his mouth alleviating my worry over how this situation has just gone down.

I turn my attention to his friends, wanting to bridge that gap, and *not* wanting my own to embarrass me again.

"So, since we're on the topic of work. Logan, Bryce tells me you're in marketing . . ." It's more awkward than I'd like and Ángel mumbles something under his breath about this not being a networking event, but it's the best I can scrape together when my mind is full of half smiles and sad eyes.

"Yeah, we went into college with a single goal in mind—one that was harebrained and not something we should have planned whole degrees around but here we are. Bryce was going to get the business degree, I would get the marketing degree, and together we'd open a hobby shop."

"What kind of hobbies?" Farren asks Logan and I could kiss her in gratitude.

"Magic." Logan and Gabrielle's lips twitch with their suppressed mirth.

"Like MAGIC: The Gathering?" Farren asks and the two finally let their laughs free. Bryce chuckles softly beside me and I find myself relaxing at the sound.

"No, that would certainly have been easier, more popular, and far more lucrative." Logan takes a bite of his noodle dish.

"Wait, so, actual magic?" I ask Bryce and his large hand comes up to cover his eyes, a groan escaping him.

"Yes. Actual magic."

"That's so fun!" I can't help the tone of my voice. It's part excitement and part just thinking this is the cutest damn thing I've heard.

Bryce peeks out at me between his fingers as if he's surprised at my reaction and I can only imagine what an interest in magic would have been like as a teenaged boy. Somehow I doubt vapid young people would have thought it was very cool.

"I used to be really into collecting old items, especially art and photographs. For a long time I thought I'd become a restorer but there's not a lot of money in the arts, and computers seemed to be the ship everyone was boarding, so I went along with it. Also didn't help that my mom was getting sick of all my 'creepy old crap' lying around and running me out to markets and thrift stores on weekends. I'll tell you what though, twelve-year-olds who like antiquing aren't the height of cool." I'm breathless by the time I'm done speaking.

By the end of my uncharacteristic sharing Bryce's hand has dropped from his face and his mouth is curving up at the image of pre-teen me shouldering old ladies out of the way at antique flea markets.

"So, it's no wonder you're constantly enamored with Historic Dulaney and that apartment of yours. Even though every stair creaks and the water heater works at the speed of a Model-T. I kind of feel bad now that I didn't take you to one of the properties I was looking at. It was a Brownstone that had been in the same family for over a hundred years," Bryce says.

Something in my expression must betray my hidden disappointment at missing out and fright at being pegged so solidly. I love my new apartment and the floors that countless generations have walked. I love wandering Main Street and its offshoots to stare at the buildings that have seen more life than I ever will.

This isn't something I've thought about in over a decade. I put it away, tucked into its own box to gather dust in the dead end hallways of my memories. Saved and cataloged right along with people I encountered in that season of my life and the faces I kept searching for in antique tins of photographs that I knew would be impossible to pinpoint—the ones that echoed my own.

How much of Mom discouraging my hobby was because she was fed up with it and how much was her recognizing a yearning and hunger she didn't know how to fill?

"Miss Metropolitan has a soft spot for lost, forgotten things. I never would have seen it coming, your vibe is very . . ." Ángel pokes fun, lighthearted of course, but it's enough to make me bristle.

"Modern," Sebastian finishes the sentence and the two nod at each other.

"It's been a long time." There's nothing else I can say when I'm being tossed into the sea of unresolved feelings I thought I'd left behind along with my childish longing and unpopular hobby.

"I think it's great and if you're interested, I know of a really awesome antique mall up near the state line on the way to Gettysburg," Bryce says quietly, only for me, and he bumps his shoulder against mine in camaraderie.

His arm is warm against mine, and even closer than it was before. It would be simple enough for me to drop my hand from my lap to tangle with his where it dangles between us. But that would be seeking comfort where I shouldn't.

Although the reasons against that are growing weaker as my attraction and admiration for him build.

How many more slips, how many innocent touches until I embarrass us both?

Dinner wraps up soon after and I'm a little more withdrawn as I say goodbye to my friends. Ángel pulls me into a tight hug and apologizes for picking at a scab he had no idea existed and I assure him we're good. Maybe it's better having someone else know, getting it off my shoulders with my safe person. Maybe it's healthier that way?

"Tonight has just been a lot. I'm trying to make this work and bringing so many pieces of my life together in one night has taken it out of me."

"Speaking of—have you told your family about the move and the job yet?"

"Not yet."

His bleached brow rises and his mouth puckers as he tells me without words that I'm being ridiculous. "You should tell them while it's still on your own terms. You don't want to wait until it becomes a necessity and things get even more strained because of it."

"Yes, Doctor Reyes."

He ignores my eyeroll and his expression becomes cheeky. "While we're talking about what the doctor ordered. Jump that man's bones before I do."

"You're a mess. I am *not* going to sleep with my boss. Besides, I don't think you're his type."

Ángel doesn't even have to say it for me to know what he's thinking. "Don't worry, I'm not selfish. I wouldn't hog him."

"Stop trying to bait me. Besides, I don't share." My sentiment gives more away than I'd like because Ángel looks like the cat that caught the canary before he turns to leave.

I want to call after him and clarify that I didn't mean it the way he took it but I'd only be lying to both of us. Farren and Sebastian each bid me goodbye while I'm still standing shell shocked that I admitted to my best friend that I want my boss, just for myself.

"You ready to head out?" Bryce asks and I come back to myself and an empty sidewalk, our friends dispersed back to their lives.

"Sure." I follow behind him on the way to the car and he looks over his shoulder at me every couple of feet as if he's checking that I'm still with him and I wish I could tell him to stop.

Stop looking at me. Stop seeing me. Stop being so fucking kind and cute, and considerate, and on my mind every day. Stop giving me pieces of your life in such a small way that I look up and realize the picture is getting clearer with every day and only more beautiful for it.

We do our little dance of him opening the door for me and

waiting until I'm situated before he shuts it for me. He settles into his side and the car beeps as he powers it up.

We're on the beltway before he breaks the silence. "Do you want to talk about it?"

"Sorry?" It what? There are so many 'its' right now. I can only hope he doesn't mean my ill-advised interest in him that's slowly smoldering into something more with every brush of his skin against mine.

"Whatever made you stop antiquing."

Fuck.

That's not an easier topic and time seems to slow, my heartrate pulsing heavily in my ears before I decide to divulge. My chest is so heavy with past hurts that part of me wants to shed some of it, share the weight.

"Some of it was interest, and appreciation for beautiful things, but Ángel was right. I have a soft spot for lost, forgotten things because sometimes that's what I feel like. My mother got tired of my scavenging, of me wondering about lives I might have lived and people I might have belonged to if they hadn't adopted me. If I'd been . . . kept by the parents I'm tied to by biology."

His blinker clicks as he merges onto our exit and I brave a look over at him. His face is a study in chiaroscuro, the darkness of night juxtaposed with bright headlights passing us. This time when he glances over at me I'm not worried about the repercussions of him doing it while he's driving and more like I'm afraid of what I'll see there.

"You're adopted?"

I nod, my throat tight at the admission that I've never made to anyone before. The irrational inadequacy that's trailed me my whole life, that I've been trying to outrun and outperform and disprove, hangs between us suspended in my silence.

He seems to be weighing his words before he speaks and it takes a few moments of tension before he does.

"That's their loss."

I suck a shocked breath between my teeth, the air catching in my lungs. Out of everything I could have envisioned him saying, that never sprang to mind. Too close. He's too close to being able to completely disarm me with words alone and I change the subject before he can burrow any deeper into the crack in my armor.

"What made you stop enjoying magic?"

His gaze moves back to the road and I watch his fingers curl around the steering wheel, clenching around the leather before he huffs out a breath and expels the reason like he has to get it out before he changes his mind.

"My ex, Stephanie, considered it childish. She was looking for a man with a portfolio and a hefty 401K, and a ten-year plan for the future. The kind of person I tried but failed to be and our marriage ended for it. After she left, I looked up and it had been years since I'd touched anything that made me feel alive, since I visited my family or made time for friends that were mine and not *ours*."

The escape room, Logan, it all falls into place and I realize he's got just as much to prove as I do, just as much baggage making him doubt himself and his worth when what was his world told him he wasn't enough.

There's no fitting way to respond other than to take a page out of his book.

"That's her loss."

# CHAPTER  8

*THAT'S HER LOSS.*

Rachel turning my phrase against me feels like a blow to my ribs and I have to swallow the emotion welling. She's just reciprocating. Logically, I know she wouldn't be saying this if I hadn't uttered something similar but the wounded part of me wants to believe it, believe *her* and that she means it.

"Sounds like they've done a number on us, huh?" Her statement is dry, barely even humorous, but it's enough to pull a chuckle from me.

"So, you've had a little more experience with this than I have. Does it get better? Do we ever get to a point where we stop searching for our worth in others?" I look over at her again, finding it harder and harder to avoid it as every day goes by.

What if I miss a smile? What if the sun catches on her hair and lights it up with gold and I don't see it?

"I'll tell you if I find out and you do the same if you get there before I do, deal?" she asks. Our jokes are barely that but after the heaviness of our confessions it's necessary. Drowning in her big, dark eyes, I lick my dry lips before I answer.

"Promise."

The rest of the drive is quiet. I contemplate this evening and I'm sure she's doing the same. Every moment, from Logan's whispered, "She's stunning" and Gabrielle poking him in the ribs for his lack of subtlety, to the scent of her hair as we looked over the will together in the escape room. Each brush of her arm against mine at dinner set my nerve endings on fire and the way her face had fallen during dinner— I acknowledge and quickly set aside the way seeing her look that sad made something inside of me clench.

It's joined by the niggling sense of watching her interact with Ángel, the easy intimacy between them, and despite her just calling him her best friend I can't help but wonder if there's more there. My inner voice that sounds suspiciously jealous pipes up that Ángel's statement upset her and I'm the one smoothing it over. He might have gotten to hug her but I get to see her almost daily.

*Because you're her boss and if you hit on her you'll be no better than the asshole she left D.C. to get away from.*

Have I already overstepped? I can't help the urge to be near her. Somehow I live in those moments with her hand in mine, that touch intoxicating even if it's just for a second, even if it's just under the guise of helping her. She's everywhere. Rachel Mackey is a thunderstorm and I am cracked earth begging to be quenched by her.

I park outside her building, step around the car to get the door for her, all so I can have her soft hand curl around mine. This time I take it a step further. I walk her to the robin's egg blue wood leading up to her apartment and she pauses with her hand on the knob.

Turning those large dark eyes on me, I swallow, wishing I was better at this. If I were anyone else I'd know what to say, how close to stand, when to push or pull. I've never been good at gauging the mood or picking up on context clues. Stephanie and her departure, the one that surprised me but felt like an inevitability for her, is only proof of how much I miss. I've never been at ease in this kind of scenario in my whole life.

Somehow, Rachel doesn't make me feel . . . off. Tumbled around and spit out, and aching for the equilibrium of her touch, but never wrong. Every moment with her feels strangely right and I'm terrified to jeopardize it.

"I had a lovely time meeting your friends," she says, barely above a whisper, struggling to fit her key into the slot.

Downtown is quiet, streetlights leaving golden pools spilling from them every couple of yards and perhaps it's the safety of the night around us, bathing us in darkness like a blanket of quiet words and loud longing, but I make my move.

Stepping closer so that I can feel her back pressed against my front, barely, but enough to steal the breath from my lungs. Reaching over, I cover her hand with mine and help her guide the metal home. Trailing my fingertips down the back of her hand, I ghost them over her forearm before taking a step back to clear my mind from the wayward thoughts bursting forth.

She smells like spice, botanicals with a bite. It's subtle, the escape room dulling some of it, but now with the early summer breeze and the proximity of her body to mine, her scent floods my brain and I want nothing more than to drown in her.

"So did I," I respond after too long. I know it's been too long because I have to swallow and moisten my lips to speak, parched.

"Bryce . . ." Something hangs suspended in the way she says my name—plaintive and breathless, and something else—something I want to reach out for and hold with both hands, but I could have this wrong.

I could have all of this wrong and then I'll make a mess of it for both her and me. There's no HR department, no protection. Just my mom's guidance and a contract I got from Google, and this sick pang in my stomach wishing I'd met her under any circumstances but these.

"Rachel?"

She cants backwards, her fingers gripping the keys now freed from the lock, and she's a hair's breadth from my body. I'm torn. Part of me waits, begging her to make the first move so that I can't be responsible for the blow up to come. The other part, the one that's been growing louder and louder since Stephanie called me meek, wants to prove the opposite, to inhabit the confidence I never felt comfortable enough to step into.

It's the second part that takes over, just for a moment. My hands wrap around her biceps, goosebumps rising on her skin at the touch. She shivers, though I doubt it's from the cold and I can only hope I'm reading this right. Weeks of glances, and the barest of touches, if she feels even a quarter of what I do—if she wants this even an iota as much as me—it might be worth risking.

Stepping forward, solid against her, I breathe her in and whisper my false confidence into her hair.

"I need you to be sure. I can't read you or this. I don't want to make a mess of things or misunderstand. I need words." My voice is deeper and riddled with gravel, forced through my nerves and the words leave me at her mercy.

Her head falls back against me, her breath hot against my collar, and she shivers in response. Her hand comes up to cover mine where it rests on her arm. I wait a beat, for her to say something, anything. A car rushing by us pulls me out of the cocoon of desire sweeping through me. Now isn't the time. I need to process my feelings and what they mean for both of us —if there were to be an us. I have to be prepared for whatever outcome, whichever path we go down . . . together or separately.

Planting a kiss against her temple, I whisper against her skin. "Goodnight, Rachel."

Her touch slips from my hand and I walk away without a backward glance, my mind full of half-formed images of her and me, and everything I'd do with her if she said the words.

*You're her boss. She's off limits. You're trying not to be like every other person who treated her like everything other than her own person. You don't get to decide to want her and then expect her to welcome your attention. You're her boss. She's off limits.*

But what if she wasn't? What if Rachel Mackey said the word and I followed her up those stairs and past every one of my insecurities? What if I was brave enough?

*Brave enough to get hurt again?*

My brain is bound and determined to ruin it for me, self doubt creeping in and reminding me of the suckerpunch that was my last relationship.

Though, Rachel and I don't necessarily *need* to have a relationship. I could be casual. I can do casual, if that's what she wants.

*Can you? Mr. Monogamous Dawson who's only been with two women, one of whom was his wife. You're sure* you *can do casual?*

If that's the only way I can get an invitation to cross this painful line drawn in the sand, the one protecting us both, I'll take what I can get. Even though I'm sure Rachel Mackey would *casually* wreck me if I gave her the chance. All I can do is hope, and wait.

THERE'S A CERTAIN PAINFUL BEAUTY IN IT BEING A SATURDAY NIGHT. I leave her at her doorstep and then I have two full days to overthink every second because of her work schedule. I could call or text. But my bravery left when I did and I can't help feeling like

I've messed this up before it even started. I make up for it by working myself into exhaustion at the theater, starting with the process of ridding the space of its musty and old interiors.

Sweat dripping, and making me absolutely miserable, I head out to the hardware store multiple times over Sunday and Monday to find the right way to unbolt the seats from the floor.

On Tuesday morning, earlier than I'd usually be communicating with Rachel about the day ahead, I find a text message from her, sent at a ridiculous time last night.

RACHEL

Hey, I'm not feeling too hot. Is it okay if I work on some actual coding and ideas today and I can present them more formally once I'm done?

No worries.

I'm starting with clearing the space before it's usable and it's been a mess of physical labor. Knowing that the "after" is being taken care of is a huge relief.

Take the week to work on it and we can evaluate together after that?

Perfect. I'll keep you updated!

Same! Have a good week 😊

You too!

Oh god, I sent an emoji. I've never been the kind of person to do that but I'm petrified that she'll misconstrue my tone. It's always my fear that I'm either not understanding the underlying mood to an encounter or sure I'm interpreting people correctly, or I'm worried I'm not coming across correctly. Most of the time though I feel totally oblivious and worried I'm missing something crucial.

The slow death between me and Stephanie only served to amp all that up and in the face of something so new, so unformed and barely there with Rachel feels like a wisp of smoke, or a soap bubble. One wrong move and it'll dissipate.

So, I wait but mostly I hide. My hands ache at the end of the day, dust chokes the back of my throat from carpets older than I am and leave my sinuses miserable. The dumpster behind the theater is full of discarded seats and parts of the floor that have ripped up with them. I've got one room gutted and feeling pretty good about my prospects. My days start and end with this space and I collapse into bed after scarfing down the food my mother leaves in the microwave for me.

I should join them for dinner. I should make more of an effort. But the hyperfixation has kicked in and I need to see this motivation through to the end before I lose it. Though there's nothing like procrastinating something to get me to focus on something else. If I put off thinking about Rachel and the non-thing that happened between us then it only serves as fuel to get the job done.

*Of course this has nothing to do with the fact that the sooner you get stuff done and the business up and running, the sooner she won't be your employee anymore.*

My inner bitterness crops up, taunting and teasing me more so than usual the last few days. I've never been able to lie to myself, to hide from my thoughts, no matter how close to the vest I keep everything. Part of why I'm avoiding my parents is because I know they'll see through it in less than a minute. Though that comes with the perk of knowing me my whole life. So, I wallow in silence and work until my knees ache from kneeling and my hands are a mess that'll eventually become calluses. One can only hope.

By the next Thursday, Logan steps in to pull me from my misery.

"What are you doing on Saturday?" His voice comes through the speaker phone as I try to undo a stripped screw.

"More of the same. I've been trying to get the rooms empty so we can start actually making something of this dump." I grunt as the wrench slips and my hand bangs against the metal keeping the chair in place. Stifling a curse under my breath, I inhale so deep the air rattles in my lungs.

"You know, I've been thinking. Maybe a room themed after something local? Or lean into the theater aspect and do movie-inspired ones," Logan suggests.

"I'll bring it up to Rachel but I like the sound of it. It'll be unique at the very least."

Logan sighs. "I didn't mean to give you more work. I was actually calling to tell you to take a break."

"Can't today, or the next week. I'm at a crucial point." It's a lie. I could break whenever I want but I still don't know what to say. All that talk about processing the conflicting feelings roiling within me and all I've done is brood instead.

"Fine. Then the Saturday after. Two weeks should be far enough in advance for your calendar to allow it. It's Pride and Kate—my neighbor that came with us to that bad escape room which set all this shit into motion—she's a bit apprehensive about going single, especially since she's sure to run into her ex-girlfriend and her new partner. I told her we'd be there for moral support."

Grimacing from the pain radiating across my knuckles and the prospect of putting on my "people" face in a huge group of strangers, I fight with myself to say yes. The only thing I hate more than the idea of hot, sweaty bodies and large crowds is disappointing the people I care about.

"What time?" I ask.

"It starts around ten a.m. but you can cut out whenever you want. I just—"

"You want to be there for your friend. She came out to support me at your request, so I'll do the same. I'll be there."

"You're the best. Has anyone told you lately that you're the best?" Logan asks.

*That's her loss.* Rachel's words clang in my mind. "Not quite." But not far off. Hearing that . . . hearing that I'm something that would hurt to lose fizzes inside of me.

"The set up starts at the park and runs along the riverwalk. I'll meet you at the big oak at ten."

"Big oak at ten. Anything else I should know?" The pain is a throb that sends sharp stinging bolts through my fingers when I try to straighten them out. Turns out punching the metal legs of a bolted down chair is a colossally bad idea.

"Do you own anything rainbow?" Logan asks.

"No? Should I find something?" I manage between trying to push my knuckle against my mouth, as if kissing it away like my mother would've when I was younger will actually do something.

"Don't worry. I got you. See you there!"

Before I can ask or worry about what that means, Logan has hung up and it's becoming increasingly clear that the rest of today's work is a wash. My knuckles are busted. Kissing away the pain didn't work but my mother will have some peroxide or something to clean it at the very least.

Locking up behind me and plopping down heavily onto the driver's seat, I take the long way home. If that happens to include a jaunt past a particular blue door, that's no one's business but mine.

If my parents are surprised to see me home at a reasonable time, or entering through the front door instead of escaping up to the garage apartment, it's overtaken by their concern once they see my hand.

"*Bryce Locke Dawson,*" my mother admonishes, running water over a paper towel to press on my knuckles.

"What happened?" my dad asks from his perch on the bar stool at the kitchen island. His owlish eyes blink at me with worry behind his glasses, brows drawn low, and I realize with clarity that this is probably what I'll look like when I'm older. Give or take a few things I inherited from mom.

Someday I'll be sitting at my own table, with or without someone else to share it with, glasses perched on my nose and my face lined with all the emotions I let slip past my facade.

"Got into a fight with one of the theater chairs bolted to the ground. The chair won."

My dad barks out a laugh and my mother just shakes her head, tutting as she rushes over with the first aid kit. Cleaning the creases of my knuckles, bruises already forming, the cuts sting as she passes an antibacterial over them.

"How's the renovation going?" Mom asks, bent over my hand.

"It's slow. I underestimated how much needed to get done, but I hope I can still make it work by December. Six-ish months should be enough, in theory."

"I can't believe it's been two months already. How's it going? How's that girl you hired getting on?" My dad manages it between bites of mini pretzels, always grazing.

"*Woman*, Dad. She's a woman, not a girl, as I've mentioned before. And it's . . . going."

I stare down at my hand, my mom slathering on some kind of ointment then pressing gauze to my knuckles, before bandaging them up. I'm sure it's overkill but being cared for feels so nice I'm not going to argue. Besides, it gives me the excuse not to answer my dad's last question, and I can only hope he doesn't pick up on me avoiding it.

My dad huffs, the meaning behind it indecipherable, and when I turn to him again he schools his face into something neutral before offering me some of his pretzels.

My mom pats my forearm, apparently finished with her impromptu nursing. "You should invite her over for dinner."

She must anticipate that I'll protest because she carries on without a moment's hesitation in her mom voice, "I'm sure she's lonely away from everything and everyone she knows. Dulaney might be coming home to you, but she's still finding her footing."

Theresa Dawson throws in a sharp look to emphasize her feelings and I wilt under her gaze.

"I'll ask her if she has a preference on time or any kind of food issues."

My dad laughs at how quick I folded and when my mother trains her sharp expression on him he sobers immediately, winking at me as soon as she's gone back to her task of staring into the refrigerator as if dinner is going to jump out at her if she looks long enough.

"No one tells you when you're growing up that the worst part of adulthood will be trying to come up with meals, every meal, every day, for the rest of your life," Mom grumbles, opening drawers, condiments clinking in the refrigerator door.

"What I'm hearing is, we're going out for dinner." My dad pops another pretzel into his mouth, eyes twinkling with hope.

My parents play this game constantly. She'll try to be responsible and he'll be waiting in the wings to enable whatever thawing she eventually shows. It works because mom gets what she wants without feeling like she has to ask for it—something both she and I struggle with—and dad gets to pretend all the good ideas are his.

"I think dinner out sounds great. I'll come with you," I say, leaning into my dad's coaxing.

"And we're going to pretend it's not because you'll get a free meal out of it?" My dad teases and when I shrug he throws a pretzel at me, the mini twist bouncing off my arm and onto the floor.

"Okay, enough you two. We'll go out." Mom acts like it's a chore, playing her part perfectly but the Cheshire grin at the end is new and something about it has my stomach clenching with nerves.

"Why don't you invite Rachel? It'll be less cozy if we meet her outside of our house for the first time."

It doesn't escape my notice that my mom said 'for the first time' as in 'of many' and I sputter for a moment before acquiescing.

*Wow. Doing great at standing up for yourself. So not meek at all.*

Shut up.

I shoot over the text before I can think too hard about it, or before my mother takes it upon herself to send the text for me.

> Hey, sorry to bother you.

> I'm going out to dinner with my parents and they were asking about you.

> Would you like to grab something to eat with us?

> No pressure.

> (Or some because my mom has been curious about you for weeks and it's driving me up the wall. Save me.)

I hold my breath when I shoot it off into the ether.

"She might be busy. Even though she doesn't have friends in Dulaney yet, she's got some really nice friends in D.C. They might have made plans."

"Oh, you've met her friends?" My mom asks, eyebrow quirking up at my dad and his lips purse to hold back his laughter.

"Not like that. She's my employee. It's professional. We tried out an escape room with Logan and Gabrielle, and Rachel's friends." My tone is terser than I'd like and I regret it immediately.

After an exhausting day, in pain and frustrated at more than just the task ahead of me, it's really hard to police how things come out of my mouth.

"We're just teasing, son. You've been happier the last few months than we've seen you in quite a long time. We only wondered if she was part of it. We won't rib you for it again." My dad gives me a sad smile and I pull in a shaky breath with my nod. Ready to remind them again that she might not say yes when her text comes through.

RACHEL

Rachel to the rescue.

When and where? I'm starving.

My smile must speak for me because my dad leaves his pretzels behind and heads out of the kitchen with a, "I'll get the keys."

My mother peeks over at the phone I've left unguarded and I scramble to grab it before she can see what I said about her.

"Tell her we'll meet her at Stacked in fifteen to twenty. Hopefully it's enough notice for her. I know you mentioned at some point she doesn't have a car so downtown is best, unless you want us to pick her up on the way somewhere else?"

My mom with unfettered access to Rachel—a captive audience —for an undetermined amount of time while we're confined in a small space?

"Stacked is great."

I SURGE TO MY FEET WHEN SHE ENTERS THE RESTAURANT, SLIGHTLY windswept, an apology already on her lips for being late when she's perfectly on time. My parents are just over excited and early.

Her eyes are on mine, a question in them as she gets closer, and I don't dare hug her even though I want to. We've never crossed that line, not really, unless you count me catching her. I'd rather not do it for the first time in front of my parents. Instead, I step out from the table to stand beside her, my hand hovering over her lower back and wishing I could close that inch distance to touch her.

"Rachel, this is my mom, Theresa, and my dad, Frank."

She turns her questioning gaze from me, morphing her expression into a bright smile that I'm close enough to tell doesn't quite reach her eyes, and she sticks her hand out to shake each of theirs.

"Nice to meet you!"

Pulling her chair out for her, I help her scoot in before I take my place beside her, facing my dad and I want to shake my head at the excitement glinting in his eyes. Mom always said he was like Gene Kelly when she met him; he had that movie star sparkle in his gaze and a smooth mouth to go with it. For an awkward and shy Theresa, it was just who she needed to step out of her shell.

"So, Rachel, Bryce tells me you're a developer. How are you finding the change from D.C. to here? Not just in the job requirements but living as well?"

And I wish my mom had stayed shy Theresa because I can already tell she's had these questions fired up and ready to go since I hired Rachel.

"It's lovely here. I can definitely see the benefit of bringing something like the escape room into a community like this. There's a healthy amount of foot traffic by the old theater, especially on the weekends, so between people who are familiar with Dulaney and what it offers, and others who are popping in for a weekend escape, it'll be a good venture. I've been enjoying the charm." It sounds almost practiced, and if I hadn't just spent weeks with her I would have taken it at face value, but I've played the sound of her voice over and over in my mind and I can tell there's something just a little too stiff about it.

In fact, her whole body seems kind of tense. Posture perfect, in an outfit far too nice for an American-style casual restaurant like Stacked and I haven't seen her like this since the first time we met to do our interview.

*She's nervous*, I realize.

"Rachel has an interest in history and antiques." I offer it as a way to deflect their eyes off of her and I feel the catch in her breathing in how her arm brushes mine, by the time their attention is on her again she's got her armor back and glinting prettier than ever.

"You'll have to take her up to the antique mall." My mom doesn't wait for me to agree or ask whether I'd be open to it. She's decided it's the right move based on the situation in front of her. Interest plus opportunity plus attraction equals antique date.

"Oh, it's not a bother, really. It's been a while since I've indulged in it seriously, but it has been fun to see a lot of the history in town."

"Speaking of history." Dad winks at me as he pitches in to shift the conversation away from Rachel and I'll never be upset at how well Frank Dawson can read the mood of a crowd, down to the last person. Or maybe he's just picking up on how tense I am worrying about Rachel. "Theresa and I had our first date at the theater you all are renovating."

Subject switched over and Rachel no longer in the hot seat, our food arrives and I am content to sit back and watch. My dad and Rachel do the majority of talking, jumping from thing to thing, eventually landing on music and I know my dad is in his element.

"A fun little fact I've learned over the last few weeks is that you put Jimmy Buffet's Margaritaville into a minor key and it's the most depressing thing you've ever heard in your life." Rachel's observation blows my dad's mind.

"It's a breezy beach song. How can it possibly be depressing?" As somewhat of a yacht rock aficionado, he's running through all the lyrics he can remember. It's like watching a kid learn that Santa isn't real.

"He's singing about wasting away in an alcohol-fueled haze after his wife left him on their vacation, and when you take away the steel drum and the beach vibes, it's kind of a punch to the gut."

My dad sputters at her statement and I chuckle. It's rare that he has nothing to say. Gift of the gab and all that, but Rachel's disarmed him and my mom's smug smile mirrors my own. Neither one of us have been good at thwarting my dad when he's on a roll. My mom and I get too stuck on arguing our specific point, and dad just pirouettes around it onto something else, pivoting the argument as many times as needed to win.

"Didn't peg you for a Jimmy Buffet kind of gal," my dad eventually manages and she grins, a real one for the first time tonight, that devastating dimple cutting into her cheek.

"Oh, I'm not. The bar my best friend works at has a Tropical Tuesdays thing in the summer and because a lot of the Hill is in recess in August it gets quieter than usual, so I keep him company. It's a lot of Margaritaville, and Escape, and drinks with umbrellas."

"Ángel?" I ask, trying not to bristle with an unfamiliar jealousy and Rachel nods.

It never hit me with Stephanie— jealousy. At first, I think part of me was just so happy someone looked at me with interest after bumbling my way through most of high school and college. There was a hint of being starstruck, until there wasn't. But I always thought I wasn't enough of a prize to feel like I could, or *wanted*, a claim over her. She transcended me and I put her up on a pedestal, and the distance between us only grew.

This *thing* with Rachel, this unnamed, hungry thing feels so different. I've wanted to touch Rachel, to *know* her, since the first time we met. And not because she batted her eyelashes at me to get what she needed out of the exchange. Rachel takes an interest in *me* as a person.

Anxious energy builds up in my body as I think about the moment outside her door and my fingers clench into a fist before I remember my mishap today. Needless to say, pain shoots through my injured hand and I hiss a strained breath.

"Oh no. What happened?" Rachel's tone shifts, concern bleeding through the mirth left from her victory over my dad.

"It's nothing," I say, brushing it off and trying to hide my hand on my lap.

"He hurt his hand. I patched it up as best as I could." My mom betrays me and I shoot her a look, hoping she knows exactly how unimpressed I am with her right then.

"Bryce?" It's the pleading in her voice, the open worry in her eyes that has me lifting my hand for her to view.

It's not the one next to her, slightly out of reach, but she leans over and cradles it carefully in both of hers. Inspecting it, though nothing is visible because of the bandages.

"When?"

"Today."

Our clipped words might sound cold but I'm filled with a heat that won't diffuse. Every second of her hands on mine, and something about the bite of pain and the softness of her touch, is torture in the best way.

"How?"

"Renovations. My hand slipped while I was working and . . ." I shrug, because what else is there to say when the result is evident.

"Was someone there with you?"

I can't lie to her, and she sees it in my hesitation to answer anyway, so there's no point even trying.

"*Bryce*." There are leagues wrapped up in that one word. Disappointment, worry, frustration, hurt. "If I'd have known you've been doing it all alone . . ."

"It's my responsibility. There's absolutely nothing in your contract about physical labor. I couldn't possibly ask or expect—"

Before I can keep defending my choices, she's talking again. "Screw the contract. You got hurt and I bet you drove yourself with that hand. It could have been broken. No." She shakes her head, dark hair swinging with the movement and I want to touch it so badly, see if it feels as soft as it looks. "No more. From now on if one of us is going to be at the theater, both of us will be there. I can help with the reno, or program while you're working. Heaven forbid you were up on a ladder and fell or something."

Her seriousness and stern words, the way she sounds almost protective nearly do me in and I have to deflect before the emotion overwhelms me.

"Oh, and you'd know all about ladders and falling." My mouth quirks up on the side, the reference to her ill-advised decorating technique.

"That was *one* time." She rolls her eyes and her mirth is back, light spilling through the crack in my chest.

"I think it's a good idea, hon. You shouldn't be there all alone. And if you need help with anything, please let us know." My mother's voice pulls me out of the moment and I realize with startling clarity that my hand is still within Rachel's grasp and I had completely forgotten we were even in the middle of a dinner.

Rachel covers her shock better and carefully extracts her hands from mine, nodding at my mom, pleased to have backup.

"It's settled then. You'll take two weeks to rest your hand before you even *think* of doing more, and when you do, I'll be there." The promise and threat in there makes my stomach flip and I grin like a fool, covering it with a bite of my food when I catch my dad's eyes on me.

"Next Monday," I urge. I can't afford to wait much longer than that.

"That's only ten days." I try to give him a stern look but he just smiles and I give in after a bit. "Only if you go to urgent care or something and have them do a proper X-Ray and tetanus shot. Think of the workman's comp you'd have to pay out."

This time I roll my eyes at her. "I'm the workman and the boss. I'd have to pay myself."

"OSHA violation then."

"I'll go if you stop threatening me with lawsuits."

"Next Monday it is."

We share a smile and then the check's arrived and we're saying our goodbyes but I'm still thinking about the way my hand tingles from her touch. She shakes hands with my parents again, avoiding my injured one so it becomes some strange squeeze instead, closer to holding my hand than anything else.

She sweeps from the restaurant much the same way she entered it, only this time the air is thinner, *less* without her here. Or perhaps it's just me deflating after all of the excitement.

Walking to the car, I'm lost in my mind. I buckle up in the back, ignoring the pain in my hand and catch my dad's eyes in the rearview mirror. It's not until we pull up to the urgent care in town that I know has late hours that the silence is broken.

"We really like her." My mom says it so simply, as if remarking on the weather or something just as inane, but we all know it isn't. Her favor isn't easily curried, and for her to feel sure enough to speak for my father as well, it means something. The fact that she *never* said anything even close to this about Stephanie gives it even more weight.

"Not that it means anything, because she is just my *employee*," I stress as I get out of the car. "But that's good to know."

"If you step back for a moment, take in the big picture, you'll notice that the lines you keep drawing in the sand between you are too small to mean much." My mom's words halt me, halfway to the doors and tossed from the car window. "Call her whatever you like, employee or not, maybe it's time you think about just what it is holding you back. Because your father and I both know it's not some contract that'll run out within six months."

Swallowing past the dryness in my throat, the tumbleweed of thoughts whirling within my mind, I have nothing to say. Because they're not wrong, and I'm scared to look too closely at that. But maybe it's time I stop being so scared. Who exactly am I holding back for?

"I'll be out as soon as I'm done," I say in lieu of an actual answer and step into harsh overhead lighting—antiseptic, and a throbbing in my hand, head, and the traitorous heart hidden behind the cracked mess in my chest. Terrified to feel its insistent beat, thrumming with the thought of Rachel and what could be. Quiet, but there nonetheless.

# CHAPTER  9

I HELD HIS HAND. I HELD HIS HAND IN FRONT OF HIS PARENTS AND probably made a complete fool of myself. And I've fixated on it for days. It's time to call in reinforcements because I am so far out of my depth and in over my head that I can barely breathe without thinking about his scent and how I've missed it. All day Friday, and culminating in a moment of weakness where I woke up on Saturday, flushed and aching from a very vivid dream.

He was right there, so close his warmth seeped through all my clothing and my mind ran away with the image of us that close, that heat at its apex between us. He opened the door, metaphorically and physically, and I've been locked in my apartment with nothing but want and conflict inside of me since. *I need you to be sure*, he'd said and it stilled me. Because as sure as I am that this thing, this arcing energy between us may be magnificent to explore, I am not sure that I'm ready.

Between looming job insecurity if giving in proves a mistake, and the fact that I haven't been with anyone since Riley in any meaningful way despite all the Fridays at Public Service, it's scary to let myself picture the possibility of Bryce.

So, despite the fact that I know what he'll tell me—*Or maybe because of it*—I call Ángel.

"What's wrong?" His voice is thick with sleep and I should've thought about it before I called him at 8 a.m. on a Saturday morning after his Friday night shift.

"Nothing." My voice breaks on the second syllable and he gives a big sigh as I hear him shift in bed.

"Rachel, I'm barely awake and in a bed that isn't my own. What's up?"

"*Oh*. Shit. I'm sorry. I didn't mean to interrupt."

I hear more rustling and then another low voice, mumbling.

"My friend is having a crisis. I'm sorry, but I'm going to have to go." Ángel sounds further away, as if he's turned his head away from the phone.

"It's not a crisis, per se. I just—I might have held his hand last week, and there might have been a moment where he had me crowded against my front door. I need you to talk me out of it. I need you to be the voice of reason right now because all my normal excuses for not giving in just aren't cutting it anymore." I'm rambling, tripping over the words and as they leave my mouth I can tell how ridiculous I sound.

"Calm down. It's going to be okay. No need to panic." Confusion spreads through me at his reaction.

"I'm freaking out a little but I don't think it counts as a panic?"

"Just let me grab my things. Hold on." The sound does that thing where he gets quieter and I hear him whisper to his companion, "I'm sorry. It's bad. I have to go but I'll call you, okay?"

The stranger must agree because I hear Ángel's belt buckle jingle as he dresses himself, the phone likely pressed between his shoulder and ear.

"You are *not* using me as an excuse right now," I grit it out but without much anger behind it. It's not the first time we've rescued each other.

A door slams behind him and Ángel gives a sigh of what I can only assume is relief.

"Impeccable timing, as always. Thanks for that. I fell asleep by accident. The shift was a total bear last night. Your fuckwit of an ex-boss was there. I served him out of a dirty glass."

"While that's very sweet of you, I don't want you to get fired because you're retaliating on my behalf."

On my back, staring at the ceiling and the crown molding, and the stained glass Tiffany-esque light fixture above my bed, unlit in the early morning, I can't fight the push and pull within me.

I want this. I want Bryce. Dulaney and escape rooms, and large hands covering my own. A solid body at my back that makes me feel like I'm safe, infallible and worthwhile just for who I am and not what I can achieve.

"Now, what's going on with you and Brycey Boy?" The vocal quality changes.

"Are you in your car?"

"Yes?"

"Come over? I haven't left the apartment in over a week, since I went to meet Bryce's parents and I'm going a little stir crazy thinking about him all the time."

He whistles, the sound sucked in between his lips. "You met his *parents*."

"It's not like that. He's just mentioned me, I guess, and they were curious." Don't read too much into it. It might have been exactly that. I need to take it at face value because the alternative is too scary to contemplate.

"Rachel, when's the last time you met your bosses' parents? Hell, even a colleague's parents?"

"Shut up."

"I'll grab some gear and meet you outside your place, just shoot me the address. Looks like there's a Pride Parade downtown today."

My breath shudders out of me, taking some of the tension with it.

"Thank you, thank you! How come you know about the parade?"

"I have my ways," he says, his tone dropping into something teasing and mysterious.

"Be serious."

"Because I joined a stupid neighborhood group when you moved so I could make sure everything was okay. Sue me. You go get yourself showered and dressed the fuck up. If we're doing Pride, we're doing it right. I'll see you in like ninety minutes. Be ready." Ángel doesn't wait for my response before hanging up, and I text him my address.

Relief and giddiness at breaking my routine, and hopefully getting Bryce off my mind, spurs me out of bed.

By the time Ángel arrives, decked out in tight jean shorts, rainbow chaps, and some kind of rainbow fringed denim vest with no shirt underneath, I'm ready. Clearly we should have discussed better beforehand because we have two very different vibes going on right now. He's even gone and used Overtone to turn his bleached hair Barbie pink.

Ángel takes in my loosely curled hair, spilling over my shoulders, and my pink, purple, and dark blue bi flag colored sundress I had made a couple of years ago but haven't had the chance to wear.

"*Nice.*"

"You too. Though I'm not sure if Dulaney is ready." My smirk has him giving me a cheeky grin in response.

"This old thing? Just something I had laying around." He

holds his elbow out for me to take, like a courtly gentleman, not a half-naked take on a cowboy.

The June sun bakes down on us, kissing the tops of my shoulders and my nose as we walk toward the park. Downtown teems with people in various colorful shades and levels of risque clothing. Ángel doesn't stand out as much as I teased. As we approach, music increases in volume, a heart pounding pop song blaring from a stage and walkway.

Stalls are set up all along the riverwalk, selling clothing and jewelry, refreshment stations, and even a booth to register to vote with a local representative campaigning. I'm handed one of those silicone wristbands at the arched balloon entrance to the park, like the LiveStrong ones I remember from when I was a kid, only this one is marked with Dulaney Pride.

We peruse the little stalls and Ángel talks me into the kitschiest Maryland crab earrings done up in the bi flag colors instead of the Maryland yellow, black, red and white.

"Blue crabs are a whole culture here, even though Dulaney isn't on the Bay. Between crabs, Old Bay seasoning, and the Maryland flag, repping any of those is practically a personality trait that screams 'I'm from Maryland.' I've never seen anything like it," I say as we walk past the third seller stocking some kind of state-themed merch.

"State 'Pride', in more than one way. It's sweet, kind of, how much they care. What would it be like to feel so strongly about something so inconsequential?" Ángel muses and I turn toward him to argue, to defend this community and the people who have been nothing but kind and caring to me—to tell him that it can't be inconsequential if it means something to them—when I collide with a solid body and my breath is knocked from my lungs.

I grunt out an oof, and strong hands wrap around the tops of my arms to keep me from toppling backward. Staring into a strong chest, covered (mostly) by a rainbow tank top that looks a hair too small. A smattering of light brown chest hair peeks out at the top and I follow the freckles up the muscled arms holding me, over his brawny shoulders, and up some more. It's a functional strength. Grounded. It's the kind of body people swooned over before superheroes bodies became something vaguely scary. Solid without being "cut" and dehydrated to death.

"*Bryce*," I breathe.

He blinks once, twice, behind those glasses and I've never given much thought to how hot glasses could be until this man.

"Rachel." It's deep in a way that makes me shiver despite the summer sun, and the smile he gives me is boyish, only adding to the flush in my cheeks.

"Didn't think I'd be running into you today." I try to reorient myself but he hasn't let go and my heart is a drumline marching through my chest.

"Literally," Ángel murmurs beside me and Bryce's gaze travels over to my friend. The soft expression hardens into something neutral and I can't help but wonder if there's something else there. Does Bryce only look at me that way? Or is it Ángel specifically that has his attitude changing? Bryce looks between me and Ángel before swallowing hard. Is he . . . *jealous*? No. That's ridiculous. It can't be, but . . .

"Nice to see you again," Bryce says, his hands sliding down my arms before he steps back and I feel strangely bereft at the loss of contact.

"Same," Logan says and I peek around Bryce to see him standing there with what can only be called a cheeky grin on his face.

"And who is your other friend?" Ángel asks Logan.

"Kate, Ángel." Logan points between them. "Ángel, Kate."

"Good. Now that the introductions are done, why don't you show me where I can get something cold to drink and we'll leave these two to catch up," Ángel—the *traitor*—says to Logan and

Kate and they're walking off even though Ángel and I know full well where to find a cold drink. Given we got one half an hour ago.

"*Stupid Ángel, and his stupid meddling,*" I whisper under my breath. Not quiet enough because Bryce gives a little laugh.

"Meddling, huh? And why would he feel the need to do that?"

I stare at his throat, the strong column speckled with a few freckles I'd love to kiss. Every single one.

"It could have something to do with the fact that you're very good looking and single." I shrug as if it's no big deal.

Bryce's thumb and forefinger lightly lift my chin so that I'm staring up into those golden flecked eyes. "*Very* good looking, huh? According to Ángel or according to you?"

I've never seen him look this confident, this teasing. I try to break his gaze, heat burning up my neck and cheeks, and it's ridiculous that a *man* is making me feel this way. Ugh.

"Both," I admit.

His chuckle is infectious and I chase it with one of my own. Hand dropping from my chin, he traces the back of his fingers down my neck and over my arm.

"Words, Rachel." Bryce reminds me of that night outside my door.

"Bryce . . . I want to, I just don't know how it'll impact us working together."

"So, put that aside for now. If it was just you and me, no escape room between us, would you be holding back?" His voice is soft, plaintive.

"No, but—" I start but don't get to finish.

"—but we're not at work right now. We are just two people at a parade. We can overthink this again on Monday. Right now I want to hold the hand of a stunning woman who's had me off kilter since the first time I met her."

"It's mutual," I admit, my resolve crumbling under the

warmth of his eyes on me and the tingle where his touch just was. I want more.

He must be able to tell that I've given in because his uninjured hand twines with mine and he kisses the back of it before letting it drop between us. Connected.

Fuck me for finding it so sweet and unexpected. Especially given how hard we've been trying to avoid each other.

"So. Hungry?" He looks down at me as if he hasn't just asked something with a double meaning I'm not ready to reveal. But he must see it in my eyes because his smile is smug and the sight of it has my core curling in anticipation.

Two can play at that game. Stroking my thumb against his hand I smile up at him, the edges sharp with competition. "Famished."

The blush that pinks his cheeks is worth it.

We walk the path along the riverwalk, thankfully shaded because my shoulders are starting to prickle from the sun's attention. Bryce raises my hand to his lips again while we wait at a crosswalk. Colorful people, chatter and the rumble of far-off music fills the air. He tugs me along, on the car side of the one-way street, his body a shield between me and anything that might harm.

Bryce does this constantly, without thinking. It's innate. I thought it was just courtesy but maybe there's more there. Maybe he feels . . . protective? The idea has butterflies dancing up my chest. I've never been the kind of person to be coddled, to *let* herself need anything or anyone. Self-reliance was an early life lesson. So what is it about this man that has me entertaining the idea of just letting myself unravel?

We both get hotdogs and bottled soda from a cart and find a shady spot beneath a yew tree away from the bustle of people. Grass tickling the back of my legs and Bryce's hot hand on my thigh, atop my dress, it feels like a perfect summer day. Dulaney and Bryce, this moment and this spot, are right. I know then that even if things between us implode, even if I lose this, I won't go back to D.C. Not when the time away has afforded me the chance to breathe.

My chest doesn't cave in from the stress of Lakin-Cole everyday. My eyes aren't blurry from staring at the same screen for eight plus hours stuck in a cubicle. I don't have to go to bars just to feel something. Just wandering down the tree-covered streets of Dulaney, the riverwalk and the multitude of people taking a moment of peace has brought me a quiet I never thought I could have.

"What's got you so deep in thought?" Bryce asks, pulling me from my reflection and when I turn to face him, he's got a glob of ketchup at the corner of his mouth.

I wipe it away with my thumb, chuckling. "You're a mess." My laugh dies on my tongue when I suck the sauce off my finger.

His eyes track the movement, pupils dilated and hiding that honey and warmth from his irises. Hunger, unsated by our lunch, burns in his gaze and I know that something between us is about to shift.

"Words?" It's gravel. It's smoke and danger, and everything I've been trying to avoid for the last few months because my subconscious knows once I take that step, I'll never find my way back unscathed.

"*Yes*," I say and we surge closer, his hands gripping my waist.

Swinging my leg over to straddle his thick thighs, Bryce lifts his hold to envelop my face in both of his hands, the bandage on his injured one jarring in texture after the heat of his skin but I don't have time to worry about it. Because he's tugged me closer and my hands are on his chest, feeling the rapid rise and fall of his breath, and the thunder of his heartbeat beneath them.

His mouth finds mine, too desperate to be tentative. Nips of his teeth sting against my bottom lip, a deep grumble from his mouth like he's sampling and savoring a bite of something divine. Arms wrapping around my waist, and caging me against his chest, Bryce's embrace is all encompassing. Like a dam breaking, everything we've restrained spills forth into one starved meeting of mouths.

A wolf whistle behind me has us stiffening and I realize with startling clarity that although we aren't on the main riverwalk, we're still in public.

"I guess you didn't need my help deciding, after all," Ángel says and I can hear the malicious glee in his tone.

Burying my face against Bryce's neck, his grasp around me softens so that he's tracing his fingertips along my spine in an attempt to soothe me.

"Come on, Rachel. I'm heading back home and I'd like to say goodbye before I leave."

Whether he's genuinely trying to save my dignity or to embarrass the shit out of me, I can't tell, but I ease myself off of Bryce's lap with a quick peck to his cheek and head toward my friend.

Logan, Kate, and Ángel are on the paved path not too far from our spot under the tree. Logan raises an eyebrow at Bryce, his expression what I could only describe as a shit-eating grin, and I don't dare glance back at Bryce because my face is already aflame with mortification at being caught.

Ángel pulls me in for a quick hug, whispering a frenzied, "I better get all the details later." Then he's gone. Rainbow fringe draped across his shoulders swaying as he walks, I've never wanted to cuss my friend out more.

But he's just saved me in a way. Neither Bryce nor I should have reacted like that in public and the second we try again, I'm sure this thing between us will be like pouring lighter fluid onto a barely banked fire.

"You're welcome to hang out with us, Rachel." Logan's statement pulls my attention away from Ángel's departing figure and by now Bryce is standing beside his friend, a question in his eyes I'm not sure I can answer.

"I appreciate that but I actually think I'm going to head out. Too much sun. I've likely already got a sunburn and I don't want to add heatstroke to that list as well. But it's kind of you to offer."

I can't meet Bryce's eyes because if I do my strength will falter. I need to get the hell out of here before I climb him like a tree in front of all of these people.

"I'll walk you home?" Bryce offers and I give him a sweet smile as he breaks away from his friends to get close to me.

"I don't want to cut your time short. You haven't taken a break in a while. Have some fun with your friends and I'll see you Monday, bright and early at the theater."

I want to hug him, press my face against his chest and feel his arms wrap around me until all I can sense is him. Nothing else. No one else. So, I turn away instead, making it two steps before he catches my hand and tugs me back to him.

The backs of his fingers brush against my cheek and he leans down to plant a sweet, fleeting kiss against my lips. So tender compared to before.

"That's what I meant to do for our first kiss." His words ghost across my lips and I lean into him, eager for more.

But Bryce keeps his head about him and steps back. "I'll see you Monday."

Our hands stretch between us as I walk away, until we have no choice but to break the connection and all I can do is nod.

Staring back up at that Tiffany light fixture once I'm in my bedroom again, sweat stuck to my skin and sunburn exasperating the feeling, I imagine that sound he made against my mouth and I squirm.

God, what am I going to do?

MONDAY TURNS INTO FRIDAY WHEN THE WATER PIPES GIVE IN AND rusty liquid in the men's bathrooms bursts through the tile—corroded metal that's been ready to blow for a while—and Bryce is forced to call in a team of plumbers. We can't do any demo while they're working since they need to check the restrooms and the line at the same time. The last thing we need is one of the rooms flooding.

Still, I email Bryce some of my room ideas, layouts, and places where a tech element can enhance the experience. Everything from a horror movie room, equipped with a remote controlled fog machine, spooky preset sound effects that the room controller can deploy at any time, and the ghostly projections of the dead that came before . . . all the way through a Christmas themed room that should be perfect for the December opener.

I've got lists of equipment and the start of clues for different pieces. We want a blend of practical and technological. Magnetic trap doors but also phones to ring at specific times that require information to be spoken into the receiver to work. It's comprehensive and it's kept me sane as this thing between us keeps growing larger and larger in my mind.

Even outside of D.C., I can still bury my feelings in work. I'm not quite sure what to make of that fact.

Thankfully, by Friday, Bryce has a way to distract us both from the fact that our hands are tied and setbacks keep happening.

BRYCE

Want to go to that antique mall I mentioned?

My heart in my chest, excitement and the slightest pinch of pain—the reminder of past hurts—spreads between my ribs like the insulation foam Bryce picked out for the attic, as soon as we're good to go again. I should say no. It's not work related and we haven't really had time to talk about what happened.

Rather, I've been too nervous and he's been caught up in damage control where the building is concerned. But perhaps antiquing could be a way for us to test the waters, see if we have compatibility besides attraction.

> Sounds like a plan. When were you thinking?

Would 30 minutes be too soon?

I'm in town finishing up with the plumber

Seeing your face would go a long way to making the day better.

How am I supposed to keep my cool when he says shit like that? Rushing down the stairs, I flip the deadlock and my hand grips the railing as I careen up the steep stairs.

> 30 is fine. Door's unlocked for you in case I'm not ready when you get here.

Shutting my laptop, I don't even spare it a glance on the coffee table as I rush to the bathroom. My messy bun, summer pajamas that consist of a too-big and almost threadbare George-town T-shirt and a pair of short bottoms that I lost the top to over a year ago stare back at me in the mirror. Time to get to work.

Rushing through a shower, scrubbing my teeth, I'm in the middle of braiding my wet hair when I hear Bryce call from the front door.

"I'll be right out! Feel free to get yourself something to drink from the fridge if you're thirsty!"

My eyes are a little wild, the steam from my shower still clinging to the edges of the mirror as I stare at my reflection. No need to pinch my cheeks like one of those old-fashioned movie characters. They are plenty flushed as it is.

When I walk out, Bryce is leaning in the arched opening between the kitchen and living area. "It's really come together. You've done a fantastic job." He points to the room with his bottle of water to emphasize his point and the praise lights me up from within.

"Thank you. It's such a great space, I just tried to play to its strengths. Hopefully I'll be able to pick up a piece or two today that'll enhance it more." The stuff I brought with me from D.C. doesn't all fit and a lot of it has been relegated to the attic space Mr. Collins offered for me to use on that first day.

"Hmm," he hums around a swig and I watch his throat work around the swallow, a droplet of water dripping down the corner of his mouth and down his neck.

*Lick it off*, my inner voice urges and it's getting harder and harder to ignore her.

As if he can feel my gaze burning him, he shoots me a little smile. "Hello."

My attention is pulled from his throat and I huff out a chuckle at being caught staring. Bryce stalks forward, a few strides and he's in front of me, placing a cool kiss against my lips. The water he drank might not have a taste but somehow his kiss quenches and refreshes me all the same. His large hand spanning my cheek, Bryce deepens the kiss and I swear to god my knees tremble.

It's the hardest thing I've had to do until now, but I pull away.

"Hello to you too," I say, the words little more than air since he's robbed me of speech. "As lovely as this is, I have a feeling that if we keep going we'll never make it to antiquing."

Some of his ardor cools, a simmer but still there, and he gestures for me to lead the way out of the apartment. It's a routine I'm familiar with by now, his car parked in my spot that never gets used except by Bryce. He comes around to open my door, as always, only this time he tucks a stray hair that's escaped my braid behind my ear, clearing it from my face before he shuts the door and puts a brief distance between us.

The drive north toward Gettysburg is loaded with tension and the space between us feels like a chasm. We've been in his car plenty, but now that I know what his mouth feels like on mine—how his hands can grip and span, and move over my skin—the air separating our bodies is an unwelcome intrusion.

Farmland, wineries and cows dot the landscape blurring past us. As we cross over a portion of the Maryland Appalachian mountains, the trees surround us, verdant, and sunlight dapples the dashboard as it tries to reach out through the space between leaves. Some local station plays low and Bryce hums along quietly. He looks more relaxed than I've seen him in a while, and considering the fact that our progress has taken a heavy dent, it's surprising.

As if he feels me examining him, his attention breaks away from the road to give me a quick questioning glance.

"What's on your mind?" he asks.

"You." We both chuckle at the speed at which I say it and I speak again to clarify. "What I mean to say is, you look kind of relaxed. It's nice. If a little baffling."

"Turns out I'm way less high strung when I stop fighting the urge to touch you. Keeping my distance was exhausting, frankly." It's said without humor and the earnestness in his words have butterflies rioting in my stomach.

"I get it—guess we're both being honest here. Pretending to be unaffected didn't go very well for me, either. Still, I'm not sure where we're at or where we're going with this."

He takes an exit toward a little town, just below the Pennsylvania border, a mixture of typical and cute. A gas station and dollar store, and then a historic downtown. The juxtaposition is strange when you think about it but not unusual for towns like this. Past remembrance and present convenience meet in jarring contrast.

"We are here, and we're going on a date. That's all we need to focus on right now. I don't know about you but I'm tired of over-thinking this. One day at a time, yeah?" Bryce says and smiles.

The last time I agreed to something like that I ended up strad-dling him out in the open. It feels dangerous to say yes but Bryce is quickly becoming a weakness—an anomaly where my pragma-tism is concerned.

But he's taking me antiquing.

"Fine. I just want to make it known that spontaneity and flying by the seat of my pants isn't really my style."

"Isn't it?" he teases before we get out of the car. Entwining our hands, we walk toward the double doors of an unassuming, squat but long building. Closer in appearance to a warehouse than the cute old houses, estate sales, and flea markets I used to haunt.

"What do you mean? I'm always called the solid one. The dependable one."

"Rachel, you're the ship, not the anchor. You know, you can be both. There's more to you than you give yourself credit for. You moved out here with barely any notice and you've taken it all in stride. Every set back, every challenge. Don't hold yourself back because you're trying to embody something you've been told to be. What they think of you isn't who you are."

And with that fucking bomb, we walk into the building and I'm immediately assaulted with the scent of old books, aging metal, and the slight musk and dust that comes with old things being cooped up for too long.

Rows stretch on either side of me and I can't decide where to start. Mind full of the thought of lives lived and what they might have been like, I tentatively touch. An old Kellog wall-mounted telephone that families might have used to call in big news to each other lays on its side.

A mannequin is decked out in a twenties evening gown, beads and chains draped around its neck. What party did that dress see? The hot press of people in their version of a night club? A strong body against it as they danced the night away, gin on their tongues and smoke in the air?

Bryce lets me roam, trailing behind, and I'm only vaguely aware of him. I snake down every aisle, entranced.

"Paintings, photographs, and letters are over here," he says, and it's like coming up for air. The focus that had zeroed in on the shiny things in front of me is diverted toward what young me would've raced to.

Carding through black and white photographs, some in sleeves for protection, others worn down by age and touch, I lose track of time. Until Bryce pulls me back to reality again.

"You've met my parents. Tell me about you, how you grew up and your parents."

He already knows the bit I don't tell anyone. How much worse could the rest be?

"I grew up an only child so the focus was on me, blinding like a spotlight but distant the same way. The better I did at school the prouder my parents were. I never felt as good as I did when I achieved something for them. It was such a high. Top of the class —my mom took me out on a solo movie date. Just me and her. It meant a lot because she worked most days as a receptionist for our local doctor, weekends included and free time was usually reserved for catching up on life."

A few geriatric ladies bustle along, oohing and aahing at the items around us, including the photos I've neglected since this conversation started. Bryce twines his fingers through mine as he leads me to a less busy corner of the building and I take a deep breath before I dive deeper.

"My mom wanted to study medicine but growing up they never had the means. She made it her mission to make sure I had it better than she or my dad did. Etiquette, and manners, and how to act in front of the doctor she worked for and his people so they wouldn't suspect we were less well-off than we seemed. My dad didn't care as much as she did—my mother is a *forceful* woman who directed the two of us—but they both insisted I go to college."

My hand shakes in his and Bryce tugs me close in a hug. "We don't have to talk about this if you don't want to.

"No, it's okay." The words get lost against his chest but he hears me anyway. "All this to say that they loved me. I know that. I know how much they sacrificed for me to succeed and so it's hard for me not to feel guilty when I don't live up to that ideal. The least I can do after they adopted, and cared for me—made sure I got a chance to get ahead in life—is make sure their time and money and love wasn't wasted. But it's so hard to hide myself from them. My sexuality. My doubts. All the years of aching to be seen by them and now I avoid speaking to them if I can. Texts a few times a month, if that. We don't know how to speak to each other outside of the safe, expected topics."

"I hate that you feel like that. I get it though. Not with my parents but with others—my ex especially. I felt like I had a role to play, a script to follow, to please her. Tick the right boxes, say the right things, and maybe she'd be happy with me. Yet the more I tried, the less happy *I* became. I'm sorry that you've been unable to be your full self because of fear of disappointing the ones you love most," Bryce says.

I capture his mouth in a quick kiss, aching at knowing that he can relate. No one should.

We're so close, chest to chest, and the air is filled with dust and the sweet scent of old parchment, and something that's all Bryce.

I'm not sure how he does it but he's disarmed me again. In public. It's like the world fades away when it's just me and him and it would be so easy to get lost in it—in him.

"I'm sorry that someone made you feel that way too. If it's any consolation, I think you're fantastic just the way you are," I say. My cheeks flame and I can't believe that I still have it in me to blush over giving someone a compliment.

The embarrassment is assuaged by Bryce's slightly pink flush at the words. "I feel the same way about you."

I'm so ready to kiss him again but then I hear conversation coming closer, another customer on the way to our secluded little corner surrounded by history.

"We should—uh—we should try to get some things. A historic Dulaney room should have some authentic items, don't you think?" I ask, trying to distract myself and him from the roar of butterflies swarming in my chest.

"Lead the way."

Bryce and I walk down each aisle, chatting about lighter things. We float ideas for the historic room and by the time we're ready to ring up we've got a decent grouping of items on our rolling platform cart. I've even grabbed a few things for the apartment.

The ride back to town is quiet, the silence between us easy as the local station drums on low. Bryce is humming along again and I can't help the glances I steal. If someone asks me later when I started to like Bryce, I'll tell them it was during the numerous car rides over the last few months. Something about the proximity, the accidental brushes as we sit side-by-side, and the countless conversations from silly to serious have cemented it for me.

I like him. A lot. Enough to consider risking more than I have in a while. I'm just not sure I'm brave enough to voice it. Yet.

We get back to my apartment and opt for delivery instead of going out, and then curl up together on my couch. The window unit is going full blast and as much as I hate the heat radiating off of Bryce, it feels nice to have him so solid against me. We pretend to pay attention to the medical show I've been binge watching, and I butt in every now and then to try and get him up to speed on all the drama. He nods and laughs, trying his best to take it in, but the way he traces the lines on my palm as we watch lets me know his attention is as divided as my own.

"I do really like the lamp." Bryce points at my new purchase as two of the doctors on-screen start making out in an on-call room.

Sitting on a steamer wardrobe trunk I picked up as well is a beautiful Tiffany-style lamp. Almost like stained glass, similar to the one in my bedroom. It'll be stunning when lit up in the dark.

"Thank you for helping me find it. I think we got a pretty good haul." I press a kiss to his cheek. "I'm especially excited for some of the stuff we got for the room. We can lean into the theater history and have it be something tied directly to it rather than just generic Dulaney. I'll have to print out things like a cast list and vintage posters, but I think we can pull it off."

"I have faith in you. In us and this whole endeavor. I'm glad you're the one helping me bring this to life."

His confidence in me and what we're doing—what I'm contributing—is heady and the feeling of pride at pleasing him swirls low in my belly.

Bryce's phone buzzes multiple times and he takes the call, and judging by his face, it's not good. Disentangling himself from the couch, he paces, stalking down the little hallway making unhappy noises and when he hangs up all the joy from today seems to have been sucked right out of him.

"Everything okay?" I ask.

"The repairs have really cut into my budget and I'm worried with the way things are going and how quickly the money is disappearing that we won't make it to our original opening date. December seemed so perfect but what if I don't have enough capital to get us there?" Bryce plops down on the couch beside me again and I thread my fingers between his, giving them a squeeze.

"So we scrap one or two room ideas for now—maybe the

176

Dulaney one—and tighten the rest up to focus on our strongest ones. Maybe we can stretch the money that way—scale it down a little? I'm here. I'll help however I can," I say.

Even if it means I won't be getting the months of pay I'd been planning on. I can worry about my options after, right now the task ahead is daunting and getting ever closer.

"You're amazing. I hate to say so but I'm grateful your old job didn't work out. I'm not sure I would have made it this far without you."

My stomach does a little flip at the words and I don't know what to say because I don't want to admit that I feel similarly grateful that Keith was a Grade-A asshole because getting to know Bryce has been the perfect balm to that hurt.

We pretend to watch more TV, until it becomes unnecessary because *our* show of being unaffected fails when Bryce kisses me. His mouth slants over mine and his hand moves to cradle the back of my neck—fingers splaying into my hair.

It's like the park all over again, heat sweeping up in me—and him—to the point that somehow I'm beneath him on the couch and he's hovering over me as he nips down my neck. We're both breathless and being surrounded by him feels overwhelming in the best way.

Bryce whispers my name into the crook of my neck, one of his hands on my waist and the other holding him up so he doesn't crush me.

We should stop. I know we should. There's still too much in the air and he's dealing with a stressful situation. I don't want to dive into this without consideration even though it feels like my brain has melted and I'm relegated to nothing but sensation.

It continues for a few more fraught seconds before I gather myself enough to speak.

"We should stop. It's getting late." It's little more than a whisper and I hardly recognize my voice given how husky it sounds. It's the most cliche excuse but I can't come up with better when he's left me little more than a puddle.

Bryce pulls away from me, his pupils overwhelming those warm honey flecks in his eyes and it's reassuring to know he's as affected as I am. Our chests heave with breath and every time they do I feel his sternum press against my breasts.

"You're right." Bryce shuts his eyes, taking a deep inhale through his nose to come down. "You're right."

I don't know if he's repeating it to acknowledge what I've said or if it's to convince himself of the words. Still, he pulls himself off of me and I feel strangely bereft. Sitting up, I tug on my clothes to right them and fluff my hair out of my face.

His hair is mussed from my hands raking through it and I want to giggle at the sight. I can only imagine what his parents will think when he arrives home—if he happens to cross paths with them.

"I'll see you soon at the theater?" Bryce asks, heading over to and lingering in the archway of the living room.

"I'll see you soon. Thanks for the date," I say and am pleased to note the slight flush of his neck.

"Any time. Lock the door behind me."

I nod, staying right where I'm at because I know if I get close to him now, if I follow him to the door, there will be more kissing and it'll be impossible to pull away next time.

And I know I desperately want there to be a next time.

# CHAPTER  10

SHE HAS A SMUDGE ACROSS THE BRIDGE OF HER NOSE AND IT TAKES everything in me not to swipe it away with my thumb. The past weeks have been torture. The ones since Pride and our date even more so. June melts into July as we buckle down to finish this project and the only stress relief I find is with my mouth against hers, pushing my mind to a blissful blank.

All the conversations in the car, the way her face lights up when she talks about her ideas, leave a heavy feeling in my stomach that's getting harder and harder to ignore. Even with the additional week apart for my hand to heal and the bathroom fiasco. Besides, I have no idea if she's even planning to stick around. Maybe sex will complicate things too much.

*Maybe you should just let yourself have something for once. Be selfish. Take what you need and stop second guessing. Stop sitting with your tail between your legs, begging to be seen and hoping she will take the initiative so you don't have to admit that you want something.*

It's ridiculous that I thought she was anything like Stephanie in the beginning. Beyond the occasional professional smooth appearance, which has gotten less and less frequent since our work got more physical, the two couldn't be more different. Where Stephanie cared about appearance for appearance sake, Rachel just wants to make her parents proud. Stephanie only seemed to want me around as a symbol but Rachel treats me like a person.

I never realized how big that difference felt until she came into my life. I'm dangerously close to something there's no coming back from and the last thing I want to do is ruin the business relationship, and friendship, we're building because I'm in too deep. Maybe this is casual for her. There's too much at stake. If we don't launch within the next two months, I will have sunk all this money into the business with nothing to show for it.

"You okay? You seem to be thinking *really* hard about something over there," Rachel says it with a lightness I don't feel but the smile on her face is enough to coax one onto mine.

"Just worried about the launch."

"We'll pull it off. Even if it means all-nighters and recruiting whoever we can to help. My stubbornness won't allow for anything but success. This is well thought out and there's interest. Believe in yourself, Bryce. I do."

Her words have me blushing so hot my cheeks throb with heat, although that could also just be the ninety-five degree day. Gutting the place on the hottest day of the summer so far is a dangerous endeavor considering we don't have the AC worked out yet, but time is not on our side.

I finished the room I was working on alone and now the signature room—the biggest and most elaborate of them—is slowly coming together, or rather apart. I've got two rows of seats unscrewed from the ground and Rachel is slowly peeling the weird industrial-type carpet crap from the walls so we can improve the soundproofing. The yellow glue underneath it is a different story. I underestimated just how much physical labor this would require but after weeks of hard work at least I've built up some calluses.

"Do you know if we have any industrial-strength stripper or anything? I'm scraping these off but the glue is tacked on so thick the edge of the scraper is near useless." Rachel lifts up the offending tool and I grimace at the yellow-brown gunk.

"I think we have some paint stripper in the supply room just off of the kitchen that might work on that."

She nods and sets her scraper down on the floor, atop a pile of charcoal carpet squares that served as soundproofing but are so old they do little but look horrendous now. Halfway up the walkway the image of her on her TV stand hanging curtains springs to mind and I chime in.

"If it's out of reach just call me over, I'll help you out." The last thing I need is for her determination to do everything herself to get her injured.

She must know what I'm thinking about because she smirks and agrees before she struts out of the room and it takes me a full minute to get the image of her in those shorts out of my mind.

*Shapely legs, wrapped around my waist, her body pressed against a wall and the salt of her skin on my lips.*

No. I need to behave. I've been trying to keep my head about me so that my focus doesn't shift from the business to Rachel. Because I worry that she will pull me in so strongly I'll sink, forgetting how to breathe. There have been a few slip-ups. Lingering touches and hungry kisses that we've been able to brush off—taking it slow—but this is something else. I need to get myself under control before she comes back. Maybe I can hold out until the opening? So we don't get distracted?

"*Bryce*," she yells but the sound is faint given the distance, and I hope she's calling for my height and not because she's gotten herself into a scrape.

I rush toward the supply room, her back to me and she's up on her tiptoes, calf muscles straining as she tries to reach. The light from the hallway throws her into relief, and I'm surprised she was able to find anything at all in the dim room. In my haste I don't see the paint bucket propped up against the door until I've effectively kicked it into the supply room.

*"Son of a—"*

The door snaps shut behind me, darkness swallowing us until there's no light but the sliver under the door and the soft glow of her phone screen from one of the shelves.

"Oh, no." Rachel's grim tone pulls me out of the pain radiating out from my toes.

All I can think about is that Lord of the Rings fact that every fan loves to toss out about Viggo Mortenson as throbbing pulses through my big toe.

"'Oh no,' I've hurt myself or 'Oh, no,' something else?" I grit out between my teeth.

"Nothing to panic about." Despite her words I can hear her breathing pick up in intensity, and catch before she exhales. "Let me just try my phone and I'll—"

The light from her screen uplights her face and I see her worry her lip between her teeth and her brows lower in concern before she looks up at me. Her frown shifts into concern as her gaze flits across my face, looking torn on whether or not to finish that sentence.

"What is it? What's wrong?" Unbidden I take a step closer to her so that her hands touch my chest and I can stare down at the screen in them.

"I was checking for signal . . ." It's feeble and from my vantage point I can make out the angry symbol even upside down. "But there's no service in here."

It's then that my breath catches in my throat and anxiety spikes so quickly I'm surprised I'm still outwardly fine.

Turning, my body brushing against hers and keeping me grounded, I try the door. Tugging on the handle, I shove with my shoulder a few times but it doesn't budge. The room is basically a broom closet, closing in on the both of us. Despite my typically cool head, my straightforward way of thinking and ability to detach, I panic.

The dark closes in on me, that sliver of light under the door and Rachel's phone light the only things reminding me that I'm not being swallowed by an abyss.

"Bryce, it's okay. We're going to figure it out. Why don't you take a step back and I'll give it a try as well." Her hand is small and soothing on my arm and I focus every thought on that point of contact. She turns on her phone flashlight to try and get a better look at the door.

Claustrophobia sneaks up on me. Everything is too close; I need out. I need to take a breath untainted by dust and old cleaning products. Not even Rachel's scent is enough to drown it out. This is my worst nightmare. Although, it could be worse. I could be alone.

Noting my distress, Rachel tries the door, a similar jiggle, shove combination that makes no difference. Then she gets more aggressive with the handle, frustration in her voice. "Come on. Come *on!*"

A metallic clink sounds, the limited visibility heightening the sensation of my hearing. My heart soars for a moment and then gets stuck in my throat when I see the horror on her face. In her grasp is the handle. No longer attached to the door.

"Oh god. Oh no. Fuck." My hands are shaking now. The expletive is so unlike me that it must tip her off because she's there. Handle on the ground, she sets her phone down on one of the shelves so the flashlight illuminates some of the space. Her hands hover over me, unsure.

My breath saws in and out of my chest and I know I should

slow it down. Hyperventilating helps neither of us in this situation. Cooler heads prevail. But my mind fled when the door shut and left my body in charge. It's hard to tell if the darkness at the edges of my vision is from the lack of oxygen or just the lack of light around me.

"Bryce." Her voice is soft, coaxing.

I wish I could respond, but I'm choking on the lack of air and my shaking fingers grasp at my neck in desperation. On the verge of clawing at my throat, she grabs my hands with a strength I wasn't expecting.

"I'm here. You're okay. You're safe. I'm here," she says it over and over, like a mantra that I try to cling to but everything is fuzzy.

"I need you to sit down. We need to get your head between your legs." She tugs me and my body complies, nothing left in me to fight when the overwhelm has taken me over.

Concrete that's only barely colder than the hot air around me is a new sensation, one that gives me a shred of something to ground me. It should be counter productive, putting my head down and making myself smaller, but somehow it helps. As if I'm no longer in the space at all.

Rachel's hand traces up and down my spine, just on the edge of tickling, and I focus on that. On her quiet shushes and sweet tone. I don't make out the words but this is probably what a wild animal feels like when someone is trying to coax it out into the open.

"We're going to be fine. We'll get out of here, I promise."

I latch onto that, working to slow my breathing to something other than gasps and eventually things calm. My face is wet with tears when I lean back, my head against the wall behind me, and I wipe them away with my forearm.

Little catches betray me, but her hand is on my knee, stroking her thumb back and forth and I am grateful she's here.

"Rachel," I croak. "I'm sorry."

"What are you apologizing for? If anything it's me that needs to apologize. If I hadn't called you over for help, if I'd warned you about the paint can this wouldn't have happened. If I hadn't tugged on the handle too hard . . ." she says, her voice glum. "This is my fault."

I cover her hand on my knee with my own and she gives a big sigh.

"We need a plan but first I have to make sure you're okay," she says, concern laced through every word.

"I'm fine. Or at the very least, I will be. This used to happen way more when I was younger. I've found coping skills and stuff to help but yeah. Dark plus small space equals claustrophobia and panic. I never did get the hang of escape art the way I did the other aspects of magic."

"Is the coping skill to avoid small, dark spaces?" There's a hint of teasing in her voice and I lo—adore her for it. Distraction is a great way out of a heightened state.

"Pretty much. Am I that obvious?" My chuckle is as dry as my throat and I wish we had some water in here.

"Not obvious, but I've been around you for a while now. Long enough to learn some of your tells and tendencies."

"Oh yeah? Care to share?"

It's intimate in here. Coming back to myself she's sitting in front of me, her back against the door but her hand is on me and our bodies are so close it wouldn't take much to touch her.

"You overthink a lot. There are these moments where I can see your mind whirring as if you're constructing what you're going to say word for word before it comes out. You doubt yourself and I don't know if it's innate or learned from somewhere, because your parents seem to think you are the best thing to walk the earth."

Emotion sits heavy on my throat, not dissimilar to panic, and

I'm not sure I'm ready to be stripped bare like this. But she keeps going, peeling me away like she's the paint stripper and I'm being exposed for the first time in thirty years.

"You care deeply about the people in your life, just from the way you talk about them and seeing you with your friends. You're courteous and considerate, sometimes to the point that I worry it's at your own expense."

She takes a deep breath before she dives into the next statement and I brace for impact.

"Sometimes I wonder what it would be like to make you smile so big the corners of your eyes crinkle. I've come close. When we first met, that was my first thought, that you looked like you'd forgotten how to smile and how badly I wanted to be the one to make you do it."

Her nervous huff of a chuckle slips between us and I know she intended it as a way to release the pressure between us, but it's done nothing to quell the feelings rising within me.

"God, it's so hot in here. I'm not . . . I might have to shed a layer because it's getting a bit unbearable in here." She's rambling and she tugs her top over her head, exposing the tank top she's wearing as an undershirt. It clings to her, a bead of sweat highlighted by the flashlight, meandering down her neck and between her—no. I cannot think of that right now. We're stuck in here and I need to get my shit together.

"Distract me, please? I don't do well with heat. Hopefully something breaks it soon." Her hand returns to my leg and the first day of scouting locations comes to mind, when I divulged my fear and she reciprocated.

I find my own voice, wanting to be seen by her but wanting to escape too. If I'm talking about her then she'll stop talking about me.

"I hated how beautiful you were. It hit me in the stomach when you walked through that coffee shop door and I wasn't prepared for it. That whole first meeting I kept trying to find ways to focus and not screw it up so that you'd stay," I say. She says nothing for a moment so I fill the silence. "You've got your own quirks, too."

"Oh, been studying me?" Her voice is kind of breathless and I love that I've affected her even a little.

"I study everyone. It makes it easier to know what response they'll be expecting from me and how to convey myself correctly. So yes, in a way."

I slip her hand from my knee, twining our fingers together so I'm holding it.

"You push yourself, likely because you feel the need to prove your worth through what you can produce or show externally. You have a carefully constructed image, professional but friendly. I've never seen you ruffled even though I know for a fact this has to have been hard for you," I say.

Her fingers tighten around mine and if I don't get this out now I won't have the courage again. Something about being in the cocoon with her . . .

"No one has seen all the sides to you. Ángel probably most but not all. As if you're keeping some things just for you, protecting those parts and yourself. I know you want to make your parents proud and prove you belong, as if you've never really felt comfortable anywhere you couldn't show yourself useful."

Lifting her hand in mine, I plant a kiss on the back of it. "I don't want that from you. There's nothing to earn with me. You see me as a person, not a faceless name on the payroll, not a trophy or doll to move around within your life to your satisfaction. These past couple months with you have brought me so much light and I can only hope that I've given you even a fraction of that." My throat tightens as I speak, the confession getting dangerously close to being too open.

"You've given me peace," Rachel responds before I can spiral.

"Safety. I know it sounds stupid and I know no one wants to hear that they're solid or safe but that's something I've always had to be for others and I've never been able to just *breathe*. When the burden of keeping everyone around you happy falls on you, there's no time to fall apart. With you, I feel like I could."

Stephanie's words from months ago spring to the surface, weaker now, less hurtful. She called me a dining room table, spitting my attempt to be dependable and stable back into my face. Hearing that Rachel appreciates something Stephanie made out to be a failing fills me with something I'm not ready to examine too closely.

"I hope that makes sense. Being in Dulaney, being with you, doing this"—she gestures at the general area around us and I know she means what we're building—"It's made me feel like myself for the first time. You're right about me not knowing where I belong, trying to be the 'right' version of myself so that I might—for the first time in months the need to present, to *perform*, isn't there."

Her big brown eyes are shimmering with unshed tears and she worries her bottom lip between her teeth when she's done talking.

"I don't know where this is going, or if you think you might want to stick around Dulaney once we've got the business going, but if you did . . . if you stay, I'd be here to catch you if you fall. Think about it." I smirk, hoping she picks up on the second meaning there.

I don't want her to fall apart, and I'm careful to phrase it that way.

"Is that a dig at my potentially risky behavior and balance issues? Because if so, that's not very nice." She sticks out her tongue but there's no heat behind her words.

"Catching you that day . . ." I take a breath, amping myself up to go for this, to lean into the flirting. "Nice wasn't exactly on my mind with you in my arms."

Her eyes dart from mine down to my lips and it's ridiculous how desire can make me go from panicked to desperate in a wholly different way mere minutes later.

"Care to share?" It's cheeky but breathless, her words giving her away and letting me know she's just as on edge about it as I am.

Coming off of my panic attack, the adrenaline still clinging on slightly, or perhaps that's just my latent fear needing to be redirected, I take another risk. Leaning toward her, my hand cupping her jaw as I approach, I wait for her to stop me.

She doesn't and our lips meet. Not as tentative as it should be. Something about Rachel tips me over from sane and level-headed into something different—a stranger in my own skin. Want and fear twist in my stomach, both begging to be freed, clawing up my chest. As much as I ache for her, this broom closet is not the time nor place.

"Let's get out of here and I'll show you." I barely recognize my own voice, the intent behind my words, a gravel I've never used on anyone.

"Challenge accepted." Rachel's grin is wicked, that dimple cutting into her cheek and I'll never tire of seeing it, knowing I had a part in it being shown off.

We rise to our feet, her body brushing against mine and it's torture, knowing I can't indulge right now no matter how much I want to. Not while my anxiety is barely contained and Rachel's fanning herself because the heat is getting to her. I'm not far behind. Stuck in this little closet, no air, on the hottest day of the summer so far is a sure recipe for disaster. If we don't get water soon we'll overheat and dehydrate.

"We can't shove it open. The handle is useless. What other options can you think of?" I muse aloud and Rachel barks out a laugh.

"What's so funny? We're stuck."

"*Exactly!*" She giggles and I'm worried that the heat is getting to her head. "We need to *escape* the storage room. This is too perfect. If we'd been bad I'd say it's borderline Karmic but you're good and I've been on my best behavior here in Dulaney. So that's not it."

It *is* kind of ironic. "Huh."

Rachel waves the phone flashlight around, searching the shelves and I do the same.

"Okay. I found a hammer, a screwdriver, and a bunch of old rags." Her haul is on the shelf at her eye level.

"I've got the paint stripper you were looking for." We both chuckle, and then her list of items permeates the haze of my brain. "Wait. I have an idea. Shine your light on the actual door."

Although it's heavier, not a hollow door that we'd be able to brute force down, the hinges are on the inside and I give her a smacking kiss against where I know that dimple hides. "You're brilliant."

"What are we doing?" Rachel asks.

"We can take the door off the hinges by dislodging those pins. We can knock them out with the hammer and screwdriver and then theoretically we should be able to get out."

She hands me both tools and I start with the top one, my height an advantage here and this way Rachel doesn't have to stand on a bucket or something. Because she totally would. Hates asking for help.

Except she did, and it got us into this, so maybe I understand why she refrains from doing so most of the time.

Knocking the first peg out takes a couple of tries but I'm able to pry it out once it's shimmied out of its confines. Rachel gives a little excited whoop, gripping my bicep in excitement and damn if it doesn't make me want to rush through this escape. The second and third pegs are easier once I get the hang of it.

All three pegs rest against Rachel's palm and I look down at her for a moment before we try it. "You ready?" I ask.

She doesn't wait to respond, merely pushes against the door and it gives. Dropping to the floor outside with a heavy thud, light streams in, almost blinding. The pegs clink to the floor as she drops them and she rushes out of the room, hopping around the door, and I follow.

"I'm sorry that happened, and that I freaked out. I'm just—" I stammer behind her, my courage leaving me as the brightness steals the intimacy of our confined space. But she doesn't even let me finish.

Turning, surging up onto her toes, Rachel's arms wrap around my neck. One hand gripping the back of my hair, she tugs me down to meet her and I'm lost. Hands splayed around her waist, the back of her tank top scrunched in my grip, I savor her. Our mouths are hot and wet, the little mewling sound she makes when I nip at her bottom lip only drives it higher.

Before I lose my rationality, before we do something we can't come back from, I disengage. Just enough space between us so I can speak.

"Are we doing this? Because I need to know what you expect and what you want. This was a high stress situation and I want to make sure you feel—"

Again, her mouth slots over mine to shut me up and it's kind of becoming my favorite thing.

"This has nothing to do with the closet. I want you. In whatever way you're ready for. Don't doubt that, Bryce. I know things are confusing and up in the air between us, but please know I've wanted you since we first met and you've done me absolutely no favors in helping me get over that." Her words are rough, whispered an inch away from the seam of my lips and the heat in me rages into an inferno.

"I'd invite you over to my place but I'm back with my parents until I find something else." It's supposed to be a bit of a joke, a way to clear the tension that's near choking, but I don't quite manage.

"You parked at my place anyway, remember? When you came to pick me up this morning it was early and we were under the misapprehension that it was a nice day out—not this heat hell."

I walk her backward, kissing her every few feet, trying to keep control until we get out of here.

"We need to shut off the lights and equipment. We have to lock up." The disappointment in my voice has her laughing again but it's enough to make our pragmatic sides slip back into place for a moment.

Within five minutes we're at the doors, padlock in hand ready to chain the place back up. Only when we step outside it's a downpour. I can't help the smart comment that comes out of my mouth as she steps into a puddle immediately upon exiting.

"You said you wanted something to break the heat. Here it is." Gesturing out at the street, our little overhang barely covers us.

"I didn't know I'd be hoping for a storm!" She shouts it above the sound of rain pelting the ground.

"We're going to have to make a break for it."

My hand wraps around hers, both of us jogging down the sidewalk and within a block we are completely soaked. Crossing the street feels hazardous and I can only hope that cars are following the lights because visibility is incredibly poor. Rachel's hand in mine is a grounding force, the heat of her skin against my palm feels like so much more than I thought I'd get.

This might turn out to be a big mistake but I'm tired of playing it safe. I'm through making the smart choice, the expected choice. Rachel's reminded me what it feels like to actually want something for myself—selfish and unashamed about it.

We make it to her blue door, the lock clicking and she kicks the bottom of the door to get it to open while it's swollen with moisture. Then we're trying our best not to fall on her steep stairs. I make her go ahead of me, so that if she slips I'll be able to catch her before she can get hurt. By the time we're through her door, our shoes kicked off and discarded beside it, we're kissing again.

It's hungry. It's frustrated from the frequent stopping and starting and constantly being out of reach. She gives as good as she gets. Fingernails digging into my back through my sodden shirt, the material clinging, Rachel's got her head thrown back as I burn a trail down the side of her neck.

"Please?" she asks and I feel the words against my lips, vibrating through her throat as I nip and suck at her skin.

"Words, Rachel."

"I want you." It's a growl, and I feel bad for asking but I never want to misconstrue this. Whatever is between us, I want to make sure I understand completely before I take that step. "We're sopping wet. I wanted to take it slow. I've thought about this for so long and I want to do this right."

Her fingernails give my back a reprieve only for her to card her fingers through my hair and give the slightest tug.

"You're driving me up the wall here." Her voice is barely more than a whisper.

I know what she means but my mind stutters on the image of driving into her, *against* the wall, those legs wrapped around my waist like I'd imagined earlier in the day. Still, I only get one time to make the right first impression. If this goes poorly it could be over before it's even started.

"Do you trust me?" I ask and she pulls back to stare at me with a question in her eyes.

"What do you—"

This time I'm the one to cut the words off with my mouth, giving a searing kiss before I pull away to repeat. "Do. You. Trust. Me?"

"Yes."

My grin splits my face, joy at hearing it and lust at wanting to show her just how much her trust will be rewarded. I've never been the one who took charge in the bedroom, Steph was always too controlling for that, but something about Rachel—the way she looks at me like I'm capable and strong makes me want to prove that.

Walking to her bathroom, I tug Rachel by the hand to ensure she follows. Droplets leave a trail over the wood floors but I don't care right now. We'll deal with it later.

She's got a massive and deep claw foot tub and I send up a silent thanks to whoever owns the building because this is perfect. I would have made a shower work but this . . .

Drawing the bath, hot water pouring from the tap and filling the tub, I pour a little bit of the bubble bath under the spray. Foaming, the steam fills the room and makes my glasses even more useless than the rain did.

She giggles at the sight of my lenses fogging up and carefully removes them from my face to set down beside the sink. Stepping closer to her, I crowd her against the countertop, the shadow of us in the foggy mirror doing something dangerous to me. I sweep her wet hair over one shoulder and bend down to press my lips against the curve of where it meets her neck.

Rachel's breath catches, her hands splaying out on the counter and I thread my fingers over hers, raising one to loop around my neck. Kissing against the pulse point in her wrist, the rush of water behind us and the intoxicating feel of her against me making it really hard for me to take it slow the way I'd like to.

"I've been dreaming about this, about you. Even today while we were working. Your legs in those shorts . . ." The words are a rasp against her ear lobe.

"You're not the only one." She pulls her hand out from under mine and runs her fingertips over my forearm. "These have been on my mind for weeks. It's embarrassing how much power your forearms have over my thinking ability. Your hands too."

As much as it pains me, I glance over at the tub and step away to shut off the water before it gets too high. The air is thick with steam and desire, and I can't believe this is happening right now.

Without saying anything we close the distance between us, her hands in my hair and our mouths tasting. My hand snakes up under her tank top, palming her in my hand. Swiping the pad of my thumb against her nipple, I relish the taste of her moan. Rachel doesn't stay still for long, tugging at my shirt, urging me to lift it over my head once she's reached as far as she can at her height.

The fabric hits the floor with a wet thud, closely followed by her tank top joining the fray so that she's in her nearly translucent bra. I've never been more grateful for a summer storm. Kissing down her neck, over her collar bone, she tastes like rain. Sinking down to my knees before her, my mouth blazes its way down her body.

My lips against her stomach have her sucking in a breath and I grip her hips in my hands before pressing my forehead to her abdomen.

"What are you doing to me?" I whisper, lost.

"No different than what you're doing to me. *Please*, Bryce."

No more prompting needed, I slip her shorts down her hips and kiss every inch of newly bared skin. Her hands grip my hair and the closer I get to the apex between her legs, the tighter the pull.

"You're so beautiful," I say. Staring up at her from my knees, her face flushes. Her nipples strain against the sodden material that hides nothing anymore.

Rachel's hand drifts down to cup my face, her thumb stroking over the stubble of my cheek. "Your turn."

I rise with great reluctance, desperate to taste her, but there will be time for that later if I have any say in the matter.

When I was younger I might have been more self conscious about my body, but I'm beyond the point of caring. My cock is achingly hard and I'll leave it up to Rachel to decide whether she finds me attractive or not—forearms notwithstanding.

She bites her bottom lip, hands skating over my chest and shoulders. "Fuck."

I take it as a good sign, pressing myself against her body until the heat of her is flush with my front. Sampling her, tasting the salt on her skin dulled by rainwater and steam, I plant kisses along her jaw until I reach her ear.

"I'm going to take my time with you. Until you're needy. Until you ache for me to fill you." It's a promise, laced with a little bit of that danger she's stoked in me. There's a darker edge than I'm used to because I've wanted this for so long and the prospect of getting something I thought I never would . . . it leaves me fraught—desperate for all she's willing to give and anxious that this is the only time I'll have her.

As complacent as I am—as willing to go with a stronger opinion—she makes me want to call the shots. Rachel makes me feel more. Better. Sure.

She moans at the words and I take it as an invitation to continue. Unclasping her bra I suck just beneath her ear, making a small mark before I speak. "I don't know what this is. I've never felt it this keenly—this need—and I'm asking you to promise me that you'll tell me if any of this is too much. I haven't been with anyone since . . ."

I let the confession hang between us. "In fact, I've only ever been with her and one other person in college. So when I say the thought of you has plagued me for weeks, edging me to the brink, it would be an understatement. I just want to make sure you are fine with this before I lose my head and the last shred of my self control."

She laughs, breathy, and I feel it against my mouth. "You still have self control? That makes one of us."

Rachel steps back a little, breaking the contact of my mouth against her neck so she can look me in the eye. "I'm a big girl, Bryce. I can handle it and you. I've had partners of both sexes, in case my bi pride dress wasn't enough of an indicator. But I'm responsible. I get checked regularly. I'm on birth control. And I want this—with you."

That's it. The last clear moment. Whatever happens from here will be pure feeling and instinct, and that deep-seated yearning I've tried to ignore.

"Take them off. I want to see you." I lean against the lip of the tub, eager.

Rachel's pupils are so dilated, her tongue darting out to wet her lips, but she doesn't shy away. Tugging them down her hips and over her thighs, she steps out of her underwear and stands naked before me. It's the most tempting sight in the world.

"God, woman. You're killing me. I'll never be able to focus at work now that I know what you look like under those dresses and shorts."

Her grin is feral, that dimple that I've lived to coax doing little to soften the sharp look she gives me.

"Tit for tat." She gestures toward me and I comply, kicking the boxer briefs over to the rest of the pile of clothes we've made.

A few feet between us, we assess each other, the hunger only growing. I hold my hand out for her, beckoning. I step into the water first, hissing a little at the temperature but I adjust almost immediately. Still holding onto her hand, I help her step over the tall side of the tub.

Settling into the water, Rachel's back to my front, nestled between my thighs, I finally let myself explore. Fingertips ghosting over her sides, the water lapping over our bodies is a sensory experience that's nearly overwhelming when combined with touch.

One hand on her breast, the other moving down her stomach and over her thighs until I rest it at the juncture.

"*Bryce.*" I'm not sure if it's a warning or a plea.

"Words."

"Touch me."

I stroke my pinky against the side of her thigh and I swear she growls.

"Manners," I say and suck another mark against the back of her neck.

"Touch. Me. *Please.*" She grits out between her teeth and it's enough.

My thumb strokes over her clit until she arches against me slightly, her breath catching in the back of her throat. "*Good girl.*"

# CHAPTER  11

*OH GOD. HIS PRAISE FLOWS THROUGH ME LIKE MOLTEN HONEY,* warming my core and even without the water to help his fingers glide over me, my desire would be more than enough. Thrumming against me, I'm a hairpin trigger away from losing it. The slow touches, his sinful mouth on my neck—fuck the things those neck kisses make me want to do to him—it's got me close to the edge already.

I'm ready to fall. Poised on the edge of pleasure. And then he stops. Lathering his hands with soap, he drags the suds over my arms and neck. Over my breasts and stomach.

"What are you doing?" It's supposed to sound demanding but instead comes out as a whine.

"Keeping my promise. Taking my time. Touching every inch of you. Take your pick."

"But I was close." This time it's definitely a whine and I'm not sorry.

"And you will be again, but we worked hard today and we're

going to wash the day from our bodies. Then, we'll wander over to your bedroom and I'll put my mouth on you to push you even higher."

"You know, I never took you for a tease."

His hands still on the outside of my thighs. "It's not teasing when I'm not done yet. And I am so far from done."

"You know, I don't know why anyone would think you're quiet or unassuming. The way you're talking right now . . ." I taper off, part of me begging him to keep going like this. I trust him enough to let go, to give him free rein and let that hint of his forcefulness take over.

His thumb swipes over my nipple again, pulling a hiss from me at the sensation of smooth water and work-roughened hands.

"I lay the blame at your feet. You make me want to be more confident. More assured. Demanding even. The way you look up at me like you have faith in me and what I'm doing—you have no idea what that does to a person."

It makes my heart ache in my chest a little to hear it and I wish I could see his face. Is it open? Vulnerable? Does he look as disheveled as I do? I wish I could meet whoever it was that made him doubt himself and his worth, because the Bryce that I know is kind and capable, and eager to learn. And there's something about that control, that competency, that's fucking hot to me.

"You're not the only one affected by whatever this is. Something about you softens my edges, makes me . . . vulnerable. I'm not the kind to yield easily, and when I do it's usually because I have a plan to get things another way. With you, I'm tired of pushing, of trying so hard to be the image people have of me. With you I just want to be me. Bare."

I need to see him.

I shift away from him even though the loss of contact is the last thing I want. Carefully turning to avoid spilling water over the edge, I face Bryce and straddle him. His hardness is proportional, and that means it's a little intimidating. Despite how much I want to, I don't sink down onto him. Instead it rests between us and I plant a sweet kiss against his lips.

This time I'm the one that lathers body wash between my palms, touching him wherever I can. Over the broad shoulders and wide expanse of his chest. His sides that I learn are slightly ticklish, and finally I grasp him in my hand. Pumping up once, twice. Bryce sucks a breath between his teeth and I can see the veins in his neck straining.

"Clean enough for you?" I ask, cheeky. Knowing that I do this —that my touch has this kind of power—is a heady thing.

"Rachel Mackey, you're playing a dangerous game. I said I was going to take my time. That won't happen if you keep doing that."

I bite my bottom lip to suppress a chuckle and stroke him again, swiping the pad of my thumb over his tip. "Doing this?"

His hips press up beneath me. His large hands are wrapped around the edge of the tub, knuckles white from the strain of holding back.

"Out. Now." He grits and those golden-flecked eyes flash with something that makes my belly clench in anticipation. It would be easy enough to keep teasing, to push him toward pleasure and stop the way he'd done with me but I want this as much as he does and pretending not to is a waste of time.

Water sluices down my body as I stand. Wrapping a towel around me, I hand Bryce another, and we both make quick work of drying our bodies. This time I'm the one that's tugging him along, toward my bedroom.

Once the bed is within reach, Bryce wraps his hands around my waist and pulls me close. Our faces are a hairsbreadth apart. His breath is as erratic as mine and I can feel the hammering of his heartbeat against my skin.

"You're sure?" His eyes plead with me, the desire there barely held back.

"I'm sure."

Walking me backward, the back of my legs hit the mattress and he urges me down. My curiosity gets the better of me and I lean up on my elbows to look at him. Bryce is on his knees again, something that makes me fucking feral, and his hands spread my thighs.

His stubble scratches the inside of my thighs as he kisses down along them. The window AC rattles softly on the other side of the room and the cold air, combined with his kisses, sends goose-bumps along my skin—my nipples hardening from cold and need. I'm about to ask, to scoot back and invite him onto the bed with me when his mouth slots over me.

Tongue tracing before he sucks me into his mouth, I mewl. My muscles tighten as he coaxes me higher again. My fingers splay through his hair, half dry, and I grip the strands when he spreads me with one finger. Heat pools in my core, pleasure sending sparks through my body that culminates in a moan when he adds another finger.

Curling them, stroking, he moves his thumb over my clit as he sucks a mark onto my thigh. I should tell him not to do that, especially when he's already left a couple on my neck, but I don't care. I want him so much. His lips on mine—his touch on my skin—and his mark on me as a testament to the fact that he wants me just as desperately.

Part of me is mad that I've waited this long to have him, to let myself have him. Another is grateful that we had a foundation to build off of because the last few months with him have been a study in patience and longing, and to see it come to fruition after so much waiting makes it so much sweeter.

"I'm getting close," I say and when Bryce pulls away I want to kick myself for doing so.

"Scoot back."

Shuffling up the bed toward my pillows, Bryce stalks over me. His muscles flex beside my head as he holds himself up and I take another moment to enjoy the sight of him. No pretty and perfectly cut muscles, rather the solid kind of mass that comes with strength over appearance. Golden brown chest hair dusts across his pecs and narrows down to a strip over his stomach and below.

I was right.

His freckles cover most of his body, little flecks I'll take the time to kiss if he'll let me. Bryce's lips are plump, swollen from the ferocity of our kisses, and the sheen of me on his mouth sends a blush spreading all the way up my body.

Resting on his forearm, his other stretches between our bodies to notch him against me. Rubbing his head up and down, over my clit and through the wetness between my legs, Bryce leans forward. Just enough.

My hands grip his back as he moves, agonizingly slowly, inching in deeper with each shallow thrust. I want him to get it over with. To put me out of my misery because all I want to do is fall apart around him and this tightrope of desire that I'm on has me breathless.

"Please. I'm ready. Please." I don't even try to inject humor into it. He was right when he said he'd have me begging.

"You're ready?" His voice is a dark question against the shell of my ear as he shifts in and out again, stubbornly refusing to sink all the way inside.

I nod frantically against him.

"Since you asked so nicely." The words don't have time to permeate the mush that is my mind right now before he surges all the way inside. It's exquisite. The stretch of him inside me, pleasure with the slightest hint of being near the limit.

He grunts against my ear and I wrap my legs around him. Mouth against my neck again, he thrusts as he kisses. "Fuck."

The swearing is so unlike him and it brings me incredible pleasure to watch him descend into something baser.

"Your legs wrapped around me. Your moans against my skin. So beautiful." His voice is husky and makes me ache even more. He lifts up slightly to look at me, his eyes glazed with desire and I'm sure mine are the same. Bryce looks down between us, at his pelvis flush against mine, and it elicits another groan. "You take me so well," he praises.

The words have me fluttering against him and he picks up speed at the sensation. Gripping my thighs with his big hands, Bryce increases the intensity of his thrusts until the bedframe makes a lewd squeak with every up thrust. Our skin slaps together, my moans and his grunts, and the rattle of cold air so overwhelming I can hardly stand it.

"Do you like this?" Bryce asks and coupled with the ferocity of his movements it sounds darker than a mere question.

"Yes!"

"You like me touching you, hmm?" His hand grips my bouncing breast. "Stretching you?"

His thumb rubs across my overstimulated nipple and I shut my eyes against the pleasure, my neck straining backwards as I arch into him. Rising onto his knees, without breaking the connection between us, Bryce grips my hip with one hand and strums his touch across my clit again.

I'm incoherent by this point. Everything heightened. Sensation and need building toward something explosive and I know I'm close. But I don't want him to stop. I can't handle it if he stops again.

"You like me marking your skin with my mouth?" Bryce punctuates it with a gentle touch against my neck, the back of his fingers tracing over the love bites he's given me. "Like knowing that whenever someone looks at them, they'll know I made you mine?"

I don't know what it is. This kind of intensity feels simultaneously surprising and also makes so much sense. Bryce holds back in almost every aspect of his life. He's deferred to others for so long. It makes sense that now, with his walls down, the depth of what he wants is finally clear. If I am finally me with him, then perhaps it's the same for him. Perhaps he feels safe enough to expose what he's unable to ask for under normal circumstances— too scared to take.

"Is that what you want? For me to be yours?" I manage, panting between the words.

"Fuck yes. All of you. Mine."

And just like that I shatter. Pleasure rolls over me in waves and Bryce folds himself against me again, covering my body with his. He swallows my scream against his lips and his thrusts grow erratic.

"Please," I beg against his lips.

"Please what?" It's harsh, undercut by the desperation of his breathing.

"Please come for me."

His hands tighten on my sides, so strong I wonder if their impression will bruise my skin. "Where do you want it?"

It doesn't matter much to me. We'll have to shower or something after this anyway, given we've worked up a sweat again, but I have an inkling of what he'd prefer. Taking the risk, trusting my gut, I dig my fingernails into the skin on his back. Half circles to mark him the way he's done me.

"Inside."

My guess pays off because he whimpers, "Yes, fuck, yes," against my skin and within a few thrusts he's buried himself all the way. His body tenses as his own pleasure crests and drags him over. And he fills me.

Careful not to drop on top of me, Bryce wraps his arms around my back and turns us over so that I'm laying on top of him, strad-dling his still-hard cock. The stretch combined with gravity has me moaning again. And when some of him escapes, his release and mine, against my thigh I can't help but shudder.

His hands are gentle on my back now, tracing lazy patterns against my skin as our hearts slow. Depleted.

"That was—" I rasp, my voice a little raw from screaming my release into his kiss.

"—phenomenal." Bryce finishes my thought and I can't help but agree. I've had great sex before but this, this was something else.

I've never let myself be "taken," always stuck in my head and the need for control. Relinquishing that to Bryce, letting myself be and feel without overthinking it—I don't know that I've had anything better.

His stomach growls below mine and we both laugh, more of him slipping out as I do so and some primal part of me relishes it.

"I'd ask 'what now' but I think your stomach answered for me," I say.

"Sorry. Guess I worked up quite an appetite." His joke has me grinning like a fool and I love this. Humor and ease. Sober and before dark. Being with Bryce like this is so unlike me and I can't help but wonder if I could have this—all of this.

Days at the escape room, nights in bed, laughs in between.

With that slightly alarming thought, I extricate myself, reluctant but resolved.

"Let's clean up and order something." I'm at the door already, looking over my shoulder at him and it's a stunning sight.

His bulk, his height, taking up most of my bed where he's splayed. His hair is an absolute mess from my hands, his eyes hooded and a lazy smile on his face. He's never looked hotter to me.

"See something you like?" His smile turns to a smirk.

"We've got to eat something. Gotta keep your strength up. I'm not done with you just yet." And that thought is a little scary but if I bury it beneath the physical maybe I can postpone the panic.

"Is that a promise or a threat?" Bryce asks.

"Both."

I slip into the shower, knowing it doesn't matter how much water I use, Bryce Dawson will remain on my skin. My body is tender where his hands have touched and gripped, my core a slight ache letting me know exactly where he's been. I take the time to center myself, to tuck away my traitorous feelings before they bloom into something uncontrollable. Like the mint that nearly took over my mother's back garden one year, Bryce threatens to overwhelm, and I can't let myself consider that yet.

Not when it's so tentative between us. Not until we're done with the escape room and I can know without a doubt that this isn't just the rush of a shared project, of feeling valued and respected.

Bryce waits for me to emerge before he kisses my cheek and steps under the spray. I dress, choosing soft material that won't affect my sensitive skin.

Clean, bones languid, I settle onto the sofa and pull up delivery options near me while I wait. My apartment smells like him and it's only once he walks out in nothing but a towel slung low on his hips that I realize our clothes are soaked and he has no others.

"Oh. Let me get our stuff into the wash. I totally forgot."

Gathering the piles of clothes off of my bathroom floor, I chuck them into the washer as quickly as I can, and the old machine grinds as it starts.

"You in the mood for any particular kind of food?" Bryce asks from the living room.

"Whatever you'd like. I trust you."

He's on the couch, the towel still wrapped around him, and I settle down beside him.

"My washer and dryer are really slow, sorry."

He quirks an eyebrow at me, "And what does that mean, exactly?"

Words. Of course. He needs me to say it.

"That means it would be better if you gave them time to dry properly. It'll be late once they're done. Maybe you should stay." My cheeks flame and my attempt at being coy about it is totally ruined by me blushing like a fool. I drop my gaze down to my hands, wringing them in my lap.

How can I be so confident about sex and so unsure about what comes after?

Bryce tips my head up, his finger crooked under my chin to urge me to look at him.

"I'd love to stay," he says, quiet and devastating, and tucks me into his side.

Our food arrives shortly after we order, the scent of sweet tomato sauce and savory cheese sending my own stomach growling, and we devour the pizza in front of the TV.

"What do you mean you've never seen Smallville?" Bryce sounds aghast.

"Exactly what I said." Taking another bite of my slice, I suppress a grin at his expression.

He takes the remote from my hand and pulls it up. "That is something we are going to remedy right now."

The theme song comes on, something missing from recent shows, and I watch the light of the screen flicker across Bryce's face as sunset steals the daytime. Content. I am so content. He laughs against my side at how ridiculous the early 2000s special effects look, that rumble passing through his body and to mine.

Later, with his clothes dry and folded, he puts his boxer briefs back on and I strip down to an oversized shirt and underwear. Melting into the bed, both of us are tired from the exertion of renovation, stress from being locked in, and the exhilaration of the storm and what followed.

Bryce tucks himself behind me, enveloping me. His knee between my legs, arm slung over my side to splay across my stomach, Bryce spoons me from behind and I know I'm in trouble.

Because I've never felt safer or happier than right here in his arms. Sleep drags us under and the last thing I'm aware of before it takes me is Bryce's whispering, "Good night" and the press of a kiss against the top of my head.

ONE UNEXPECTED PERK TO FALLING ASLEEP NEXT TO YOUR HALF-naked boss is that forgetting to set an alarm is a non-issue. Can't be late to work if they are too. Sunlight streams through the crack between my curtains and somehow in sleep we've migrated from spooning to me partially on top of him. Leg thrown over his hips and my head on his chest, Bryce's breath is a gentle ebb and flow beneath my ear.

I let myself smile, bask in the warmth of him against me, for a moment.

And then I realize what's woken me. An insistent buzzing on the bedside table vibrates a phone across the surface. Shifting, trying to extricate myself without waking him, I fail spectacularly. I've barely rolled over and grabbed the phone before he hauls me back against his body, tucking his head against my body and protesting the start of the day.

"Phone call," I whisper, though it's useless since we're both awake now.

"Yours or mine?" His morning voice is husky in a way that makes heat pool in my core again, wanting to hear him do more of that dirty talk from last night. Because, wow. Unexpected but so hot.

The caller ID reads "Mom" but the black rectangle is indistinguishable otherwise. Rooting around the table for the other, I press the home screen on the one that's not ringing and the lock screen is his.

"It's mine." The call drops and my stomach sinks as I note the seven missed calls from her. I remember the texts from a few weeks ago that I ignored because I was too scared to tell her the truth and too tired to keep lying. Distance and omission seemed safest. I'm not quite sure about that now.

Immediately dialing back, it only rings once before she's on the other end. "You better be dead or dying!"

"I was asleep. What's up?" I should probably take this call in another room, but Bryce's hand has snuck under my tshirt and he's trailing his fingertips over my stomach in a way that gives me butterflies.

"Asleep? At nine on a workday?" Pulling the phone from my ear I check, and sure enough we've slept in. I can still hear my mom's tinny voice even without it pressed against my face. "I have been outside your apartment since seven hoping to catch you before you went into the office. Imagine my surprise when some random person answers the door and tells me he has no idea who 'Rachel' is."

Oh shit. Fuck. Okay. No. Wait. I never expected them to drive into D.C. especially not without warning. It's terrible of me that I still haven't told them, given it's been months now, but between the sporadic contact and my aversion to disappointing them . . . I was content to just let the time slip by and cross that bridge when the time came.

Apparently that time is now.

"So, uh, there's something I should probably tell you."

"Are you *with* someone right now?" I don't know how she

knows. Bryce hasn't made a sound. Maybe it's that uncanny sixth sense that mothers seem to have or maybe she's just going down a mental list of possibilities.

"That's not what I need to tell you." Frustration mounts at her changing the subject.

"But you *are* with someone? In bed with someone?" Of all the things to focus on.

I do the only thing I can think of to steer the conversation back on track: blurt out the truth and wait for the fallout.

"I don't live or work in D.C. anymore."

There's a beat of silence on the other end and I'm holding my breath, bracing.

"*What?!*" Her voice is shrill and it's the worst case scenario. Elizabeth Mackey doesn't raise her voice like that often. She communicates far better through sighs and disappointment. Anger is a rare beast and one that's never easily contained before it wreaks havoc.

"Okay, I need you to listen to me for a moment without losing it, please. I know I have no right to ask that of you since I didn't tell you what was going on and you're understandably upset. But it was important to me."

I can hear her huffing and puffing on the other end of the line, likely pacing wherever she's at.

"Talk," Mom bites out between her teeth.

"I got passed over for a promotion at Lakin-Cole. Again. And then my new boss sexually harassed me and I just—I couldn't stay there." Despite asking her to keep her cool, I'm the one getting elevated. "They treated me like crap. Overlooked everything I did. So, I quit and found something else. It's so fulfilling. I get to be creative and actually collaborate with the business owner. I'm getting a stake in the company. It just required me to move to Maryland."

"Still software development?" I hate that that's her question.

Not "Are you doing okay? Are you liking it? Do they treat you well?" Just, "Are you using your degree for its intended purpose?"

"Among other things. It plays a role."

"What *exactly* is the role?" Fuck that stupid sixth sense and my mother's ability to sniff out a partial or untruth from a mile away.

"It's design. Software and physical."

"Physical? Rachel, stop beating around the bush and just tell me. You asked me to listen, so speak."

My agitation is so high I can feel my heartbeat in my head. Bryce is dragging soothing swipes of his thumb along my skin but it's not enough to combat the panic building. The reason I never wanted to have this conversation in the first place and have avoided it desperately.

"It's for an escape room. I'm collaborating on and designing an escape room, okay."

She gives one dry chuckle and my stomach drops.

"You left a six-figure income in Washington D.C. at a company you've been at for nearly a decade because of some *man*? Slunk off to god knows where in Maryland to lick your wounds, likely taking the first job you could. I thought I raised you better than that."

Acid eats up my esophagus as she dismisses it all, boils it down to my weakness. *My* inability to put up with it like I should have been able to.

"I'm putting myself first, Mom. Lakin-Cole didn't give a damn about me and neither did anyone there. *This* is exactly why I didn't want to tell you. I knew you wouldn't get it— would just consider me emotional and weak for leaving, but I'm not."

"So your solution is to be selfish? Your father and I worked ourselves to the bone at the same company for thirty plus years to pay for you to be great, all the way up to now still paying off your school—to support you when you were starting out, only for you to throw it away."

My breath gets stuck somewhere between my ribs, chest achingly tight. "I'm not throwing anything away. Just because I'm not on the path you picked doesn't mean it's the wrong thing. I'm still able to pay my half of the student loans and the rest of my bills. Besides, no one stays at one company for thirty years any more. Corporate culture isn't what it was in the nineties!"

Bryce's frown is so severe that a line cuts in between his brows. I never seen him angry like this before and despite the rage radiating off him at my expense, he moves my hair back with a gentle touch so he can plant a soft kiss on the top of my shoulder. His hold on me tightens and I can feel the shiver running through him as he tries to balance between supportive and righteously tense. It's a study in caring—a juxtaposition that I never knew I needed until now.

"Why can't you just be happy that I'm happy? Does that mean nothing to you?" My voice has lost its forcefulness, the quiet broken part of me asking what I've been afraid to for so long.

"Of course your happiness is important to me. I just don't want you to make a huge mistake."

"It's my mistake to make. Which, for the record, this is *not* a mistake. But even if it was, it's not up to you. I'm a grown woman who can make choices for herself and I have kept myself amiable, and proper, and never stepped a toe out of line because disappointing anyone feels like the worst thing in the world. But I can't keep living to appease everyone else. Including you, Mom." My voice has risen, emotion leaking through in wobbles and breaks on the words and I hate that I can't keep myself unaffected, hate knowing that she won't accept this kind of reaction.

There's only silence on the other end and I try to picture what this must be like for her but I can't. Because I've never fought her on something like this before. I've folded every time. The closest was when I insisted on D.C. both for college and after, but I was able to convince her with the numbers. Showing her my worth on a piece of paper, to someone's bottom line.

This. This she won't understand. Elizabeth Mackey doesn't *do* choices driven by emotion. She's meticulous and careful. She thinks everything through, all the diverging paths and possibilities. And I'm included in that. Tucked into the plan *she* has deemed best, without asking anyone else what they think.

"Well. Sounds like you have it all figured out." She's got that tone, the one that lets me know she's exasperated and about to shut down. "We'll talk again when you're less emotional. I can't discuss things with you when you're like this."

The last statement throws me over the edge and my fear and sorrow fall to the wayside as anger surges forth.

"Don't bother. I'm done hiding my emotions because you're not willing to accept them. And done living my life for you like I owe you something. *You* adopted me. I didn't ask for this and I've spent my whole life trying to prove to you that it was worth it. That *I* was worth it. I can't do it anymore."

I wait. Perched on the edge of uncertainty, and hope, and heartbreak. I wait for her to say the words I've aspired to my whole life.

"All I've ever done was love you and take care of you. But fine. If that's how you feel then I'll leave you to your mistake."

The call cuts out and I set my phone back onto the side table with a gentleness that belies my current state. Then I hear him against my ear, echoing the words I soothed him with yesterday. "Shh, it's okay. You're okay. You're safe."

And I realize that I'm sobbing, shaking against him, my hands freezing despite the summer morning. I turn in the cradle of his arms and bury my face against his chest. Crying for me now and the little girl I was, and the hole in my chest I've had all this time hoping she would fill it if only I was good enough.

"It hurts," I manage between sobs.

"I know. I'm here." Bryce envelops me, until the sunlight from the morning isn't visible and all I can see and feel is him. I love that he's not trying to fix this. He's not trash talking my mom or trying to cheer me up with a misplaced joke.

Bryce holds me while I cry, just letting me have this moment, this feeling I've been hiding and keeping contained for so long. When he says "It's okay," I know it's not him trying to convince me that the situation is fine. He's giving me permission to fall apart, there to catch me just like he promised, though this was never the way I pictured it happening when I made that statement.

Minutes pass, my crying calming to the occasional catch in my breathing—sticky tears on my face and his chest.

"I got my gunk all over you, I'm sorry." My nose is stuffy from the force of my crying and he just leans me back to look me in the eye.

Brushing a strand of hair out of my face behind my ear, he wipes away the tear tracks on my cheek. "I don't mind."

"Well, you've seen the whole gamut of emotion from me. Scared off yet?" I ask it as jokingly as I can but my chest aches, hoping against hope that I'm not too much for this man. Because as tentative as things are between us, Bryce has carved himself into me, just the tiniest nick but permanent in how he's changed me and the way I think.

Six months ago I wouldn't have dreamed about telling my mom off. Six months ago I'd still been languishing in a thankless job and picking up people in bars. Six months ago I kept myself so compartmentalized that it felt like no one knew me or cared to.

Bryce Dawson is a rogue wave—sneaking up on me and upending me in the space of mere moments. A ripple on the horizon that I never saw coming, and now I'm not sure which way is up. I'm content to let him rock me back to shore. Wherever that ends up being remains to be seen.

"Never. The ways you scare me have nothing to do with you letting yourself be human and everything to do with how you leave me off balance whenever I'm around you," he says.

"Now who's the one who should be careful with heights," I tease. Trying to pretend at being nonchalant when what he said has me wanting to clutch at my chest and the kernel of hope that burns there.

Bryce grabs my hand, lifting my palm to his mouth and planting a soft kiss there, quiet words woven into my skin when he speaks. "Be careful with me."

No mirth in his eyes, just the vulnerability I've been running away from. If I don't let anyone close they can't hurt me has been somewhat of a mantra, a life's motto so to speak. Because I wouldn't let myself want him, Bryce got closer than anyone else has, because I didn't think I needed to protect myself against him. He wasn't a threat to my carefully constructed house of cards. Until now.

Now, with him asking for care from me—consideration for him and his feelings—there's no more running unless I plan to hurt him.

"I will," I vow.

His cheeks flush and rise with a smile that crinkles the corners of his eyes. So strange seeing him without his glasses but the sight is so much more potent face-to-face with nothing to detract from the intense warmth in his eyes.

This time when the buzzing on the bedside table announces a message, more shuffling vibrations, it's his. Handing him the phone, he considers whatever is on his screen for a moment before looking over at me.

"My mom," he says, shaking his head. "She says they just

heard back with an invoice. Do you mind if I call her real quick? I'd like you to hear whatever is going on as well."

"Sure," I say.

"Is this a good time?" his mother asks and the consideration in her tone when compared to my own mother makes my chest clench.

"That depends, is it good news or bad news?" Bryce asks.

His mother breathes in deeply and it's almost like Bryce's whole body deflates before she speaks. "The bill for the bathroom renovations came in now that they're done and it's . . . hefty. You might want to take a look at the financials as a whole and make some calls on how you'd like to proceed."

Bryce's sigh is so big it jostles me and I kiss the spot over his heart to try and calm him.

"Give it to me straight, Mom. I might have a degree in finance but you've had the experience of actually owning a business."

"The quicker you open, the quicker you can earn money. It doesn't have to be perfect from the start, or even as big as you planned. Get a feel for it and then expand more once business picks up. That way you're maximizing your resources and time."

It's not all that different from what I'd suggested before—cutting down rooms. This just gives the additional pressure of an earlier opening as well.

His brows are low and severe over those beautiful eyes, the honey dull under stress. I trail my fingertips over his cheek, then smoothing the line between his eyebrows with my thumb and I get the tiniest quirk on the side of his mouth as a reward.

"Okay." Bryce sighs again, a huge exhalation of air followed by a double inhalation, the stutter of air rushing back into his lungs. "Okay. I'll be dropping back home in a few and we can look at the numbers. Once I've dealt with that, once we've decided, we'll jump in immediately."

"I'll see you soon, hon."

"See ya," he says, tone morose, before hanging up and leaning over me to set the phone back down.

This time he's the one that tucks his head against my breasts, holding on as I feel his body tremble slightly. Not tears, but anxiety.

"We'll figure it out," I soothe. "We'll make it work and I'll do whatever you need to make it happen."

"Is it okay if I come back here once we've formulated a concrete plan? To go over those room ideas you had in depth?" His voice is muffled against my shirt and I stroke my fingers through his hair to try and combat the tightness of his muscles.

"You're welcome any time, Bryce. Seriously. For what it's worth, I think your mom is right. If you have to move up the deadline, focusing on two or three rooms instead of all of them will be a great way to get a feel for what works and what doesn't while you get the hang of it all."

He kisses the middle of my sternum, the heat of his lips scorching through my shirt so it might as well not even be there. Unbeknownst to him, the touch is right where he's managed to burrow into me. A crack. A hairline fracture. A weakness that he could exploit if I let him.

Fuck, I want to let him.

"Text me, keep me updated. If it works out, I'd love to have a meal with you and go over stuff?" I urge and all it does is make him tighten his arms around me. Stubborn. As if he can hide here and the world won't intrude. "Bryce . . ."

"Don't wanna." It's so pouty I can't help the laugh that spreads through my body and his answering one fills me with warmth along every nerve ending.

"Gotta."

This time when he sighs it's over dramatic and for show. "Fine. But I'd like the record to show that I am *not* pleased with this turn of events. I was having a perfectly lovely sleep and I'd planned to pick up where we left off last night." The hunger is there, peeking out in his last statement.

"Patience is a virtue. One that will be rewarded. Work first, then play."

Bryce rolls away from me, taking some of the comforter with him and the sight of him—shirtless and disheveled, wrapped up in my covers, his face still soft with sleep—makes me wish for more. More of this. With him.

It isn't until he's dressed—leaving with a goodbye kiss that slips a little too close to stoking the flames from last night—and out of the door that I have a startling realization.

If the deadline moves up and we have to rush through getting Locke Box open, that means . . .

My time with him is slipping away faster than I'm ready for and soon I—*we*—will have to make a choice on whether or not there's a place for me after. If there is an after for us at all.

# CHAPTER 12

LEAVING RACHEL THERE, HAIR MUSSED FROM SEX AND SLEEP, HER LIPS soft and swollen, is the hardest thing I've had to do in ages. I'm not sure whether it's from exhausting ourselves and the stress of yesterday, or just the comfort of her pressed against me, but I've slept better than I have for months. She's ruinous.

It would be easy to let her all the way in. Hell, I'm pretty sure I already have and I'm just kidding myself to think otherwise. Rachel's already become a comfortable part of my day, so right to be there that I've never thought to question it. Now she's on my mind all the time. I find myself looking around for her whenever something happens, like I'm searching to lock eyes with her so we can share a look or a laugh. Rachel's snuck in the way night swallows sunset until I'm bathed in it. Slowly, then encompassing.

Seeing her hurting this morning—my heart twinges in my chest at the broken sound of her sobs and I would have given anything in that moment to squeeze her tight enough that it glued all her broken pieces back together.

My mind is stuffed full of her, cotton wool making me fuzzy and my thoughts sluggish. The drive home is silent, forgetting that I even have a radio when all I can focus on is her and what my mom said on the phone.

I knew the repairs would set me back but I've been operating in denial. Expecting things to work themselves out. I underestimated how hard this would be. I'm used to being able to set my mind to something and push myself through anything to make it happen. But life doesn't care about how well I can fixate and overwork myself. The universe doesn't dwell on my inexplicable belief that as long as I pretend I'm fine everything else around me will be too.

Summer is well and truly underway. Verdant branches hang heavy over the streets downtown, casting shadows in an arch of leaves. Parks are packed with summer little league camps, families basking in the sun, and people walking their dogs. Morning melts under the promise of another scorching day. By the time I pull up to my parents house, I can smell a hint of smoke in the air. Margaritaville spills from the backyard speakers, grill going, relaxation-mode on full blast. All I can think about is the interaction between Rachel and my parents, and how easy she made it look.

Following the little smoke signal, I enter through the side gate to see my dad behind the grill, happily humming along to the marimbas and upbeat steel drums, and Jimmy Buffet's rampant alcohol dependence.

"Well, well, well. Look at who finally decided to show up."

There's a heavy pause in which I fight the urge to defend myself, before he smirks at me and the tension fades. I'm a grown man. There's no need for explanation. Although my mom probably won't be as quick to let it go.

My father clicks his tongs shut, resting them on the side of the grill. Standing on a perfectly manicured lawn, he's in open-toed shoes again and my mom is going to kill him if she sees. There's a push and pull between them, she tries her best to wrangle him away from impulse and danger, and he runs full speed ahead at whatever sparks joy.

"How's it coming?" I gesture at the grill.

"Just about done. Maybe fifteen or so."

In theory fifteen minutes should be no big deal, but in direct sunlight it's a less pleasant concept. Dulaney is sweaty. It's high humidity and bug bites and cicadas. Most people don't think of Maryland as particularly humid compared to places in the Deep South but on days like today—ninety-some degrees and desperate for a thunderstorm—it feels like breathing through a wet sock.

But my parents are proud to live here. They know every one of their neighbors. They spend as much time in the grocery store chatting as they do shopping. I never thought I'd be back here. At least not in a permanent capacity and yet I find the prospect is kind of invigorating. The echo of my youth and the fact that I'm realizing at least part of a dream I'd let die has injected some spirit back into my life and myself. Now that I'm not spending every moment of the day pretending to be the version of me I think people want, there's so much more room to enjoy things.

By the time the food's ready, my skin is dotted with perspiration and I'm dying for a glass of something cool. I follow my father into the kitchen through the sliding glass doors, the blessed cold lick of the air conditioner wicking the sweat from my brow and back. My mother's behind the island, hair piled up on her head in a messy bun that's gotten so much grayer. Even over the last few months. Or maybe I'm just extra aware of how much older my parents have gotten since I've moved back in with them and noticed the changes.

Time with Stephanie meant less time with them, and now that I see them every day, the difference between the last time I lived here and now is stark. The lines beside my dad's eyes are carved deep and stay there, even when he's not smiling. My mom's gentle hands are dotted with spots, her veins like tributaries flowing through thinner skin as she dishes the food onto our plates.

Mom waits until I'm into my first bite of a burger before she pounces.

"So, should I even bother asking where you were last night?"

I choke on a piece of lettuce, grasping for my glass of water and coughing through clearing my airway before I answer. "Why don't you just ask me what you really want to know? Neither you nor dad really care that I didn't come home. You're just curious about the why."

Both of them give me sheepish grins, and I wait it out to see who will be brave enough to call me out on it directly.

"Ooh, okay. We'll ask you some one word questions and then guess." My dad sounds way too excited about it but I don't mind. These moments won't last forever and even though it's embarrassing, I've missed having them around to give me a hard time.

"Were you working all night?" My mom asks.

"No."

"Were you with Logan?" My dad tries.

"Nope."

"Was it a date?" The twinkle in my mom's eye is a little alarming.

"In a way."

My mom backhands my shoulder to scold me for being so vague. They share a look, that weird silent communication between them that comes with thirty-plus years of marriage, and the grin on my father's face is borderline diabolical. "It was Rachel."

My cheeks flame and I take another sip of water to try and play it off. "That wasn't a question."

"We didn't need to ask. It's all over your face." Frank Dawson laughs like I'm the funniest joke he's ever heard and my mom shakes her head at him.

"For the record, we really like her. She seems like a lovely woman—smart, driven, but still kind and approachable," my mom says.

I can't help but feel like my mother listed those first two attributes, ones that could have been ascribed to Stephanie, only to make sure she could juxtapose them with the qualities Rachel has that my ex lacked.

Clearing my throat, working up the courage, I nod. "It's barely anything. We'll see what happens, especially considering the escape room. Which—speaking of—how bad is it?"

The mirth on their faces disappears. "It's not great. Crunching the numbers, accounting for operating costs for the first three months, repair and renovation costs, you'll have to open by the end of August or beginning of September in order to make it work. And that's with the diminished room count I mentioned. Do you think that's doable for you? Six weeks or so? Since you're working on most of this yourself?"

My temples radiate with a headache that's rapidly formed. Between being overheated and stressed there's no avoiding it.

"Do I have a choice? I've already sunk half my savings and the money from the house sale into this. I've signed a year-long lease on the building and we've gutted one and a half rooms already. No, I've just got to push through. I might just have to ask for help wherever I can get it."

My mom pats my hand, no doubt having noticed it's turned into a fist. "Your dad and I are here and although we aren't as spry as we once were, give us some painting or organizing. Heck, Logan will probably come as well if you told him what's going on."

"And there's Rachel. She's already been amazing from what you've told us and what we've seen," Dad chimes in.

"I just don't want to ask too much of her. The lines are blurring between us and the last thing I want is for her to think I'm exploiting that change to get more work out of her. She's been such a help. I couldn't do it without her."

"Just make sure you show her that. I know you struggle with articulating what you're feeling. Like me, you're a person of action when words fail. I'm sure she already knows, but keep showing her how much her work means, and how much you admire her as a person, and you'll be fine." My mom's statement has me huffing out a shuddering breath.

Because she's not wrong. Expressing my emotions in the right words has never been my strong suit. Which is a freaking joke when considering I suck at picking up physical or other subtle cues myself anyway. Communication is a struggle. No wonder I missed my marriage falling apart when I leaned on Steph's words alone.

"Yes, but also, she deserves more than that. I have to at least try to say it as well as just showing it. I don't want to make the same mistakes again." It seemed unfathomable to me when Steph first asked for a divorce that I would ever want to be with someone again—to put myself in a position to be vulnerable and potentially get hurt. But maybe things are changing.

"Good. But for what it's worth, Rachel isn't Stephanie. And you aren't the man you were with Steph. You've grown. I've never seen you this confident or sure of yourself. Even when doubting this endeavor, you're pushing through. I'm proud of you." My dad looks suspiciously emotional, a bit of moisture shining behind those glasses of his.

"Okay, okay. Enough mushiness. My food is getting cold and I need to get over to the theater as soon as possible if we're going to kick this thing into high gear."

The rest of the meal is less heavy, small comments and plans that have no big bearing on anything. The stress of it all is already clawing up my throat and I can't let myself panic two days in a row. Once I've helped my mother load the dishes, and freshened up, I drive back over to the theater.

> Hey, I'm back over at work if you'd like to join.

> I understand if you don't. It was a rough morning.

> But I'd love to see your face. It's been too long already.

RACHEL

> Give me thirty to get ready and head over!

I try to keep my cool while I unbolt the chain on the doors and get set up for the day, preparing to finish gutting the second room. I've got a little under two months to pull this all together before money falls prey to time and I can't afford not to finish. By the time I've ripped up another row of seats, Rachel arrives with a cooler bag full of water bottles and snacks.

"I figured we were going to be here for a while, so I brought provisions." Her cheeks heat as she holds the bag up, the first thing either of us have said since I left her bed this morning.

"You're amazing. I'd hug you but my hands are dirty." I hold up the evidence, black streaks and dust on my hands and forearms.

"Not just your hands. You've got some on your forehead from wiping sweat." She laughs at me, sets the bag down, and gives me a quick peck on the mouth before straightening up with her game face on.

"So, what's the plan?" Rachel asks, prying more of the glued down wall covering. This time she's got the stripper and scraper ready to go.

"According to the financials we have just under two months to pull stuff together if I'm going to be able to keep things going.

We won't do all the rooms now. Just two or three to start and then as we gain more interest and earn money to cover operating costs, there will be a chance to expand per our original plan."

Rachel considers this for a moment, her hand stilling midair before she continues with her task. "Which three do you think we should focus on? If you and I can narrow that down I'll be able to start looking for locks, props, and mapping the puzzles to fit the room specs."

"I liked the idea of a historic Dulaney one, but Logan brought up a good point a while ago as well. We could theme a few of the rooms to movies, like a nod to the theater itself, and that could be a good draw."

"What if we use the theater's history? I think I saw that this used to be a stage theater before it got chopped into smaller rooms for movies. What if we fabricate a mystery around the theater itself and that way we can add Dulaney touches but still have it feel unique to this space?" Her brows are furrowed low over those gorgeous dark eyes and I am transfixed by watching her brain work.

"You're brilliant, you know that?" My words pull her out of her ruminating and she gifts me a blinding smile.

"That's why you hired me."

"I'll see about recruiting some other people to help me with the reno so you can focus on that. We need to narrow down our theme ideas. They were all so great but if we're scaling down they really have to pack a punch."

Despite being on opposite ends of the room at this point, the emptiness of it makes our voices carry easier so it feels like she's right beside me when she answers.

"I can take some of the room ideas we had and try to cross reference them with movies. We likely won't be able to mention them outright due to legalities but I'm sure we can come up with some kind of work around. That way it's on theme and feels cohesive from the start—even scaled down."

We agree and Rachel sets up a little Bluetooth speaker to fill the silence while we work. It's strangely companionable. Comfort in quiet. Steph never met a silence she couldn't fill and at the time I thought that was a good thing because that way I was off the hook. But this, being in the same room with Rachel even if we're not talking, feels peaceful in a way I can't describe—grounding.

As day succumbs to night, our bodies dotted with sweat from the summer heat outside and the exertion of work, we finally finish gutting the second room around seven PM.

"You want to grab something to eat?" I ask, Rachel and I sitting against the wall and greedily gulping down the water that's barely chilled at this point but refreshing nonetheless. We're packed up for the day and ready to go but I don't want it to be over yet.

"Looking like this?" She gestures to her work clothes, gunk and glue and dust making them look rough.

I don't even want to think about how bad I look—or smell right now.

"Fair point." One I can't dispute and I wish I knew how to ask her what I really want to. But I've never been good at that. My needs are low on the list when compared to those of others.

Once I would have considered that noble, self-sacrificing for the sake of the person I was trying to help. Now, I know it's just fear. Fear of rejection, fear of ridicule. I've kept so much of myself boxed up because I was terrified that when I finally built up the courage to ask I'd be let down. Can't have unmet expectations when you won't name them in the first place. But in doing so, shoving more and more of me down to be this blank slate of a person there only for the desires of others... I became complacent.

There is no right way to please everyone all of the time. I just wish I'd learned that lesson sooner. I might have saved myself a lot of time and energy.

"On the other hand . . ." Rachel says and pulls me from my wallowing literally and figuratively. Her small hand held out in front of me to help me up from my spot on the floor, she slides it into mine once I'm standing and we head through the exit.

"Yes?" I hope, waiting beside my car to know whether I'm staying or going.

"We could always pick something up along the way to my place, take a shower, and veg out?"

"I'd like that. Although I don't have a change of clothes."

Rachel smirks up at me and my chest tightens at the look on her face. "I have a washing machine, plus I've already seen you naked."

"Once again, fair point. This is why you are the brains of the operation."

I hold the car door for her and just before I shut the door she says my name. Resting my forearm on the roof of the car, I bend down slightly to give her my full attention.

"It might be worth bringing some clothes along for next time." Her statement is simple, no underlying tone to it that tells me it might be a joke and my stomach clenches.

"Sounds like a plan."

*Next time.*

Heart hammering in my chest, I close the distance between us, kissing her deeply for a moment, not caring that we're downtown and the cars that are out on the road are having to slightly swerve to avoid me.

I shut the door and we make the short trek over to the Greek pop-up stall at the Orthodox church down the street from her apartment. Later, showered and clad only in a towel, we eat our gyros in the kitchen and spend the rest of the night tangled together.

*Next time.*

The words pulse through me like a heartbeat as I hold her close to my body. Her soft breathing and the window unit are the perfect white noise but I can't give in to sleep. Not yet. Not when I'm lost because I've never ached so badly for more than right at this moment. More time. More touch. More of Rachel and all the next times she's willing to give.

LOGAN DROPS BY EVERY AFTERNOON HE CAN, THE TWO OF US working side-by-side to clear out the final room. Gabrielle joins when she can and by the end of July, two weeks after we had to move up the deadline, the rooms are ready for paint and the structural design elements that will make up each space.

Rachel's got the Dulaney room all figured out, as well as outlines for the other two and she's ready to present it to us all, my friends and parents included, once the last of the paint has dried. We're gathered on folding chairs in what will be the Dulaney room—the largest of the bunch—and Rachel takes a deep breath before launching into the first idea.

"The plan is to have each room themed after a movie, or in the case of the main attraction, the theater and Dulaney itself. We've settled on an adventure room, loosely based on movies like Indiana Jones and The Mummy for the first of the movie rooms. The basic premise is a trap. Not so much solving a mystery as trying to find your way out of the room before it's too late. We'll be playing with things like lighting to give the illusion of the room closing in, and torches being extinguished, as time progresses. With each ten minutes a torch will blow out and it will become more challenging to escape. This one will have a disclaimer and be geared toward more serious escapees who have done this sort of thing before." Rachel hands out a stack of stapled papers to each of us with the basic premise of the room, ideas for puzzles, and how the tech will be incorporated into the experience.

"What about the other rooms?" Logan asks, flipping through the pages.

"The room we're in right now has been nicknamed the Dulaney room and will evoke a murder mystery vibe. We're basing it on a fictional murder that took place when this was still a stage theater in the forties and caused the place to shut down. Participants will have to scour the theater for clues on who committed the murder before the killer figures out they're looking, or *they will be next.*" Rachel adds a bit of drama to the end of the sentence, the fake danger in her tone making the group laugh.

"Lastly, we've got a more entry-level room. This one is based around a heist and the participants get to be the criminals. Sometimes being bad is more fun. We're taking notes from Steven Soderbergh movies like Ocean's Eleven and Logan Lucky. They'll have to gather all the intel on breaking in, disable the alarms and cameras, and bypass all the security codes before the system comes back online."

I can't help the pride that sweeps through me as Rachel lays it all out for them—the closest people in my life and those who believe in me even when I don't believe in myself. It finally feels within reach.

This endeavor might have started as a way to prove to Steph and myself that I am more than she saw me as, but it's become so much more. This business, this time with Rachel—it's been so healing. Outside the bubble of Philadelphia and Stephanie, and the soul-sucking office nightmare that was the "family business," I feel so much more alive.

Life isn't just *happening* to me.

"So, what do you all think?" Rachel asks and I can see by the determined set of her jaw and the fear in her eyes that she's hoping for praise and terrified that her weeks of work won't garner the response she wants and deserves.

"You're a marvel. I don't know how Bryce swindled you into all this but you are killing it." Gabrielle is the first to speak and Rachel's stiffness eases under the words.

"Thank you for making this dream come to life. I know it's sappy to say but I've never seen Bryce happier and more fulfilled. No matter the outcome, you've had a tremendous impact on my son, by extension all the people in his life, and this town." My mother approaches Rachel, tugging her into a quick hug that says even more than her words do.

Mom isn't a hugger. Her physical affection is reserved for family. Heck, even Logan just gets a cheek pat, a little fake smack in greeting or when he says something ridiculous. So it just drives home how much my parents must like her.

Rachel's face flames and she nods at my mom before carrying on. "Bryce has given me your availability and I've made up a tentative schedule and duty list. Between the six of us, we should be able to pull this off in time."

Dispersing, the chatter of my loved ones discussing what they're excited for, I let myself bask in the warmth of this moment. It's happening. A year ago I was devastated by Steph changing the world as I knew it. The checklist I hid behind in order to keep me safe was pointless and in her pushing us in the right direction it became glaringly obvious just how unfulfilled I was.

I'm so grateful for it—for the spite that turned into a sort of confidence. For the pain that kept me centered. For the ability to see what's actually good for me instead of what I have to pretend my way through.

I'm grateful for Rachel and her small hand tucked into mine as we walk past the tea shop and up into her apartment. Even though it's only been a couple weeks since this thing between us finally burst free, there's a quiet comfort I don't take for granted.

It's there . . . the feeling I'm still too scared to name.

It's there through every heartbeat of hers I can feel against my skin, and the soft puff of her breathing against my neck as she sleeps.

Rachel Mackey, without even trying, has flooded every single fracture in my chest with her light. She's left an indelible mark on me that is all the more beautiful for who made it. With her touch I am a kintsugi piece of pain and growth, acceptance and affection.

And a tender fledgling love that I hope to coax into something strong and enduring.

Placing a kiss against the top of her head, I breathe in the scent of her shampoo. I'm not sure how yet, but all I know is that when this contract is up I *have* to find a way to convince her to stay.

# CHAPTER 13

IT'S EASY TO LOSE MYSELF IN THE DEMANDS OF THE LAST BIG RUSH—the final push that will make or break the last few months of my life. Somehow, in a short span of time, everything is different. I don't wake up dreading every day. I don't spend it constantly being second guessed or passed over. Bryce considers me an equal, even more sometimes when he says things about how smart or brilliant or creative I am.

The fulfillment is only rivaled by the warmth that being by his side brings.

But there's a pall, a niggle at the back of my mind. When it's dark and quiet and Bryce is asleep beside me, my thoughts race. Combing over every part of my conversation with my mother and analyzing how all the little lies by omission—from my burn out to my sexuality—and keeping my feelings to myself for so long caused it all to go wrong.

Was it during the months here in Dulaney? Before? Was it when I realized that I hated piano but kept taking lessons because she thought it would help me be more well-rounded? When I stopped looking for faces that echoed mine in photographs?

As the days stretch into a week, then two, then more . . . I ache. As much as things between us are strained, as much as I want to please her and prove my worth—I can't take it anymore. I have to be my own person. I just wish my mom could see that all the tools, all the work and time she gave served their purpose. Just because I'm not living out the life she devised for me doesn't mean it's not a good one—a great one even.

Bryce doesn't bring it up again outside of his genuine, "I'm here if you want to talk," type thing—giving me the space to work through my thoughts and feelings and I appreciate it. As we get closer to the end it's become clearer that he's the kind of person who keeps things close to the vest and needs time to process but once he does he's honest. Him affording me the same has been so helpful.

All the dude-bros and fuckboys in D.C., all the girls I dated that weren't in it as deep as I was—they all fade away under what I might consider my first healthy relationship. So far. Not that we've labeled it. I'm trying really hard not to worry about the fact that we haven't. But that's just my anxious attachment style fighting its way to the surface.

So I distract myself by working until my body aches and my brain is fuzzy. Puzzles are so much harder than I thought and I severely underestimated the amount of story that goes into this. We've had to come up with contingencies so that if people approach clues wrong they're still able to make sense of the rooms.

At night and on weekends I work on coding. On shaping the tools that will take this endeavor from good to great. Light controls and timers. Voice modifiers. Hook ups to fog machines and ringing phones. It's a carefully orchestrated mess right now and I'm terrified I won't be able to pull it all together.

"What's going on in that brain of yours?" Bryce asks, his voice thick with sleep.

Morning spills into the bedroom through the crack under the door and the space where the curtain doesn't touch the wall. It's early though; the alarms haven't gone off yet. He smells like his cologne and my shampoo and the combination is heady in a way I don't have words for.

"Just thinking about everything we need to get done." I try to brush it off and snuggle against him instead.

Bryce pulls me into the cradle of his arms, and although it's already too hot for us to be this close and stay comfortable, I allow it for the peace that it brings. When he holds me, when he kisses me or we lose ourselves in each other's bodies, it's the only time I feel like I can breathe normally.

"We'll manage it. If you need to take a break or need to reach out to someone else to help supplement the digital stuff, please do that. You don't have to work yourself into the ground to prove you can do it. I know you can. But there's something to be said for limits and knowing what they are." The words are too profound to be coming from that morning gravel making me think of everything but work.

"Pot calling the kettle black there, don't you think?" I inject a hint of teasing into my tone and in retaliation I get tickled in the ribs.

Squirming to get away, my erratic laughing leaving me breathless, Bryce is relentless. His tickles are interspersed with kisses pressed to everywhere but my mouth so I can catch my breath before he steals it again.

In that pale light, his features are soft with the smile on his face, adoration when he looks at me . . . all I want is to ask. Bryce is constantly going on about needing words from me. I don't know how to tell him I want the same. Like he alluded, I've never been very good at admitting weakness or asking for what I need.

"Good. You looked like you needed that," Bryce says as we each lay on our backs and try to get our breaths under control. The occasional huff of laughter still slips out and it's been such a long time since I laughed so hard my sides hurt.

I want this. I want this for so much longer than just this contract term and I don't know how to ask for that either when there's no telling where we stand.

My lease goes until December though—the original date. I can always try to find something else in Dulaney. If nothing comes along I'll slink back to D.C. and slot back into the corporate space. Regardless of the state of my relationship and heart, bills need to get paid.

"So did you. How have you been holding up? You've taken all the shake ups with grace but I want you to know it's okay if you're stressed. You can tell me. I know that 'boss Bryce' can't divulge when things are shaky with the business but you're more than that to me."

So much more.

He shifts onto his side, eyes combing over my face. His expression turns serious and the pit in my stomach has a gravity to it that I never noticed before.

"I'm terrified." Bryce's confession settles between us like another entity in the room and I shuffle under the covers to press a kiss against his nose.

"I don't talk about it or her much but the divorce kind of knocked me on my ass. This whole thing was a spur of the moment way to spite her and it's grown into so much more. This has gone from a far-fetched version of 'I think I can do this better than some of the others out there' to 'holy crap, this is actually happening' and I'm not sure what it's going to look like once the dust settles." The quiet of early morning, the lack of car sounds and people talking outside the window make his words swallow the silence.

I run my fingers up and down the outside of his arm, watching goosebumps form and spread, dispersing until I trail my way back and coax them out again—my small form of comfort when I'm not quite sure what to say. Because he doesn't talk about his ex much and hearing that this started as a "fuck you" has me uneasy for reasons I'm too scared to examine.

Does he still feel like that? Is all this for her sake?

"You've come so far. Don't let the echoes from the past cause you to doubt what you're doing here. Despite constant setbacks you're set to open a full three months earlier than planned. Although we won't have the December fest to use as promotion, it might be for the best. Instead of the focus being on the town we turn it to us."

Bryce catches my hand when it brushes over the back of his and brings my palm to his lips. Kiss pressed against my life line, my heart pounds. How something so innocuous and small can throw me off balance is astounding. If anything I feel less nervous when it's just sex. Not that any of this has felt like "just sex" to begin with.

"Do *you* have doubts?" Bryce asks and I'm not sure what to touch on first.

"Work, love, life? What category would you like me to answer for first?" I try to make it sound like a dry joke but something twitches in his jaw when I say the word love and my stomach does a somersault.

"All of the above?"

"I think doubt means we have something to lose. Something to want. I think doubt and fear are vital emotions because they show us what's important. The big thing to remember is that we can't let them rule everything," I say.

Sucking in a deep breath, letting the feelings I've been trying to suppress rise to the surface, I answer. "Am I worried that I fucked up my relationship with my mother beyond repair because

I was too scared to tell my parents my life was changing—that I was disappointing them? Yes."

Bryce kisses the pad of my thumb and I continue, words spewing without thought.

"Am I nervous that I might have tanked my whole career because I couldn't put up with the misogyny? Yes."

Another kiss, this one on the pad of my index finger, as if he's ticking each one off of my fingers like a list.

"Am I concerned that I'm in over my head with this escape room project and that the scope of it is more than I was ready or qualified for? Yep."

Lips on my middle finger and every touch is like a shock down my arm. But his eyes are still soft, his brow slightly furrowed as he lets me speak my piece.

"Am I terrified that this thing between us is happening and it's in this weird space between real and unreal where everything is hazy and perfect, and one wrong move could screw it all up?" My breath shudders out of my lungs. "I've never been more scared in my life."

Bryce kisses down my ring finger then threads his fingers between mine, pulling it closer so he can place another on the back of my hand.

"I get it. I'm afraid that leaving Philly and my old job, sinking all my savings and the money from selling the house into this will leave me broke and aimless. This business is everything now, my chance at independence on my own terms. I never realized it at the time but when this notion came to me I was desperately trying to escape my heartbreak and bitterness. A little on the nose, but true."

"And now?" I gather the courage to ask.

"Now I'm building something new with someone I never saw coming. I'm not great at" —he pulls air in through his lungs like he's been deprived of it—"expressing my feelings and putting them into words. It's far easier for me to shut down and logic my way out of experiencing them at all, or accidentally blurt things out in a far-too-blunt way and upset people. But there's no careful consideration and pragmatism when it comes to this, to you."

"I feel similarly. Part of me wants to analyze this to death and the other just wants to enjoy it as much and as long as I can. Being with you, doing this with you, I've never been happier and I'm scared to jeopardize it. So, for now, can we just take it a day at a time? The unknown is too scary but this—a step at a time—I can handle that." I'm a coward. If ever there was a time for me to have asked him to define this, now would have been it.

But I'd rather live in delusion for a little longer—prolong the time before the potential hurt.

"I can do that." His words are whispered against my neck, followed by his lips.

"What else can you do?" I ask, voice husky as heat rises in my stomach to replace all my fear. Burning it away like underbrush in a forest fire of desire.

"How much time do we have?" Bryce asks, his large hand skimming the curve of my waist to grip the outside of my thigh.

"Not enough."

He kisses down my neck, over my collarbone, and then his tongue darts out over my nipple, leaving me arching against him in anticipation.

"Guess I'll have to make this quick then."

As he makes his way down my body, hands and mouth worshiping every inch of skin that he encounters, my doubts fade. When he slots his mouth over my core, I cease all thought. Somewhere between my orgasm against his mouth, those hands all over me, and the stretch of him filling me, I finally relax.

We barely have a few weeks left and I'm determined to make the best of them. If that means drowning my thoughts under Bryce's body, that's fine with me.

I HAVE TO OUTSOURCE SOME OF THE WORK. AS MUCH AS IT PAINS ME to admit, Bryce was right. There are only so many hours in a day and I can't enjoy them fully—enjoy *him* fully if I keep working days at the theater and nights at home.

Sebastian is gracious enough to help out, and I offer him a percentage of my share in payment, in the hope that the return will be enough of an incentive for him since my pockets are pretty flat.

Between his help and the razor focus that comes with a deadline, we have a working prototype to test out two weeks before our soft open and I invite him and Farren, and Ángel up again to help us test some of the rooms. And, as something that I could see becoming a regular occurrence should this develop into something deep and lasting, Bryce calls his friends to do the same, effectively blending the groups. Although there's far less division now compared to the last time we hung out together.

It seems whatever Logan and Ángel got up to at Pride caused a budding friendship because the two are off to the side chatting while I triple check the locks in the room.

"So, this is what you've been working on?" Farren asks as she leans over Sebastian's shoulder to look down at the app on his phone. We've tested it a few times on our own but today is the first run through of the room in its entirety and I'm panicking.

As if he can sense my distress, Bryce comes up beside me and his hand presses against my lower back in a show of support. Something about the heat and weight of it is soothing and it gives me the push I need to keep going.

"So far it's been working out well, but today is the dress-rehearsal, so to speak. Bryce will be running the software and I'll be keeping an eye on things from above for the cameras to make sure our positioning on those makes sense. I wouldn't be surprised if you guys don't happen to escape but I hope you do. As we'll tell our customers, you have sixty minutes and unlimited clues should you choose to use them." My voice wavers slightly, belying my nerves but I clear my throat and continue. "The goal of today's test is to find any glaring holes in the software, the flow of the room, and the efficacy of the clues scattered around the space."

Gabrielle gives me a kind smile, her brown eyes crinkling at the corners into her skin and I can't deny that being around his friends, being encouraged and accepted by them, at least tentatively, feels amazing.

"As with the other escape room we did together, there are a couple different locks to look out for. We have letter locks, regular number or combination locks, and even a directional lock." Bryce lifts each type of lock as he mentions them and shows the group how to click them to finish unlocking. He looks so excited. It's adorable and I'm so glad I'm here to see this. I'm so happy I took a chance on this . . . and him. Even if it ends up only being a blip in the grand scheme of life.

"It's going to be great! Now, get out of here so we can kick this room's ass!" Logan is very enthused, punching his fist up into the air and Bryce scoffs behind me, the movement vibrating where our bodies are pressed together.

"He's right. It *is* going to be great," Bryce whispers, just for me, and I'm astonished he's not as nervous and torn up about it as I am.

"You're suspiciously calm right now?" I say as I turn to face him.

He captures my chin and lifts it so he can plant a quick kiss on my lips. "Not calm, hopeful. I'll probably crash later tonight but right now I'm trying to use the extra adrenaline for productivity rather than worry."

"Enough. We're burning daylight and I heard a rumor about a celebratory barbeque over at the Dawsons when this is done so you better hop to it. I'm hungry." Logan grumbles without any real malice and heat floods my cheeks.

It's only been a short time since we've been overt about being together but considering Logan and Ángel saw us making out in public there's been no real reason to keep it secret. Mostly it's just so we don't get distracted at work and caught up in something inappropriate.

"I'll meet up with you when they're done?" I ask and Bryce nods, him heading over to the front desk area and me to the corridor between the theater rooms where the projectors used to be, looking down into the room below.

Bryce will be watching them through the screen and texting me if any of the cameras need adjustment which I'll be able to do from here. I'll also be able to see how far the fog from the machine travels and how well the sounds spread through the room without actually being in there with them.

We're trying them in our hardest room first. It feels a little unfair but it's better to get a feel for the difficulty level that way.

Bryce hits the main lights and our teams are enveloped in darkness that's counteracted by carefully placed warm light, fake flames from torches flickering across the wall. The premise of the room is that our escapees have just nabbed their treasure and unwittingly triggered a reaction when lifting their loot off of the pedestal. Their way out has slammed shut.

Of course the real door to get out is still available and should any of them like to leave all they have to do is say so to the camera, but we wanted to keep it as immersive as possible.

A disembodied voice, deep and menacing (courtesy of Mr. Dawson who was strangely good at it despite his friendly demeanor) sounds over the speakers and Logan lets out a squeak at the unexpected noise. I stifle a laugh and try to pay attention.

"You who trespass here, who dare to plunder what does not belong to you, have evoked wrath unlike any you have ever seen. The price you pay is steep. The chance of escape, nil. Your bones will stand as warning for any others who attempt to cross into this hallowed space. Know this if you attempt to escape your fate. Others have come and all have failed. The way out is treacherous and your demise imminent."

There's a beat of silence for them to absorb the threat before the voice continues. "Goodbye, scourge of man. I await your spirits and know you will join me soon. No one steals from the Great God Dedun and lives to regret it."

A rumble passes through the room, and the remaining lights flicker with a gust of wind from the fan on the far edge of the wall, painted black to hide its existence. The preplanned timing of the effects that have been programmed in as part of the room so far is top notch. The bass from the surround sound speakers, courtesy of the theater that stood here before, passes through my chest and remains a steady thrum of doom.

"Okay. Think. *Think*. Let's start going around the treasure room to see if there's another way out," Farren urges.

Our friends trail their hands over the "walls" feeling for notches or gaps that might indicate an escape route. Logan is the first to find a clue, followed shortly by Ángel.

"I've found a keyhole of some kind. Like we're going to have to slot something in place." Logan's fingers prod at the spot in the wall that has an emblem embossed into it.

"I found a scroll and a diary from someone who 'died' here in the past and their experience trying to get out of the room. They mention the symbol on the wall and there's some kind of code here." Ángel's fingers trail over the words and the group is huddled around him, trying to read.

They gather piece by piece, splitting into pairs and small

groups as needed and it's amazing to watch something that's only lived in my head come to life beneath me.

"Rachel, can you tilt camera two down a couple of inches? I'm not getting the full space where Gabrielle is searching through the trunk. I can only see the top of her head," Bryce's voice comes through the walkie talkie portion of the app and I tilt the camera down until his voice chirps, "perfect" through the phone speaker.

Two flames have been snuffed before they unlock their first chest, filled with tools and a crude map of the room, including passages that have been sealed shut. We included a false passage to up the stakes and try to see how quickly people would move on or if they'd focus all their energy on one spot only.

"The clue says to use all our senses to try and determine which trail will lead us out and which false path will lead to our doom. Sight hasn't helped so far. Everything feels the same when we touch it and I can't see them wanting us to lick anything in the room," Logan says and the group laughs.

They're on the right track.

"How would we tell if we weren't in a manufactured room? It would either be by scent, if the air is stagnant or if there's something else . . ." Gabrielle jumps in and I want to whoop I'm so excited.

"Air!" Farren exclaims. "They can't really do scent in here but you guys felt the fans earlier. It stands to reason that the true path will have some kind of breeze that will mark it as the one that leads outside."

The group is surrounded by their clues and the tools they've amassed over the last half an hour, crouched near the ground and trying to feel for a slight breeze to determine if there is a way out. It's Sebastian that calls them over to the correct path.

They move carefully through the darkened passage into the second part of the room, closed off from the treasure area. There they find the caged-in opening to the outside with multiple locks, including a letter one that is the final barrier between them and freedom.

That lock is the secret word they have to submit—amend.

Unfortunately they get stuck at the physical puzzle that contains the word hidden within—a magnetic maze that signifies the journey they've gone through to escape. They're doing it correctly but it seems as if the magnet we chose just isn't strong enough.

More torches dim and they are down to their last one when the magnet finds its home and the scroll containing the final clue clatters to the ground.

Logan's whoop of excitement is contagious and the rest of the group have triumphant smiles on their faces as they twist the letters and unlock the way out. I rush down to the room but Bryce gets there first and Logan gives him a big hug.

"Two minutes to spare!" I say, a little breathless and very pleased despite the minor mishap. "Great job, everyone!"

Ángel walks over to me, bumps his shoulder against mine as we watch everyone else chatting about the more challenging parts and the validation they felt as each solution presented itself.

"You did it, kiddo." His praise is quiet, just for us, but the warmth that spreads through me at those words makes all these months of hard work and late nights, and all the doubt around what I did to get here worth it.

"I can't believe we pulled it off. It felt so touch-and-go for a while. This summer has been a lot and although I'd never say so to Bryce, I've had my moments of worry that it won't work."

Not just the escape rooms, but all of it. The move to Dulaney, the weeks of avoiding my feelings for Bryce, the final push through my defenses. This has felt like months of waiting for the other shoe to drop and it hasn't yet. I'm terrified to hope that it might never drop.

"What happens now?" Ángel voices my fears aloud.

"I'm not entirely sure. Technically my work is done for now. Yes, there will be more rooms but it'll be a while until he's made enough money back to sink into development again."

Ángel scoffs beside me and I turn away from the group to stare up at him. His lip curls up in a wry smile. "I didn't mean about work. I mean about him. This is different, I can tell."

"I want this. More than I did with Riley and you and I both know poorly how that ended. We've been taking it a day at a time but I can see it, you know." My breath rushes out of me, relief after it stuck in my lungs and ached at the thought of me and Bryce and the potential for the future.

"Oh yeah?" Ángel prompts, not pushing too hard, he knows me well enough now to tease things out of me. Even though I know he's doing it, I don't care. I need to tell someone. It should probably be Bryce but I'm too anxious about it.

"He makes me feel so much. Yes, there's insane attraction and there was the slight excitement of it being something we couldn't or rather wouldn't indulge in but there's more to it. Bryce listens. He lets me ramble and he watches me when he thinks I'm not looking, as if he's worried that if I notice, I'll see everything he keeps hidden. I've never felt safer, or more taken care of. You know how hard I push, how harsh I can be on myself. Bryce is constantly reminding me to think of myself as a person. I never thought that safety would be the thing that did it—"

I shake my head, drowning in memories of chasing the butterflies and heat in the city, the same ones I've felt since meeting Bryce, and then being disappointed when things fizzled in the past. "Somehow he snuck right past every single defense, just by being a soft place to land. I've never had that with someone I was seeing. I always felt like I had to be on my best behavior and anything less than perfect would mean loneliness."

"So, what I'm hearing is, I'm going to have to get real

acquainted with Dulaney and Bryce's people because you're going to be one of them," he teases.

"Don't say it like it's a chore. I can see the budding bromance between you and Logan. No doubt you bonded over how both of you love to meddle."

Ángel laughs and does nothing to dispel the accusation. The group is winding down, the outcome promising, and hunger overtaking the high of escaping.

"Dinner at the Dawsons?" Logan asks.

"I'll give my mom a call to let her know we're on our way." Bryce presses his phone to his ear and exits the room, my eyes glued to him the entire time.

"It's okay to love him. He's a good one." Ángel drops it like a bomb before leaving to join the others, filing out of the room and taking all the sound with them.

I'm rooted to the spot, the words I've been too afraid to acknowledge or voice aloud thrumming in my mind like a tattoo. It buzzes in my chest like the bass from the speakers earlier but the effects are off and the room is lit like normal. It's just me having a mini panic at the prospect of my heart no longer being all mine.

"You coming?" Bryce asks from the doorway and I can only wonder how long he's been there, watching me. Is any of the turmoil visible on my face?

"Yeah, of course. Sorry. I just got a little caught up." Clearing my throat of all the emotion I'm terrified will choke me, I thread my fingers between his, taking his outstretched hand.

Lights and electronics flicker off behind us as we go, shutting down and closing up, until we're the last ones there. Our friends have already disappeared back to the Dawsons' and are no doubt wreaking havoc over there now.

"You sure you're doing okay? You've gone really quiet," Bryce asks as we walk to his car.

His hand swallows mine, his steps shorter to keep up with me, and the summer breeze swirls the scent of him around me. My stomach aches, my chest constricting. This is so normal. I could see a thousand more walks just like this. Hand-in-hand, in step, and as close as our bodies will allow while still being able to move like normal.

"I just can't believe it's finally here. It's surreal. I can't fathom—"

*How you've snuck through my walls and rooted yourself so deeply when I hardly noticed the difference.*

"I couldn't have done it without you." Bryce lifts my hand to his lips and the light touch sets me on fire. Every nerve ending sings at the contact and I know it's over for me.

I'm in love with Bryce Locke Dawson and it happened so quietly I didn't see it until it was far too late.

BRYCE IS SWEPT UP BY HIS DAD AS SOON AS WE GET THERE, WITH barely enough time to dump our belongings in the kitchen before Frank approaches, eager to hear how his voice acting went over and the group indulges him. He really did a fantastic job and it's so sweet that Bryce is able to get his family involved. I hang back in the kitchen, scrolling through my phone in an attempt to decompress, and stuff those traitorous feelings back inside my chest.

In my email inbox is a name I never thought I'd see again.

Andrew.

My breath catches in my chest. The thrumming of blood pumping through my body overwhelms my hearing until all I can focus on is the whoosh of my breath and the throbbing of my pulse. Should I delete it? Without opening it?

Given how visceral my reaction is to just seeing his name, I can't imagine I'll react any better to the actual message. I never realized how deeply that work environment affected me until now, faced with it again.

Still, curiosity outweighs caution and I open it, despite my better judgment.

**Rachel,**

**I'd like to apologize for how things went down earlier this year. Had I realized how much the situation meant to you and how much it affected your desire to stay with Lakin-Cole, I would have reacted much differently. In the past few months it has been more than apparent how much we need and have missed you and your work.**

**If you would be amenable to rejoining the team, I'd like to offer you the position of project manager. You've more than proven yourself and I'm sorry it took us so long to see it.**

**It's waiting for you whenever you're ready. Let me know at your earliest convenience.**

**I hope to get the chance to work with you again!**

**Regards,**

**Andrew Hollis**

WHAT THE FUCK? HAVE I BEEN DROPPED INTO SOME KIND OF MIRROR dimension? There's no way Andrew typed all of that. After years of waiting and hoping for recognition, it isn't until I've stepped away that I get it?

There's no chance there isn't a catch to this. Is Keith still there? If Andrew is offering me the position then it must mean things didn't work out with him. Not that I'm surprised, given how he started off his new position all those months ago. The thought of going back—of D.C. and the grind, and my basement shoebox doesn't seem as appealing as I'd thought it might. Even with the uncertainty of my job here, I'm reluctant.

Before I can shoot off a reply to Andrew, give in to my gut reaction to tell him to fuck off, Logan slips into the kitchen.

"Here you are! Hiding in the kitchen is no way to celebrate. Theresa's got some amazing bites out back while we wait for the main event, plus a pitcher of ice cold margaritas."

"You're twisting my arm. I just needed a sec." To come to terms with my recent revelation and the giant question mark that comes next.

"Anything specific?" Logan leans against the counter, arms crossed as he settles in and waits. I want to divulge the job situation but I'm still stuck on that other shoe hanging over my head when it comes to Bryce.

"What was Stephanie like? Bryce doesn't talk about her much, understandably, but years of marriage aren't exactly easy to just set aside in a matter of months."

Logan's mouth purses at the mention of her name. "Bryce has never had an easy time with undertones and hints, and picking up on backhanded compliments or sarcasm. Steph thrived on all that. At first I'm sure it wasn't intentional but there's only so much grace you can give a person when they repeatedly set up your friend to fail and then blame them when it does."

His chest fills with a huge inhalation that he huffs out before running a hand through his hair. "Bryce was coming back here less and less, but when he did—when she was here with him—I saw it. She'd 'tease' him as she called it. Or make little remarks about Bryce's interests. Or his friends. Or his parents. Even though he might not always have read between the lines it eventually became obvious that she didn't approve of any of it. She had an image in mind for them and him. When they met, Bryce was malleable. As time went on and he became more comfortable around her . . . more set in his ways and able to stop exhausting himself to impress her, it wasn't how she wanted it."

My heart aches at the picture Logan paints. Of a marriage slowly disintegrating and one of them none the wiser until it was too late. Logan keeps going, describing an image that's painful to look at with light shone on it.

"She'd say they were all right when he felt something was off between them and asked about it. Bryce would take it at face value. Why wouldn't he believe his wife? But I guess she got tired of skirting around it and hoping he'd read her mind. He called me when she dropped it on him and the only thing he wanted to know from me was why he wasn't enough."

The ache in my chest splits to a crack. Because I get it. I know exactly what it feels like to doubt yourself like that. Professionally and personally, I get it.

"So, if this is you asking because you want to compare yourself to Steph, because you're worried that time with her overrides or outshines the depth of what he has with you. Don't."

My face must give me away because he smiles at the sight of it.

"It's that obvious, huh?" I ask, face flaming.

"You and Bryce are the only ones who seem to be missing it. I don't know what your plans are or the full extent of your feelings —and I don't want to be the first to know, that should be Bryce. All I ask is that you assume good intent when it comes to him. Nothing he does or says is with malice, even when it might come out distant. Just don't break his heart."

It's an earnest plea, one I find myself nodding to.

"You really overestimate my impact if you think I have the power to break his heart," I scoff, trying to dislodge the uncomfortable feeling in my chest brought on by his words. It's too scary to consider—to want—without getting my hopes up.

"Rachel, don't sell yourself short. If this is real for you—and I assure you it's real for him—then let go and let it happen. You don't have to overthink it. The things that are meant for us have a way of finding us if we stand still long enough."

The words fall like stones into my pristine and artificially still surface. Sinking in and rippling out. Before I can respond there's a loud ring from the counter. Someone's phone vibrates across the surface, lit up and urgent.

The joke is on my tongue about who could possibly still keep their sound on in this day and age—my mind grasping to deflect with humor—when Logan curses.

"Speak of the She-Devil."

My nerves over our unexpected heart to heart flood my senses. My breath comes just a little too shallow, and my heart thrums a touch too fast.

"He's not here. What do you want?" Logan sounds as cold as I've ever heard him. The friendliness and understanding from a few moments ago is long gone.

I'm close enough to make out the tinny sound of her answer, for the most part.

"Logan? Why are you answering his phone?" There's a pause before she continues. "Nevermind. Just tell him one of my boxes must have gotten mixed in with his and I'd like him to ship it to me. It's marked 'wedding' and it's very important that I get it back."

"Getting all sentimental? I didn't peg you for the type. Wouldn't blame you for wanting it though, remind yourself of exactly what you lost. Not doubting your choices now, are you?" It's scathing. Mocking in a way and very uncomfortable to watch.

I shouldn't be here. I shouldn't be hearing this. Then again, Logan shouldn't be answering Bryce's phone but I get it. If Ángel's ex, Jesse, called him up and I had the opportunity to run interference, I wouldn't hesitate to give him a piece of my mind and keep him far away from my friend.

She sputters on the other end and Logan latches on to her

speechlessness. "Don't even waste your breath, Steph. If that box is even here, it won't be for long."

The tone of her response can only be described as irate and most of it is lost in the muffled sound of yelling. Logan winks at me.

"He doesn't owe you shit and I'll personally burn that box if I need to. You made your choice, now keep to it. You decided you didn't want to be a part of his life anymore and you got your wish. Don't bother calling again. Don't insert yourself where you don't belong. I know you're not above that. Bryce might be too nice to tell you to fuck off, but I'm not."

He doesn't wait for a response, hanging up before she can get another word in. He's fuming, I can tell.

"Wow, Logan, tell me how you really feel about her." The attempt at levity has the intended effect and he huffs out a little laugh.

"Come on, I'm surprised Frank hasn't dragged you out by the hand yet. They'll wonder where we've been." Logan throws his arm across my shoulders like I'm one of his friends.

"If they ask, just tell them you were giving me a speech, trying to suss out what my intentions are toward your friend," I say.

The sliding door's whoosh isn't enough to draw the attention away from all the conversation and music, but the heat hits us the second we step outside.

"And what should I say if they ask me what your answer was?" Logan asks.

My eyes catch on Bryce, chatting with his dad, an icy drink swallowed up by that large hand and condensation dripping down his skin at the contact.

"Tell them the ball is in Bryce's court now but I'll play for as long as he wants to."

Bryce notices me, his eyes raking over my body and having more of an effect than the summer over the flush that spreads through me. The slow curl of his smile and the little twitch of his head inviting me over only fuel the flames.

Logan's arm drops as he heads to Gabrielle and I'm drawn to Bryce like we're tethered and one look from him is enough to tug me close.

"Everything okay? You disappeared for a bit." There's concern in his voice when he bends down to whisper it in my ear and I'm reminded of Logan saying what he asked Steph, the fear behind it.

I mean it when I say, "Now that I'm with you, I'm perfect."

There will be time to talk about Andrew's email and the call from Steph, because he deserves to know, even if Logan's trying to protect him. Bryce shouldn't be left in the dark and blindsided again. But for now I'm content to stand a little too close to him despite the heat. I'll happily enjoy the kisses he presses to the top of my head and the fingertips he trails down my arm as he talks to someone else. As if to say I'm on his mind, he's focused on me, and I find that the niggling voice in my head questioning whether he wants me or if I'm enough is quiet.

Bryce is by my side and that's all that matters.

# CHAPTER  14

OUR BIG LAUNCH DAY IS SO CLOSE AND DESPITE ALL THE HOURS AND sweat we've put into it, I feel nowhere near ready. Rachel has been a life saver, in more ways than one. If I didn't have her at my side I doubt I'd be able to do this at all. The days at the theater and the nights in her bed have morphed into my new normal and it's becoming increasingly clear that I don't want it to end.

I just have to figure out how to bring it up. We discussed taking it one day at a time but that deadline on the calendar looms and I don't think I can keep pretending to not think of the future. As much fun as living in the moment has been, I want to step in deeper.

Difficult conversations aren't my forte, as evidenced by my divorce and how it broke down over time because of miscommunications and unmet expectations. I don't want that to happen with me and Rachel. So, I'll buck up and find the words.

Curled up around her, a fan in the corner circulating the AC from the window unit and soft breathing are the only sounds early in the morning, I try not to panic. I've done something potentially stupid, and I didn't tell Rachel about my plan. It's too late though, the delivery is set for today and the opening is only a few days from now. I can only hope it will go over well.

I just have to get my 'stay-in-Dulaney-stay-with-me' speech taken care of before then. Without sounding like that medical show she's been making me watch—the same one Logan's been avoiding because he claims it's too bloody—with its whole "pick me, choose me, love me" thing. Although the drama is top notch. I'll have to tell him to suck it up on the gory bits because I'd love to be able to chat about it with him and Gabrielle—something normal and inane in the face of so much big change.

Our soft open is set for the end of the week and then it'll be out there whether I'm ready or not.

Rachel stirs in my arms, stretching against my body and pressing delectably against me. Her curves are soft against me and I will never tire of the way her scent and mine have mingled to create its own intoxicating blend that leaves me yearning and off kilter.

"Hmm, good morning." Rachel's voice is thick with sleep and unfairly hot given I have to get up.

"Good morning," I answer, pressing a kiss against her dark hair. "I'm heading over to my parents' to get a change of clothes and have a shower but I'll see you at the theater later?"

Chickening out. I could easily say that I love waking up beside her and go from there but instead I give in to my dread. I haven't practiced the words enough and my agitation only ramps up the longer I put it off. My skin feels wrong. It's too tight and something is crawling along my nerves.

"You know, you could always keep a toothbrush and a few emergency outfits here, like I said once before. Just in case of . . .

you know, emergencies," Rachel says it against my chest and I want to laugh at the halting way she says it. It's as if she's wrestling the words out against her better judgment and I know the suggestion is more than the surface level explanation she's given.

"I'll do that."

She kisses my chest and I disentangle myself with reluctance. My walk of shame outfit holds very little shame and I'm glad that she's confirmed her sincerity in inviting me to keep some things here.

*I wish you would keep me* rises traitorously in my mind and although I wish the sentiment didn't live in my thoughts, I can't deny the truth of it.

The end of summer sits heavy in the air, still clinging on despite August nearly giving way to September. Humidity and rising temperatures, even this early in the day, have me rushing to the bliss of the AC in my car. And then the cool feel of it in my room above the garage as I jump into a shower and a change of clothes. Less than a week before people other than those I know and love will be testing out this risky dream of mine.

What if it fails? What if it's nothing but a dumpster fire?

My doubt follows me to the theater and I pull up the system, ready to check the last small glitches we found when testing the rooms with a few acquaintances to make sure the feedback was unbiased. The main door clamps shut. Rachel's arrived.

"In here!" I yell.

The clack of shoes sounds and each clip gets louder as they approach the control booth.

"You didn't have to come so early. I was letting you have a lie-in before I let you know I was here," I say and turn to face her with a smile. Even though it's barely been a few hours and my anxiety is at an all time high, I'm always happy to see her.

Only, the person I'm facing isn't Rachel. My joy drains from my face and that anxiety I've been battling solidifies into something akin to dread. I knew it was too good to be true. Something was going to ruin the best thing I've ever had. I couldn't say when or how, but an innate thing inside me was expecting something to arise—to go wrong.

"Hi Bryce," Stephanie says.

*Fuck.* That's all that echoes through me. I'm not one for cursing but that word reverberates through every muscle until they're all tense and poised for danger.

"What are you doing here?" I manage to rasp, the edge I wanted to inject into the question missing.

"I called."

I shake my head, unable to dispute it when I have no knowledge of it, trying desperately to catch up. It's hard to stay present when her being here thrusts me into the past. Her perfectly coiffed blonde balayage (as she called it) cascades over her shoulders and she's made up—ready for the day. Those shoes I heard clacking down the hallway are a black pair she'd worn for me back when we were still trying to spice things up, and I can feel the ghostly imprint of those heels digging into my back. The rest of her is wrapped in a tight dress with a pencil skirt that ends just below the knee. It's poised, and dangerous.

Steph takes a deep breath and expels it hard through her nostrils. My hackles are up, my body primed with knowing that that particular reaction from her means she's deeply unhappy. It means she's gearing up for a fight and it takes everything in me not to shut down immediately.

"*Logan . . .*" she says it like a curse.

"What about Logan?" I'm so confused. Did he tell her where to find me?

"It's not—don't worry about it right now."

"What are you doing here?" I ask again, stronger this time now that confusion is overriding shock.

"So, this is your business?" Sweeping out her arms to encompass everything around her, she gestures at the last six months of my life.

"Yes."

"I'm not going to lie. I was surprised to hear about it." Steph steps further into the room and I fight the urge to back up.

"How *did* you hear about it?" Was Logan bragging? It's not unlike him to be petty when it comes to those who have seemingly wronged his friends.

"Christopher Mitchell."

"Our *banker*?" The one I called those months ago to figure out a starting point to this whole endeavor.

"I called in about something a week ago and he congratulated me on your new undertaking and hoped it was going well for you. He mentioned you'd called him a few months ago to find out about some business banking options and ultimately recommended you go somewhere local. He seemed convinced you'd made something of it though, mentioned a website. So, I checked it out and here I am. From there it wasn't hard to ask around. Apparently the town is abuzz." Steph shrugs, as if it makes sense in any way.

"So, you drove down from Philly just to see for yourself? Is that it? After the way we left things?" I can't for the life of me piece it together. "You made yourself perfectly clear the last time we saw each other."

Steph sighs. "I was hurting. I was trying to get a reaction out of you. All I ever wanted was for you to take some initiative and stand up for something. To notice me and show it. I never stopped caring and wanting the best for you. I was just tired of trying to urge you to do *anything* to make something of yourself. When I heard you'd done that here, I wanted to see it for myself."

Steph steps closer again and the room feels too small. She's close enough that if I wanted to I could reach out and touch her. I fold my arms in defiance, in an attempt to keep my distance. A few months ago I *would* have reached out. A few months ago the prospect of her here giving me some kind of validation would have had me riding a high for weeks.

Now all I have is a hollow ache in my breastbone and anxiety eating its way up my stomach.

She clearly has the same thought about touching, though she doesn't hold back. Her manicured fingers come to rest on the skin of my forearm. Thumb stroking over the hairs on my arm, the sensation is too much and unpleasant, and very much unwanted.

"Don't." It's all I manage, twisting to try and dislodge her hand.

"I have so much I want to ask. So much to say to you." She looks pleadingly up at me, the expression one I'm familiar with. It's not her genuine sad face. It's the one that usually precedes her trying to get her way. Years with her, studying every expression and nuance in tone, and I am an expert on Stephanie Dawson. If she even still goes by my last name.

"I miss you, Bryce. I didn't realize how much until you were gone. I wanted to reach out so many times but pride got in my way. I promised myself that if there was a sign—if something came along that showed you'd taken my words to heart there might be another chance for us—and I would try again. Then I heard about the business and you forging your own path. No longer complacent but ready to take on the world. I knew it was time." Steph ignores my attempt to pull away and instead she holds my forearms in each of her hands and pries my arms open, forcing me into a more vulnerable position.

She smells the same. It's been over a year since we've had anything resembling a relationship but I can't deny that there's something about that familiar cloying sweet scent that disgusts me now.

How is this happening? Why now? I would have begged to

have her coming after me when I first started this. It's too late. I open my mouth to say so, ready to set the record straight.

But she goes up onto her toes, and with the help of her heels she's much closer to me in height than she would have been otherwise. Removing my glasses and threading her hand into my hair with the other hand, she lurches forward to lay her lips onto mine. Shock slows my responses and although I am too frozen to shove her off of me, I have the wherewithal to turn my head. Her kiss deflects, more on the side of my chin than my mouth, but there's contact.

"*What the hell was that, Steph*?" I ask, removing her hands from my person.

Before she can answer another voice sounds in the small space, a mere whisper but it's enough for both of us to turn.

"*Steph*?" Rachel asks, or rather repeats with some kind of alarming note in her voice.

She sounds confused and hurt. I wish I still had my glasses on so I can see the expression on her face to make it easier to analyze. Though I don't really need to. If the situation were reversed I have a pretty good idea of what I'd be feeling right now. She's turned on her heel and is leaving by the time I've stepped away from Steph and toward the doorway.

Steph's hand grips my arm again, nails digging into the skin and whatever lingering comfort or familiarity that made me put my guard down is nowhere to be found.

"You better not be here when I come back. You ended this—us —and there's no place for you in my life."

She sputters, "Don't be like this. This isn't you."

I give a bitter chuckle, one that rises from the pit in my stomach—worsening with every second I'm delayed in going after Rachel.

"I don't give a damn about your opinion or about how you

*think* I am or should be. You don't have the right anymore. You made your bed, and I'm not in it. I won't ever be again. There's no big sign from the universe or a swell of romantic music that's supposed to set the scene for a reunion. I meant what I said. Leave. Get the hell out. Or I will have you ejected from the premises." I don't wait for a response, plucking my glasses from her grip and tearing through the theater but Rachel's already gone.

I rush out onto the sidewalk. She's already two blocks ahead and I can see her ponytail swinging from all the way over here. She's rushing with so much force. Jogging, cursing each traffic light that prevents me from following her—reaching her.

By the time I make it to that robin's egg blue door she's nowhere to be seen. But at least she didn't lock the door. I press inside, the wood sticking slightly with the humidity, and head upstairs.

I take the fact that this door isn't locked either as a good thing. Maybe she didn't expect me to come after her. Or she's inside and waiting to lay into me. Not knowing isn't enough to freeze me though, not with something this important.

Everything is as I left it this morning. The dishes from last night's dinner are still on the drying rack, forgotten in favor of kissing our way toward the bedroom. The decorative paperweight she picked up from the antique mall sits on the kitchen counter. Her bedroom door is open, if the light spilling into the hallway is any indicator and I swallow up the distance between the entryway and her bedroom in mere strides.

The bed is made, barely. Still a little rumpled. And Rachel is nowhere to be found. My heart sinks into my abdomen as I walk back toward the living space, peering into the bathroom and coming up empty again.

I'm about to sink down onto the floor from the heft of my panic when I hear it—the tiniest inhalation, shaky with tears, coming from the couch. Rachel is curled up so tightly I missed her on my first frantic surveyance.

Her large eyes look up at me and my chest aches at the sight of her crying and the doubt there.

"Rachel, please talk to me." I can't let this ruin things. I'm sure this conversation will suck, if she even is open to one, but I need to sort this out now before it's too late and she's had time to dwell.

She wipes her tears away with the back of her knuckles and takes a fortifying breath. "So, that's your ex?"

"Yeah."

"What was she doing in Dulaney?" *In the theater* goes unsaid but we both know what she means.

"She heard about the business from one of the bankers I spoke to initially and thought it was a sign to invade my life."

"It seems like a lot of effort to track you down. It must be very important to her." Rachel sniffles and her lips thin. She juts out her chin and I love that she's trying to be stubborn even with the tip of her nose being red and her cheeks shiny with tears.

"I couldn't care less about what is or isn't important to her. This is about you and me." I say and my voice shakes a little as fear climbs up my ribcage.

"About that. What exactly is this—you and me? We've been skirting around it for so long but the opening is here and my position was only ever to set Locke Box up. Where do we go from here? Because the prospect of being broke and unemployed in a few weeks is terrifying." Rachel sits in the corner of the sofa, tucking her knees up to her chest and holding them there as if it will keep her together.

"What do you want it to be? I'm not good at this. I've had almost no experience with relationships outside of Stephanie and that imploded so I'm not about to follow that blueprint. I've been trying to take it a day at a time and give you the space to decide what you want because I'm scared I'll make a mess of things again."

"I don't know. I've been freaking out for a while now and I just got an email from my old boss offering me the job that should have been mine in the first place. And all I am is confused. Do I go back, take back my lease, and follow the path that I've been on since I started college or . . . do I risk everything safe on something that isn't guaranteed?" Her words fell me and that insidious voice that loves to whisper that I'm not enough, that I'll never be enough, pipes up.

Why would she pick me? She's got what she wanted. The validation she'd been missing is here and they're eating crow.

Then again. Am I not in the same boat with Stephanie? Finally noticing me? Finally finding me worthy of her time? Somehow it lacked the luster I expected.

I know who I choose. What I choose. It's this stunning woman that blew into my life when I was at my lowest and now I want to share every joy with her. Maybe she could feel the same.

"I know it's scary. Trust me, I do. I know that thing in there with Steph looks bad. I know it must be incredibly gratifying to have your old boss have to reach out to you, to come crawling back to eat crow. But if the only thing holding you back from taking the risk is whether or not I—we—are guaranteed, then don't let it. I'm in this if you are. If you want to keep working at the escape room, great. If you want to look for something else, great. Just do it in Dulaney. Do it with me."

Rachel rises from her spot on the sofa, approaching me carefully. Those big brown eyes swallow me whole and all I can do is breathe, words hanging between us.

"You're right. I am scared. But I've been scared for months. It's just finally come to a head and I don't want to . . . I don't want to make the wrong move and lose everything I've worked for. Because it feels like I will. Whatever I choose there will be consequences. It all comes down to what I'm not willing to let go of," Rachel says.

"I'm not going to rush you into any choice right now. I just wanted you to know that nothing has changed for me. I'm still the same person I was when I woke up beside you this morning. Stephanie doesn't change that. She doesn't affect my choice. Please, take the time to think it through so you're totally sure of what you want, but at least come to the opening. You put in just as much work as I have. You should celebrate it too. Don't let whatever questions and fears sit between us deprive you of enjoying the culmination of these last few months." I pull it off. Even though telling her it's okay if she chooses something other than what I desperately want to share with her makes me want to throw up, I manage. Because it's the right thing to do.

Because if I push too hard she'll retreat. Rachel's been beholden to too many other people and their opinion of what she should or shouldn't do. She *should* get a specific degree. She *should* be grateful for the job she had in D.C. because there are others who would kill for it if she's too ungrateful. She *shouldn't* expect a promotion she's earned because she's a liability. She *shouldn't* throw away years of hard work and studies to run off to some town in Maryland to shack up with someone just as lonely and scared as she is.

"I'll come. I'll be there." Rachel nods emphatically. Whether she does so to convince herself or me is unclear.

She's right in front of me now, staring up into my face with tear tracks glistening on her cheeks and her skin strangely pallid, devoid of the blush that I relish whenever I kiss that one spot on her neck.

I content myself with something a little less risky. My hand cups her cheek, wiping away the evidence of her distress and I place a soft kiss against her swollen lips.

She tastes like salt and the best summer of my life, and I hope to whatever entity might be out there listening that she feels the same. Because I want so much more than just six months of working together and dancing around how great this could be if we let it.

I pull away, quicker than I'd like, and she's got her face tilted up toward mine. Her eyes are still shut, her lips slightly parted and it takes everything in me not to dip back down for more.

"Goodnight, Rachel. I'll see you at the opening." *Please come. Please ask me to stay. Please let what I have planned and kept to myself be enough to show you that I love you and I want this—whatever you're willing to give.*

The trip down the stairs is far less frantic than the one that preceded it and I make it home, a little shaky. Pulling up to the drive, a huge box is leaned up against my parents' front door.

"Give us a hand over here!" My dad calls through the window beside the front door and I rush over to hold onto it. Once I have a good grip, he opens the door and we slowly ease it inside.

Laying the box on its side, I tremble in anticipation and trepidation.

My father holds out the Swiss army knife he keeps in his pocket constantly—the one that's gotten us into trouble at more than one metal detector—and I slice through the tape holding the box together.

"What is it?" My mom asks, popping her head into the entryway.

"It's the sign for the front." Tugging away layers of protective foam and bubble wrap, I unearth the secret I've been keeping from everyone.

"Oh, *Bryce* . . ." My mom breathes, emotion plain in her voice.

"She saw Steph come by the theater. She saw Steph try to kiss me. I had to rush after her just to convince her to come to the opening after all that."

"What the hell is Steph doing down here?" My father asks, and I cover up the sign.

Standing, I head into the kitchen and they follow. I pour myself a glass of cold water and gulp it down, the summer heat and my desperate dash after Rachel leaving me thirsty.

"Apparently she's had a change of heart. After talking to the man who used to be our banker and finding out I've tried to make something of myself, she apparently took it as a sign that I was putting her parting words to use and it proved I wanted her in my life."

*She's not wrong. Technically.* That is sort of what this started as. My mind is quick to remind me, but it's so much more than that now.

"I told her to get out and if I found her back there I'd call the cops."

My father barks out a laugh so hearty he has to remove his glasses to wipe away a tear.

"You? My mild-mannered, sweet boy, threatened her with the cops?" my mom asks, raising her eyebrow in doubt.

"I had somewhere else to be and I am done dealing with her. It's too late and I wasn't willing to hear a single word she had to say." I shrug as if it's no big deal but we all know that Bryce from a year—two years ago would have been *grateful* that she decided to come back.

I hope I'm never that Bryce again. I've grown and from what I saw as my biggest heartbreak at the time has come my triumph. Living well is the best revenge, but more than that, it's been the closure I've needed. The months between her walking out and the day I left for Dulaney were dark and bleak. My anger and resentment, self-hatred and grief ate at me.

Now. Now, I have so much to look forward to and more that makes me happy. She doesn't even come to mind anymore.

"Do you think Rachel will like it?" I ask, my insecurity leaking through despite me trying to convince myself I'm fine with whatever she decides.

"She will. She'd be a fool not to and one thing I can say about Rachel is that she's no fool." My father's praise warms my heart. They never liked Steph, and she never cared for them.

"Would you guys mind helping me take this over to the theater? I can call Logan too if you think we need him."

"Of course we'll help you. We'll have to cover it with something until the big reveal and I have just the thing in my sewing room. You two haul it out onto the back of your father's truck in the meantime. If it's too heavy, then call Logan. The last thing we need is one of you throwing your back out just before the opening."

"Yes, Mom," and "Yes, Dear," sounds from me and my father and we chuckle at the mirrored tone of our responses.

My dad tapes the box shut again and we lug it out, heaving it up onto the bed of the truck. My mom comes out with a huge bundle of fabric in her arms, bright red and opaque, and some gold rope. Dad grabs his giant tool box as well, even though he rarely ever uses it, it's well stocked and will definitely come in handy.

"I'm going to call Logan, just in case. My hand's better but I'd rather not tempt fate or get Dad injured as well."

The drive to the theater is quiet save for my conversation with Logan and he's on his way to meet us almost immediately. I've never been more grateful that he works from home for his marketing stuff. Once I have enough capital I'll be hiring him to handle my marketing as well.

We pull up front, the truck idling next to the sidewalk and the cold air from the AC blasting out through the open doors as we stare up at what remains of the old matinee. It'll be a bear to tear down, and the new sign won't be much easier to mount either, but hopefully it'll be worth it.

"Alright, family. Let's do this!" Logan says and we jump into action.

Two days until it all comes to fruition. Two days until I show Rachel just how much she's a part of this, just as I am. And she sees exactly how I feel about her in case my words fail me.

Staring up at the matinee, resolute, I can only hope. It will have to be enough.

# CHAPTER  15

STEPHANIE. THREE SYLLABLES THAT THUNDER THROUGH MY CHEST AS I rush home and in every moment since Bryce left me here with far too much on my mind. I replay that two second image in my mind over and over. Steph's lips meeting his chin, the anger on his face as he pulls back, the way all the color left him when he saw me standing there.

I believe him. I know nothing happened. Logically I'm able to acknowledge that. But on a much deeper, gut level, all I can see is Riley blowing up multiple relationships and breaking my heart in one go.

*But Bryce isn't Riley,* my mind pipes up.

Bryce has the potential to be even more devastating.

I've never let myself get this deep or be this vulnerable with anyone else. He's saying all the right things, doing all the right things, and my fucking brain won't let me accept that it can just be that genuine. I keep waiting for the other shoe to drop. Because I'm primed for disappointment. Because if I plan for and accept the bad outcome before it's happened, it won't hurt as much when it does.

*But isn't that just a self-fulfilling thing then? You expect it so you act like it's already happened. You pull away or you hide and then it becomes real because you made it so.*

God, I hate my mind right now. Emotionally I'm lost for him. Totally knocked over and on my ass. Mentally I'm afraid of what will happen in a week, or a month, or a year. When he's so ingrained in my life that extricating myself will leave me gutted. There will be a Bryce-shaped hole if I make the room for him.

And that's part of the problem. Because there's no precedent.

He'd be the first, he's already the first person who's seen this much of me and stayed.

If there's even a chance that he's going to leave me for his gorgeous, tall, blonde bombshell of a wife then I need to know now before I give him any more sway over me.

Lying on my bed as the sun slinks across the room and under the horizon, I stare up at the ceiling and carefully weigh each pro and con.

I want so much to be able to go back to Lakin-Cole and step into the role that I rightfully earned just to spite Andrew and Keith, but I know it won't make me happy. Not really. I wasn't doing that for me. I was doing all of that to make my parents proud and to live up to an expectation.

I want to be able to stay in Dulaney and become a part of this town and its community, something I've never had but which has been amazing so far. I don't know if I want to keep working at the escape room in a host capacity but it has brought me such a sense of purpose and self. I'd hate to lose it completely.

I want Bryce. Every morning and night, and whatever falls in between. A part of me longs to just let go, to fall and let him catch me the way he did all those months ago when I was being reckless and hanging curtains while precariously standing on my console.

Those big hands will keep me safe, they'll be gentle and tender. They will ruin me with their touch. The warmth of his body against mine will see me through the winter in this apartment that desperately needs some proper ventilation and insulation. If I let him.

And I think I want to let him.

Hopefully by the opening I won't have to dwell on doubts, I'll just know what the right thing to do is.

THERE'S A LITTLE CROWD ALREADY. ÁNGEL HAS COME UP FROM D.C. to celebrate with me and although I invited my parents, they let me know that they won't be attending in a short and succinct text message response to the voicemail I left them. I can't even summon the energy to pretend it doesn't hurt. Not when all my thoughts and emotions have been tangled up in seeing Bryce again. And in appreciating months of our work finally being realized. There's a huge red cloth over where the matinee was and a shining length of ribbon across the double doors.

"This is it," Ángel whispers into my ear and his excitement is enough to pull me out of my dismal mood. "You did it!"

"You helped get me here. Thank you for the push, and the shoulder, and lending me your ear every time I freaked out about it. And Bryce. And everything before it. You're my best friend and I'm so grateful to have you in my life," I say, already a little choked up.

"Don't get all sappy on me now. One of these days you're going to make me cry and then we won't be able to be friends anymore. I can't afford to let you see how ugly a crier I am again. Last time we were drunk enough for it not to matter. It would ruin everything now." Ángel laughs and I join in.

My phone buzzes with a text from Sebastian letting me know that they've parked and he and Farren will be over at the theater momentarily.

It's early in the day, but the end of August still feels like midsummer by two in the afternoon. So an opening at 9 a.m. might not be as flashy as an opening night at the theater would be, but it'll be a boon for everyone waiting outside to catch a glimpse of what we've been working on—and enjoy the break from the heat outside.

I glance at my watch, less than five minutes to go. I should probably get closer to the doors, maybe stand near Bryce and his family, but I'm too full of nerves. I'll find him after. Once the pomp is done and the initial rush has died down, I will go to congratulate him on a job well done and hopefully by then I will have perfected the words that keep buzzing around in my head.

The murmur of the crowd around me is like a soft hum, a buzzing in the back of my subconscious and I make out none of what anyone around me is saying when Bryce steps out from the doors and ducks under the ribbon. The din picks up for a moment and then he raises his hands to try and tame the excitement long enough to address us.

Once the volume has come down he speaks. "Thank you all so much for coming out today! As some of you may know I am a Dulaney boy, born and bred, and I've been so excited to get to bring something new to the town that raised me and the community that means so much."

They are mesmerized by that baritone, as am I, and his face is alight with excitement. He's trimmed his beard slightly. He's wearing a black button up with short sleeves and khakis, very business casual, but the way it hugs his chest and those thighs is enough to make me want to salivate.

How have I gone two days without seeing him? Touching him?

I wish I was up there with him but this view is pretty stunning regardless.

"From those who used to watch me put on ridiculous magic shows with my best friend Logan"—Bryce points over to Logan off to the side and he waves at the crowd with a goofy grin on his face and Gabrielle by his side—"To the people who have come into my life more recently and have helped coddle and nourish this idea into something tangible."

Bryce nods toward someone else in the crowd and I'm pleased to note Farren and Sebastian smiling back at him broadly.

"I've been incredibly lucky to have so many people believing in me, none more than my wonderful parents who have encouraged me every step of the way, even when those steps took me off-road and away from home. I'm so glad to be back for good and to have such a strong and amazing foundation that they have laid down for me." Bryce gestures to Frank and Theresa and a couple of whoops and claps sound around me.

"But there's someone who most of you may not know, who's worked tirelessly behind the scenes and at my side since this project's inception. She's a transplant to our town, but don't hold that against her. Rachel Mackey," Bryce says and his eyes pierce right through me.

Despite wanting to blend into the crowd and hide a little until I'd built up my courage, he's got me. I wonder how long he's known I'm here. He doesn't point me out though, knowing that having a ton of eyes on me would be forcing my hand and I appreciate that he's keeping his word. He's letting me decide, even in this.

"Rachel joined the project first as a program developer for some of the tech aspects of the rooms but that very quickly grew into a partnership of ideas and enthusiasm. She has hyped me up when I doubted myself and this endeavor. She pushed me when I was being too prideful and foolish to accept and ask for help. She spent countless nights brainstorming, renovating, marketing, and breathing life into this project."

My throat is closing, eyes blurring with tears so that Bryce becomes little more than a black and tan blur until I blink them away. My hands tremble and my heart races in my chest, hope and fear and love overwhelming me. The crowd is quiet but they cease to exist to me as I stare at Bryce and he does the same. It's as if he's imbuing his speech with something else. Something deeper than gratitude.

"It literally would not exist without her. So, I made a little change without consulting her, to reflect that."

There's an "ooh" that passes through the people around me and Ángel has the audacity to elbow me in the side.

"Did you know about this?" I hiss at him.

"Nope. Lover-boy did this all by himself," Ángel whispers back.

"We've been promoting this business under the name 'Locke Box', a little play on words using my middle name. But I feel that is disingenuous when this is so much bigger than just me. Rachel deserves just as much recognition." Bryce tugs on the gold cord hanging down from the matinee and the red fabric billows down to reveal the sign outside the theater—the new home for escape rooms.

UNDER LOCKE & KEY stands out bold for everyone to see.

"It's still a pun—one playing off of Bryce "Locke" Dawson and Rachel Mac"Key"—and it was the best way I could think to thank the person who worked side by side with me, without fail. So please, give a round of applause to my partner, Rachel Mackey!" Bryce finally gestures toward me but I can barely see it through the sheen of tears that are streaking down my cheeks.

I hear applause and Ángel pulls me into a hug from the side, jostling me and shaking some more tears free.

Once the crowd quiets slightly Bryce speaks again. "Without

further ado!" and Theresa hands him a pair of large scissors that he uses to cut the ribbon spanning across the doors.

"Please join us inside for some refreshments, information on our rooms, as well as a 15% coupon off if you book today to thank you for being here to support us on opening day!" Bryce pushes the doors open and the crowd filters in.

My feet are stuck to the sidewalk. My shoes might as well have melted into the concrete. Ángel tugs at my arm to get me into motion and we end up being some of the last to enter.

The wide area that used to be the concessions, the entryway to the old theater, is packed. The posters we had discussed as ideas to represent each room are lit up in their special frames. Logan is behind the register, already helping people to book their spot and taking down email addresses for our mailing list. Bryce is mingling with the people who have been gracious enough to come out to celebrate.

I'm so lost in my own mind that time slips away and I just smile and thank each wellwisher that comes my way. Bryce is caught up with all his customers but I am acutely aware of the feel of his gaze on me. It warms from the inside out and I'm sure I've been flushed since we were outside waiting for the big reveal. There's no special speech to give him. Words elude me. Instead I'm caught up in the awe and emotional punch that comes with seeing this project become real.

Bryce has been smiling for hours, to the point that I'm sure his cheeks must be hurting. But he looks so happy and that makes something in my stomach flip. I'd kill to be the one that puts that look on his face.

Food and drink go quickly, and soon enough we're wrapping up the launch party.

"Some of our friends have been gracious enough to donate an 'escape room in a box' for one of our lucky new newsletter subscribers! So even if you don't make it out here immediately, you can get a small taste of what it might be like conceptually." Bryce rolls multiple dice onto the counter. He scans the list for the corresponding number. "Number 56, Grant Taylor!"

A short man with a band T-shirt and long hair heads up to where Bryce stands at the front counter to receive the escape room board game that Farren and Sebastian likely brought for the launch event. It can only mean that they've spoken with Bryce outside of me and our interactions together. Although some part of me wants to bristle at it and feel a little put out that I've been circumvented, it's strangely comforting to know that he gets on with my friends well enough to be able to talk to them without me driving the conversation and forcing them together.

The crowd thins until it's just our small group of family and friends. Ángel is chatting with Logan and Gabrielle. Farren and Sebastian deep in conversation with Bryce's dad, Frank. His mom, Theresa, looks a little tuckered out, gathering up the trash and I rush over to help her. Just like with Bryce, I appreciate the silence between me and Theresa because it's not awkward or heavy. It's two people working together without the need for chatter.

Soon we've got the space back to its normal appearance and we're filing out one by one. Logan and Gabrielle both give me a hug on the way out. As do Farren and Sebastian.

They all congratulate us but the words are lost in the fog that is my mind. I'm caught up in different colognes and perfumes, skin on skin and then cold AC blowing where the touch has been. I'm all sensation and no thoughts and by the time it's just me and Bryce my mouth is so dry I can barely swallow down my nerves.

"Rachel?" Bryce asks, the back of his fingers tracing down my arm to draw my attention and I startle.

"It seemed like it went really well," is what comes out of my mouth after a beat of silence and I avoid his eyes, staring at the top button of his shirt instead.

"It was fantastic. I couldn't have done it without you."

I huff, half disbelief and half humorless laugh. "You could have pulled it off."

"Not this version of it, and personally I think this is way better than anything I could have thought up on my own. Please just take the compliment and my appreciation."

"Bryce . . ."

He tips my head up to face him by lifting my chin with his knuckle. "I'm serious. I hope that you know just how serious I am."

I swallow convulsively at the heat and longing in his gaze. Bryce is holding nothing back and I feel stripped raw under those warm eyes that promise far more than I'm willing to let myself want or lose.

"The sign made that clear," I whisper. My voice is husky with repressed emotion and I am acutely aware of how alone we are in this space we've spent so many weeks in.

"I hope you weren't upset by it. It just felt right." Bryce strokes the pad of his thumb against my bottom lip and it takes everything in me not to part my lips and surge up toward him.

"Not upset. Surprised, but in a good way. Did you mean what you said? About me being your partner?" I can't look away, his eyes searching mine for something.

"I meant every word. I'd planned to discuss things with you, to offer you fifty percent of the business. My partner in work and life. You don't have to help me run it. I'm happy to support whatever it is you'd prefer to do but it's your due. As long as I have you by my side, I don't care what the circumstances are. I know Steph showing up and throwing my past in your face was upsetting—to both of us. But the only thing that is important to me is the future, and whether you're in mine." His fingertips explore the contours of my face, trailing down the sides of my neck and causing goosebumps to rise all over my body.

"And if I said I wanted to go back to Lakin-Cole?" Not that I do, but I need to know how deep this is for him before I can jump in with both feet.

"Then I'll drive down to D.C. as often as I can, or we can find a place in between D.C. and Dulaney and each commute. Don't let the job be the reason you pull away. Although, if I can be honest, I want to tell you to say no to your old boss. I want you to tell him to shove it because he didn't appreciate you until it was too late and he shouldn't reap the reward of having you back after he mistreated you in the first place."

It never even occurred to me that that was an option. In my mind it was an ultimatum, an either or. The prospect of a compromise didn't register and I'm a little ashamed to admit that. Although everything in my life this far has felt so black and white. There were rules to follow and expectations to meet, and this felt like one of them.

Knowing that Bryce wants to be with me—stay with me—no matter how we go about it gives me a courage I've lacked for months.

"I don't want to go back. I just needed to make sure you want this as much as I do. Because I really do. I want you in my apartment everyday. I want your stuff nestled up to mine and our clothes side-by-side in the closet. The bathroom will smell like your body wash after you shower and I'll breathe it in like I'll never get the chance to again every time. We'll watch more melodramatic TV dramas and game shows, and have great sex, and love each other—I hope."

Bryce smiles so big his eyes crinkle. "It's more than hope for me. I love you, Rachel. I know that. It's so deeply ingrained in me after all these weeks together it feels like an unshakable certainty. The sun rises in the east every morning. Margaritaville is a strangely sad song. No one will ever live up to Alex Trebek as a Jeopardy host, and I love Rachel Mackey."

I give a watery laugh at the comparisons, tears thick in my

throat and I have to clear it before I can respond. "I love you too, Bryce. Though it scares the hell out of me."

"We'll figure the rest out, as long as we're together that's all that matters." He leans down and sweeps me up into an overwhelming kiss

Bryce's arms are strong around my waist, hoisting me against him so that we are pressed so close together I can feel his heartbeat through our shirts. I return it with fervor, my knees trembling, and if he wasn't holding me so tight—barely touching the floor—I'm sure the shakiness would have been evident.

Feverish kisses, grasping hands. Within the span of a few breaths, Bryce is walking me backward toward one of the unoccupied rooms we've been using as storage for future ideas.

"Are we really doing this here?" I ask.

"Are you willing to wait until we've locked everything up and headed back to your place?" he challenges, staring at my mouth like he's dying for it even though we've barely just pulled apart.

I consider it for a split second. Weighing my options, the lead-heavy lust in my abdomen and my already-wet underwear make the choice for me. If I don't have him now, I'll lose my mind. "Fair enough."

And then we are nothing but a tangle of limbs and grasping hands. We divest ourselves of our clothes and I'm not sure who does what but I know it's teamwork that leaves us naked and panting.

Bryce's eyes dart around the room and land on the chaise we had bookmarked for our Pride & Prejudice/regency themed room. There's no way it'll hold up to both of us, and it's far too short for Bryce to be able to stretch out on.

"I don't know," I say, my skepticism sounding breathless given my current state.

"Trust me?" Bryce asks and the gleam in his molten eyes has me nervous to say yes. But curiosity wins out and I nod.

"Stand beside the chaise and keep your eyes forward." Bryce's voice is darker, an edge there that's excited me since the first time he took charge, and I follow his instruction.

He disappears behind me and there's rustling—fabric and metal clinking. One of the boxes of items we either didn't need or haven't unpacked yet, no doubt.

"If you want to stop at any point, let me know. But I'd like to try something." He's behind me and as soon as I nod his hand is on my arm, snaking down to my wrist.

Bryce pulls one of my arms behind my back, my fingertips ghosting along the skin there. Something cold snaps around my wrist and then clicks. The motions are repeated with my other arm until my wrists are bound behind my back by some kind of cuffs.

"You doing okay?" Bryce asks, moving around me to look me in the eye.

I'd be lying if I said I wasn't a little apprehensive but I trust him. And I'd like to see where he's going with this. "Yeah. I'm good."

"Lean your weight against the back, facing me."

It's a little awkward, but I'm able to steady myself. Only for my stomach to do a little flip when Bryce lowers to his knees in front of me. His large hands skate along the outsides of my legs, feather-light on the journey up and then squeezing when he gets to my thighs.

"Spread your legs a little."

I stare down at him, at the hunger on his face as he takes in my naked body in front and above him and although I'm at the disadvantage of not being able to touch back I feel like the one in power here. Shuffling my feet further, Bryce kisses up the inside of my knee and up along my inner thigh.

One of his hands grips my hips, keeping me steady, while he lifts the other onto his shoulder. Before I can worry about being unbalanced, his strong hold and the chaise behind me keeps me grounded. Bryce's delectable mouth moves closer and closer to where I'm aching for him and just before he gets there he looks up at me and grins. Pulling back, he removes the last holdout between him and total nudity.

"Almost forgot to take off my glasses, even though they're a mess from all the kissing." His words make me bark out a laugh at how silly it is. The juxtaposition of this man will keep me on my toes for years to come. Dominating in one moment, innocent and silly in the next.

Placing his glasses somewhere near one of the piles of clothing, he finally presses his mouth over my core and I can't stop the moan that falls from my lips even if I wanted to.

He devours. Bryce takes. This man steals the breath from the room and the heat from my skin until I'm little more than a shivering, panting mess. His hands. *Fuck*, those hands. I've drooled over them since day one and feeling them span, grab and claim pushes me even closer to the edge.

Whether it's my increasing moaning or the quiver in my leg that gives me away, Bryce leans back and releases the leg that he had draped over one of his broad shoulders. His mouth glistens and his eyes are glassy. His cock juts out, straining and hard, and seeing myself on him . . . seeing him want me makes me bite my bottom lip to hold in my whimper.

"Bend over the arm if you can." It's little more than a growl.

I'm helpless but to obey if I want to reach that peak with him, and at this point I'm near begging for it. It takes a moment of maneuvering so I don't fall on my face since I don't have my arms to assist, but I manage.

My attempts are rewarded by the feel of him spreading my knees from behind and stepping between them.

"So beautiful." It's a benediction followed by his hard heat jutting against my clit as he moves his cock along me to ease his entry.

Inch by delicious inch sinks inside and we both groan at the feel of him settling deep.

"God, you feel so good," I breathe and I'm rewarded with him retreating almost all the way out just to ease his way back.

It's slow and torturous, every drag of him against me hitting just the right spot from this position. I lose count of his thrusts in my delirium, all I can focus on is the exquisite agony that has me so close but just unable to reach. If my hands were free I'd slide one between my legs and help myself along but Bryce is the one in charge here.

It doesn't stop my little unhappy noise and he pauses.

"Are you okay? Are you hurting?" He sounds as wound tight as I feel.

"Yes. And yes."

His whole body stiffens. "I'm hurting you?" It's a little panicked and before he can pull out and end this I squeeze around him, trying to keep him buried within.

"*Fuck . . . Rachel,*" Bryce hisses.

"So close. Can't finish. Need to touch." No finesse or sex appeal injected into the words, just a breathless plea.

"No touching."

I should be embarrassed by what feels like tears slowly building out of my frustration, and the little huff I give in response to his order, but I'm too far gone to care. I try to wiggle side-to-side to get him moving again, to get some kind of friction.

"Do you need help?" He sounds smug and it makes me want to elbow him.

"Bryce, I swear to god if you don't do something about this right now," I growl.

His chuckle is half humor and half sin. The hands he's had on my waist and thighs move up to new territory. Sliding his arm under me, his left between my breasts, his hand cupping the base of my throat, Bryce lifts my torso off of the arm of the chaise so that my weight now rests on that strong arm.

His right arm trails down my stomach, down to where I'm desperate for him. Swirling the pad of his finger against my clit, he whispers right into my ear, "Is this what you need?"

"Yes," I choke out as he starts to move again.

It's lewd. It's borderline wicked the way he makes me melt and give into the pleasure. It's so quiet that all I can hear is his flesh slapping against mine and his harsh breaths in my ear as he speeds up, chasing his own high. Those gorgeous hands drive me to delirium. The fingers of his right thrum against me until I want to writhe with the pleasure of it, his left hand tightens just slightly against my throat—as if to feel the vibration of each of my moans.

Tipping my head back as far as it can go, Bryce captures my mouth and kisses toward my ear.

"Are you close for me?"

I barely recognize his voice, it's so low and dark. He sounds almost as desperate as me.

"So close. Please."

He nips at my earlobe and sets a punishing pace that I can do nothing but acquiesce to. Bryce whispers praise against the shell of my ear in a voice that's like dripping spiced honey. Sweet and biting. "Can't wait to worship you. Every day you'll let me. Want you to be mine."

"Yes, yours," I say, catching my breath for a moment before I claim him right back. "And you're mine."

"For as long as you'll have me." We make the promises we've been too scared to say out loud while joined in the most intimate sense and I feel it coming.

"Bryce . . ." I warn and he knows.

"Come for me, love. I want to feel you." He thrusts hard and deep and I wonder for a second if I'll have bruises tomorrow, from his hands or the frame beneath the padding of the chaise, before pleasure swallows me whole.

It's blinding in its intensity and if he wasn't basically holding me upright I would have melted to the floor from the force of it. I'm dimly aware of my moans and Bryce's rough grunts as he chases me over that same edge. A few moments after my bliss, as I'm settling into a body that *has* to be boneless—there's no other way—Bryce stiffens and grips me tight as his own pleasure finds him.

"You'll be the death of me." Bryce's heart races against my back, his chest heaving with breath.

"Ah, but what a sweet way to go." I chuckle tiredly and he echoes it.

"Are you okay?" Bryce asks, withdrawing and leaving me strangely bereft as he searches for something on the ground near my feet.

"I'm more than okay. I don't even feel like I have a body anymore." More silly laughter and I wonder if I'm a little punch drunk in my post-orgasm haze.

Bryce frees my wrists, lifting each to his mouth to give it a little kiss. "That was phenomenal. Thank you for trusting me."

I smile, no words available while my brain is mush. "Want to go home?"

"For tonight?" He asks and I can hear the question behind the words. Bryce wants to know my choice. Dressing, Bryce busies himself as if the act is enough to make the question seem nonchalant.

"For as long as you'd like to stay. I have a strongly-worded email to send to my asshole ex-boss to tell him that I'm far too happy with my current boss to ever consider going back. And then my current boss and I need to discuss what the future of my employment looks like now that our big project is up and running."

He ceases clothing himself, pants on but undone and his shirt the same. "Oh yeah? What else is on the agenda?" That boyish smile that I love is back and I can't stop my answering grin.

"Well, we'll need to get dinner at some point. And move his stuff over into my place. We still need to finish the season of Grey's Anatomy that we're on. Sleep has to fit in there somewhere as well." I lift a finger for each new item, listing them off.

"Sounds like you've got it all figured out but you seem to be forgetting one vital step there."

"Hmm, I don't know. I think I was pretty thorough."

Bryce stalks toward me, the heat back in his gaze and although I'm bone weary I feel the flicker of want within me respond. Dropping to his knees again, he kisses the softness of my stomach before looking down at my thighs, and the evidence of both of us trailing down the inside. "We'll need to get cleaned up and I'd love an encore of the thing we just did together."

My hands thread through his hair, clutching. "I think that can be arranged."

He stares up at me with such wonder. Love and longing are plain to see and I can't believe I almost gave this up. Because of fear and self doubt. I have an incredible man, literally at my feet, and I won't take that for granted.

I give him a hand up and we dress in silence, locking the theater up behind us and Bryce drives us the few blocks to the apartment. My key slides home in that robin's egg blue door I fell in love with on day one and as he follows me up the stairs, the thump of each of our footsteps sounds like a heartbeat.

We walk the well-worn wood from the doorway to the bath-room and worship each other in the shower until we're both spent. Naked and drying off on the bed, my head on Bryce's chest and his arm slung along my waist, I feel at peace.

Six months sounds like nothing in the scheme of things but

every day has shown me who I am, who I want to be, and who I'd like beside me for the rest of figuring life out.

All the photographs of strangers, all the promotions I chased, fade away. There's nothing to prove. No question of whether or not I'm worthy or wanted. In Bryce's embrace I feel safe and adored. We have friends that love and support us and a fledgling dream that's about to be very real. And I'm so happy that I don't have to force the smile that teases the corners of my lips.

Whatever may come, we're in it together.

# ACKNOWLEDGMENTS

Thank you to every cheerleader, shoulder to cry on, and loved one who got me through writing this draft. It took far longer than I planned and was so much harder than its predecessor, PLAYING FOR KEEPS. I would not have been able to stay the course without my wonderful husband who makes me believe in happily ever after, my family who believe in me even when I don't, and my friends whose excitement bolsters me when I falter.

Special thanks as always to my publisher, Lake Country Press! Britt and Bryan, you guys made my dream come true and I'm so lucky to not only get to work with you but to call you friends as well.

To the beta readers who dealt with me dropping chapters in fits and starts, catastrophizing, and ready to toss it in the trash—you are gems for putting up with me. Tyler, Madge, Joy, Ashley, Hannah—thank you for keeping me sane and for all your help shaping this story.

Vivian, you've outdone yourself! I'm so glad I got to work with you on the character art again. Rae, thank you for taking my amateur Canva scrapbook cover proposal and actually making it look like a beautiful cover.

To Tara, I appreciate every em dash, comma, and ellipses correction since I STILL don't know what the hell I'm doing with those, apparently. Thank you for helping to polish this book and make it shine!

Thanks to Joy, again, this time for making the inside of this book go from Google Doc to actual book. Working with you has been such a pleasure!

Last, but certainly not least, thank you to the readers—especially those of you who have been here since PLAYING FOR KEEPS! It means the world to me to hear that my characters and stories resonate with you. I hope that when you read them you know you're not alone in how you're feeling.

# ABOUT THE AUTHOR

Wife. Fangirl. Disney lover and belter of show tunes.

Overall ball of anxiety.

As a teen, Tristen escaped into her mother's trove of historical romance books and hasn't resurfaced since. Exploring new worlds through reading also fostered a hankering for travel.

When she's not working or writing about two fools falling in love, she is researching and visiting as many different places as possible.

Tristen was born and raised in South Africa but now lives in Maryland with her husband and their ever-growing book and board game shelves.

Subscribe to Tristen's newsletter

## ALSO BY TRISTEN CRONE

Playing for Keeps

I Think Olive You